They walked silently around kegs and boxes, around the station wagon, and approached the hearse with the bullet hole in the windshield. Suddenly Poly stopped.

"What's the matter?" Simon asked nervously.

"The hearse—" she whispered. "The doors are open—in the back—look. They've never been open before."

No. The hearse had always been sealed tight as a tomb. But now the double back doors were slightly ajar.

"Geraldo—" Poly whispered. Her hand was as cold as Simon's, and she clutched to get comfort as much as to give it.

Geraldo, followed by Charles, went up to the hearse and opened the doors wide.

Walking slowly, pulling back, but somehow managing to go forward, Poly and Simon followed them. The sunlight was so brilliant that it was difficult to see into the shadows within the hearse.

"Simon—" Poly whispered. It seemed that her voice had vanished.

There was something—someone—in the hearse.

Something—someone—lying there.

Cousin Forsyth.

MADELEINE L'ENGLE is the author of several books for children and young adults, including the Newbery Award–winning *A Wrinkle in Time*, which, along with *A Wind in the Door* and *A Swiftly Tilting Planet*, comprise the Time Trilogy, as well as *The Arm of the Starfish*, *The Young Unicorns*, and the Austin Family Trilogy (all available in Dell Laurel-Leaf editions). She lives in New York City.

Also Available in Laurel-Leaf Books:

DRAGONS IN THE WATERS

Madeleine L'Engle

LAUREL-LEAF BOOKS bring together under a single imprint outstanding works of fiction and nonfiction particularly suitable for young adult readers, both in and out of the classroom. Charles F. Reasoner, Professor Emeritus of Children's Literature and Reading, New York University, is consultant to this series.

Published by
Dell Publishing Co., Inc.
1 Dag Hammarskjold Plaza
New York, New York 10017

For Robert Giroux

ISBN: 0-440-91719-0

RL: 6.5

Reprinted by arrangement with
Farrar, Straus & Giroux, Inc.
Printed in the United States of America
First Laurel-Leaf printing—August 1982
Second Laurel-Leaf printing—December 1982

CONTENTS

DRAGONS
IN THE WATERS

I

THE FORK LIFT

The M.S. *Orion* was tied up at Savannah, Georgia.

Simon Renier, hands in the pockets of his old-fashioned grey shorts, looked at the small white ship with mounting excitement. He would be spending the next week on the *Orion* en route to Venezuela and already, standing on the pier in Savannah, he was farther away from home than he had ever been in his thirteen years.

It was chill this February day, with a thin rain and a biting wind. In a more sheltered part of the dock stood his cousin, Forsyth Phair, with whom he would be traveling, and his great-aunt Leonis Phair, with whom he lived, and who had come with them on the train from Charleston to see them off. Simon looked at the two of them standing under the shelter of the shed and their umbrellas and thought that if he were traveling with Aunt Leonis instead of Cousin Forsyth he would be perfectly happy.

Aunt Leonis was comfort and all-rightness in a precarious world; Cousin Forsyth he had known for barely a month, and while the distinguished-looking middle-aged man was courteous and pleasant he was not outgoing and to Simon he was still a stranger. He looked damp and uncomfortable with the rain dripping off his large black umbrella, and the collar to his dark raincoat turned up. Even the corners of his waxed moustache seemed to droop. The old woman, on the other hand, stood straight as an arrow, unperturbed by the downpour.

"Can't you come, too?" Simon had begged her.

"I'm too tired, child," the old woman had said. "At ninety I've earned the right to my rocking chair and my books. Besides, I have to stay home and take care of Boz." The old dog in pointer years was almost as old as Aunt Leonis. His proud skeleton showed under the still-glossy liver-spotted body, and Simon felt a tightening of his stomach muscles as he realized that the old hound might not be there when he returned.

He turned his face to the rain and moved farther away from Aunt Leonis and Cousin Forsyth, past the gangplank of the *Orion*, and on down the dock. All around him was activity, the tall yellow arms of the *Orion* swinging sacks of seed and grain and rice up onto the ship, to be stored in the hold. Simon watched in fascination as a large station wagon was carefully hoisted up from the dock, swung loose for a moment high in the air, then was lowered gently onto the foredeck.

On the aft deck stood the passengers who had already embarked at Brooklyn or Baltimore, eagerly watching the business of loading the freighter. A few of them waved at him, and he waved shyly back. Then he turned to watch the orange fork lifts buzzing rapidly up and down the dock, the two long tines of their forks fitting neatly into the small wooden platforms onto which bags and bales were piled. Great yellow arms swung out from the *Orion*, dropping heavy ropes which were looped around sacks and platform; the crane raised its burden to the ship's foredeck, and the highly mobile fork lift darted away, moving far more easily than an ordinary tractor, turn-

ing on a dime to reach for another load. The sailor
managing the long-angled pincers from his glassed-in
cab high up on the *Orion* swung the bags and sacks
with easy accuracy. Everywhere was bustle, and
men's shouting, and the smell of wet wood and the
salt wind from the sea. Simon would be almost sorry
when they boarded, so fascinating was the loading
procedure.

He jumped as he heard a horn, and a Land-Rover
drove onto the dock, full of children who kept piling
out, like clowns out of a car at the circus. Simon found
it difficult to keep count, but it appeared to be a
mother and father and seven children. After considerable shouting and laughing, the two older children, a
girl and a boy, sorted themselves out, managed to get
two battered suitcases from the Land-Rover, and came
to stand not far from Simon. The mother urged the
younger children back into the car, out of the rain,
and the father, rain dripping off his cap, stood leaning
in the window, talking to the mother.

The girl, banging her old suitcase against her knees,
dropped it by the gangplank and came on down the
dock toward Simon. Her brother followed. She was,
Simon guessed, maybe a year older than he was,
maybe fourteen, and probably would resent being
called a child. The boy looked younger, although he
was as tall as Simon, who guessed him to be no more
than twelve. Both brother and sister wore yellow
slickers and sou'westers, and were considerably drier
than Simon, whose fair hair was slicked wetly to his
head.

"Hello," the girl said. "Are you going on the *Orion?*"
Her accent was not quite foreign, but it was certainly

more precise than the soft Southern speech Simon was accustomed to hearing.

"Yes'm. Are you?"

"Yes. At least, Charles and Daddy and I are." She smiled, a swift spreading of sunlight over her face. "How nice to have someone our age. Daddy warned us that freighter passengers tend to be ancient. I'm Poly O'Keefe, pronounced Polly but spelled with one *l*. I'm fourteen. And this is my brother, Charles. He's twelve."

So he had been right. "I'm Simon Renier, and I'm thirteen."

Again Poly smiled, a shaft of light lifting the drab day. "You're not traveling alone, are you?"

He indicated the man and the old woman. Suddenly Cousin Forsyth stepped forward as one of the fork lifts picked up a large flat wooden crate. He watched anxiously as ropes from the *Orion* were looped around it. "Be very careful," he fussed. "It's extremely valuable. It contains an irreplaceable portrait."

The dock hands nodded indifferently as they went about their business. The fork lift backed away from the crate, which was then lifted up in the air and hung swinging between the ship and the dock.

"What's in there?" Poly asked Simon. "Your father looks as though he's about to have a heart attack." The horn of the Land-Rover tooted before Simon could answer or correct her. "We have to say goodbye!" Poly cried. "We'll be back in a minute, Simon!" and she and Charles ran across the dock, dodging loading trucks and fork lifts.

Simon watched rather wistfully while there was a tangle of hugging and kissing goodbye. Then he looked up at the *Orion* just in time to see the great crate with the portrait being safely lowered onto the deck, and Cousin Forsyth mopping his forehead with his handkerchief as though it were hot.

Aunt Leonis was still standing in the shelter of the shed and her small, not very waterproof umbrella. Simon ran over to her, skidding on the wet boards. "Where's Cousin Forsyth going?"

"He's off to make sure the portrait isn't going to get banged or crushed. I certainly can't complain about his care of it. He's overzealous, if anything." She put her gnarled old hand on his head. "You're soaking, Simon!"

"Yes, ma'am."

"You'll be boarding in a minute or two. You're old enough to take care of yourself without me, aren't you?"

"Yes, ma'am."

"And don't let Forsyth overprotect you. He can keep that for the portrait. I want you to have some fun."

He leaned lightly against her. "I'll miss you."

"It's time you got out of the nest, child. A nonagenarian is hardly a fit companion for a boy. I'm glad there are other young persons on board."

"Yes, ma'am!"

"I'm going now, Simon. I have a train to catch." She was still taller than he was. She bent down, and he kissed her softly on each cheek. For a brief moment she held him to her. Then she stood upright and gave him a little shove. "Run along, now."

Tears filled his eyes. He did not want her to see. Moving in a blur of tears and rain, he crossed the dock. He paused at the gangplank but the tears would not be held back. Poly and Charles had said their goodbyes and were hurrying along the dock toward him.

No one must see him cry.

He moved on past the gangplank, past the stern of the *Orion,* on to the very end of the dark, slippery dock. He did not see the fork lift, out of control, hurtling toward him.

Someone on deck screamed.

He felt a shove, and then both he and Poly O'Keefe were in the water.

The fork lift ground to a screeching halt, barely avoiding crashing off the dock after them.

The water was icy cold. Their clothes dragged them down.

From the deck of the *Orion* round orange life preservers were thrown into the water for them, but both Simon and Poly had managed to grab onto the pilings of the dock and were clinging to them safely. Dock hands pulled them up out of the chilling water, and they stood dank and dripping in the February rain.

The driver of the fork lift kept explaining that his accelerator had stuck.

The shivering boy and girl were surrounded by the entire O'Keefe family, by sailors and dock hands. Aunt Leonis used her umbrella to get through the mob to Simon. Through chattering teeth he said, "I'm all right, Aunt Leonis. Please don't miss your train."

The old woman turned her sharp eyes on Poly. "I saw. You saved him. If you hadn't thrown yourself at him and got him out of the path of the fork lift he'd be—" She looked at the vicious prongs of the fork lift and did not finish her sentence. She turned to the father of the family. "You will watch out for him, sir? I am gravely concerned."

Dr. O'Keefe replied, "Of course I'll keep an eye out for him. But I don't think you need worry. It was only an unfortunate accident."

Aunt Leonis looked at him sharply, but all she said was, "Where is Forsyth? If he's going to worry about the portrait to the exclusion of the boy—"

The captain of the ship came running down the gangplank, followed by a youngish man with officer's bars on his dark sleeve. "I am Captain van Leyden, and this is my first officer, Mynheer Boon."

Mynheer Boon smiled and draped heavy blankets over Poly and Simon.

Van Leyden said, "Boon will get the children aboard and help them. Order hot tea, too, please, Boon."

Simon held out his hand. "Goodbye, Aunt Leonis." His voice faltered slightly. He hoped that this would be attributed to the cold.

Aunt Leonis shook his hand formally. Then she said to Dr. O'Keefe, "I do not think that I am being just a foolish old woman." To Poly she said, "I am much obliged to you, Miss—"

"Poly O'Keefe. It wasn't anything."

Aunt Leonis said, "It was."

To Simon's surprise Charles O'Keefe looked directly at the old woman and replied, "Yes. It was."

Miss Leonis's old eyes were clouded with more than age as she watched Simon's dripping, blanket-covered form trudge damply up the gangplank. Poly O'Keefe and her brother and father were ahead of Simon; Forsyth Phair, who had emerged from the ship just in time for farewells, was behind, fussing over Simon in much the same nervous way he had fussed over the portrait. It was apparent that the boy was being taken care of. The nice Dutch officer would see to it that he got hot tea and changed to dry clothes. There was nothing more she could do. She walked slowly along the dark, wet boards of the dock.

Mrs. O'Keefe was trying to herd her excited younger children into the Land-Rover. She saw the old woman struggling along, wind tugging at her ancient umbrella. "Is there anywhere I can drop you? A Land-Rover's not the most comfortable vehicle in the world, but at least you'll be out of the rain."

Miss Leonis looked at the younger woman, and at the children, who had stopped their chattering and were staring. "Thank you. I should be much obliged if you'd take me to the railroad station. I think I may not have missed my train."

"Sandy, Dennys, help Mrs. . . . " She paused.

"Phair. Miss Leonis Phair. I can manage quite nicely myself, thank you just the same, young gentlemen." With the help of her now-furled umbrella she pulled herself briskly onto the high seat of the Land-Rover.

Mrs. O'Keefe asked, "Can we drive you any farther than the station?"

"Thank you, no. I am taking the train to Charleston."

Mrs. O'Keefe turned around in the car and looked back at her children, then smiled at the old woman. "What with all the excitement at the dock I think it very likely that you've missed your train, and I've been promising the children a visit to Charleston for ages. We'd be delighted to drive you there. Now that my husband has gone off for a month with Poly and

Charles, surely everybody else deserves a special treat."

There was a loud noise of agreement.

Miss Leonis looked at Mrs. O'Keefe, who was now smiling serenely. "I am much obliged to you. You are very kind."

"Not at all. It's you who've given us the opportunity for sightseeing, and the weather report promised sun late this afternoon, and the rain's beginning to slacken off already. Do you live right in Charleston?"

"Out in the backwoods." The old woman's next words seemed to be audible thinking, rather than conversation. "I hope I have made the right decision. It is not normal for a young boy to live all alone with an old woman." Then she pulled herself together and spoke briskly, "I would be delighted to give you a conducted tour of Charleston, and then perhaps you will drop me off on your way home—you do live north of Savannah?"

"Yes. Benne Seed Island."

Leonis Phair turned around and stared solemnly at the children. "I hope you young ones have stamina. You may find me difficult to keep up with." There was stifled giggling as she asked Mrs. O'Keefe, "Your husband will keep an eye on Simon?"

Mrs. O'Keefe turned the car away from the dock area and onto the highway. "Of course he will. He's used to having a mob of children to keep track of."

"It will make me easier in my mind. Simon has never been away from home before. And that was not a propitious beginning."

Mrs. O'Keefe said lightly, "If he and Poly needed an introduction, that was sure-fire. They're probably the best of friends by now."

Miss Leonis was silent for the next mile. Her gnarled hands held the umbrella handle, and she tapped the steel tip thoughtfully on the floorboards. Then she spoke quietly. "Your daughter saved Simon's life. I shall not forget that."

On the M.S. *Orion,* Simon and Poly in their separate cabins were changing out of their soaking clothes. Simon, alone in the double cabin he was to share with Cousin Forsyth, wondered if Dr. O'Keefe or Charles was helping Poly.

Forsyth Phair had said, "Take a good hot shower, Simon, and wash your hair. That water by the dock in which you chose to swim can hardly have been very clean."

Simon did not reply that the swim had not been of his own choosing.

"And dress in warm clothes. I don't want you coming down with a cold right at the beginning of the trip. I am very susceptible to colds."

"Yes, sir."

"I must go tend to the portrait now. One of the boards on the crate came loose as it was being loaded. Captain van Leyden says that since cabin 5 on the port side of the ship is unoccupied until Caracas, the portrait can be stored there. I certainly wouldn't trust it with the rest of the cargo." And off he fussed.

Simon stood for a long time under the hot shower, not so much to wash off the oily waters as for comfort. The noise of loading and unloading continued outside his portholes; the ship was still safely berthed in Savannah but he felt very far from home. What had seemed like a great adventure only a few hours ago now gave him a cold feeling in the pit of his stomach and an ache around his heart.

He wanted Aunt Leonis.

Not that Cousin Forsyth wasn't kind. But Simon found it odd that it was the middle-aged bachelor who had suggested that the boy accompany him on this voyage.

He got out of the shower, dried, and put on his seersucker bathrobe. Cousin Forsyth had said, 'There's no point in packing winter things. After the first or second day at sea it's going to be summer.'

Simon shivered. His soaking blazer was the warmest thing he had. "Come in," he called to a tap on the door.

It opened to a young man, barely out of boyhood, with dark hair and eyes, who was wearing a white coat. He bore a small tray with a pot of steaming tea, and some buttered rusks with Gouda cheese.

Simon smiled his thanks and asked the young man's name.

"Geraldo Enrique Armando José Ramórez. I am the assistant steward, at your service. You are Simín Renier?"

"Simon Bolivar Quentin Phair Renier. We have the same number of names. I pronounce Simon the English way instead of the Spanish way."

Geraldo poured tea for Simon, put in lemon and sugar. "But you are named after the great general?"

"Yes," Simon said, and shivered.

Geraldo looked at the boy in his inadequate cotton robe. "You have nothing warmer?"

Simon pawed through his suitcase and pulled out a lightweight sleeveless pullover.

Geraldo shook his head. "That is not enough, and it

will be tomorrow before I have your wet things cleaned and pressed." He sounded like an old man. "Drink your tea, please, while it is hot. I will return."

The steaming, lemony tea warmed Simon inside and out. He sipped and unpacked and ate the rusks and cheese and unpacked some more, taking care to leave most of the drawer and wardrobe space for Cousin Forsyth. He knew that Cousin Forsyth would have preferred a single cabin, but when they had booked passage the two single cabins on the *Orion* were already taken, one by Poly.

There was, however, plenty of room for two. The bunks were divided by a sizable chest of drawers, and Simon took the bottom drawer. Cousin Forsyth had already put his briefcase on the bunk on the inner wall, so Simon had the bunk under the two portholes. This would have been the bunk of his choosing, and he would not have felt free to take it if Cousin Forsyth had not established himself on the other.

The boy knelt on the bunk and peered through the glass. Cabin 3 was on the dock side of the ship. Sacks of grain were still being loaded deep in the hold. Sailors and dock hands shouted back and forth. Fork lifts skittered about like bugs, beetles with long sharp mandibles. He was not feeling very happy about fork lifts and he turned away. He took his small stack of paperback books out of the bottom of his suitcase and arranged them in a rack where they would be easy to reach from his bunk. Then he put out his face cloth, toothbrush, and toothpaste.

Over the two washbasins was a fan, for which there was no present need. In the radiator the steam was clanking. By the side of each washbasin was a thermos flask in a holder; Simon uncorked his and peered

in: ice water. He corked it again, sat down in one of
the two small chairs, and poured himself another cup
of tea. Then he heard a loud, deep honking: the ship
seemed to shake from the vibration, and he realized
that the *Orion* was indeed throbbing; the engines
were being revved up; they were about to sail.

He knelt on his bunk again and looked out.

On the dock the longshoremen were unhooking the
great ropes which held the *Orion* to the pier. Two
dark-uniformed sailors pulled the gangplank aboard;
two others leapt across the dark gap of water between
dock and lower deck. Slowly the dock seemed to re-
cede from the ship; the dark expanse of water dividing ship and land grew wider and wider. Sea gulls
swooped about, calling in raucous excited voices.
Deep within himself Simon felt an echoing response
of excitement. He was at sea, on his way to Venezuela.

He began to whistle, softly, a minor, haunting melody, and then to sing,

> *I met her in Venezuela,*
> *A basket on her head . . .*

He was still looking out and singing softly when
Geraldo returned with a heavy navy-blue sweater and
a fisherman's cap. "Mynheer Boon is lending you the
sweater till it is warmer. The cap is for you to keep.
You will need it to keep the sun off your nose as well
as the rain off your head." He knelt on the bunk beside Simon, not much larger than the younger boy,
and they looked at the activity on the dock becoming
small and almost unreal as Savannah drifted farther
and farther away.

In schoolboy Spanish, Simon tried to thank Geraldo, and was interrupted by a bang on the door and Poly's voice, "Here we are, Simon!" and she burst in, wearing a long plaid bathrobe which undoubtedly belonged to her father; her short, carroty hair struck out in spikes from being rubbed dry. Charles, in jeans and a red turtleneck, followed her.

"All right if we come in?" he asked.

"Oh, please do come in," Simon welcomed them, indicating Geraldo. "Do you know—"

"Oh, yes, Geraldo brought me hot tea, too, like a Herald Angel—that's what Geraldo sounds like. I used to spell it with an *H* instead of a *G*." Then she burst into a stream of Spanish so fluent that Simon found it difficult to follow.

Geraldo spoke slowly and carefully to Simon. "You understand that Geraldo begins with a *G*, which is pronounced like an *H* in Spanish? And the other passengers are all having tea in the salon. Mr. Phair would like you please to join them as soon as you're dressed."

At Geraldo's grave courtesy, Poly flushed, the red beginning at her neck and moving up her face to her forehead. "I'm sorry, Simon. I didn't think."

Under his breath Charles said, "Don't show off . . ."

Poly flung around as though to flash a reply to her brother, then stopped herself.

"It's okay," Simon assured her, "really, it's okay. And just as I was feeling smug about my Spanish, too. Teaches me how nonexistent it really is."

"We used to live in Portugal," Poly explained, "on Gaea, an island off the south coast. If you learn Portuguese, which is a stinker, it's easy to learn Spanish. Whereas it's most difficult for someone who speaks only Spanish to learn Portuguese, and—" She broke off. "Am I showing off again?"

Charles sat down on Cousin Forsyth's bunk. "It's second nature," he said, not unkindly. Then he bestowed a singularly sweet smile on his sister, on Simon and Geraldo, a slow blooming of pleasure quite different from Poly's flash of light. "Did you see us sail? Our cabins are starboard, so we almost missed it, what with you and Poly having been so suddenly in the soup."

Simon glanced at the porthole through which he had watched the land, rather than the ship, move slowly away. "It was exciting. I've never been away from home before. Even coming to Savannah was a journey for me."

"Where's home?" Poly asked.

"Near Charleston."

"Charleston, South Carolina?"

Simon's surprised look said as clearly as words, Is there any other? Then he indicated the sweater and cap. "From Geraldo. He's lending me Mynheer Boon's sweater and he's giving me the cap."

Poly spoke to Geraldo in Spanish, but this time it was slowly and carefully so that Simon would understand. "Geraldo, would you tell them, please, that Simon and I'll dress and be right along. And it's a lovely cap."

"I will tell them, Miss Poly." Then he referred to a slip of paper he pulled out of his pocket. "On the passenger list it says Pol—Polyhymnia."

"Poly, please, Geraldo."

Charles grinned. "Polyhymnia's a muse. The muse of sacred music."

Poly pulled the belt to her father's bathrobe tight in

a determined gesture. "If any of you calls me anything but Poly there'll be—there'll be murder."

"Not at the beginning of the trip," Charles said.

Geraldo picked up Simon's tea tray. "I will tell them."

"What?" Charles aked. "That there'll be murder?"

"That you will shortly be in for tea."

"Okay." Poly followed Geraldo out, but turned at the door. "I won't be more than five minutes. Hurry, Simon."

Charles asked, "Shall I stay and talk?"

"Please. Please do." Simon took clean underclothes, navy-blue shorts, and a blue cotton shirt from his drawer and went into the shower to dress.

Charles reclined on Cousin Forsyth's bunk. "If you had all the brothers and sisters Poly and I have, you wouldn't have room for modesty. But you're an Only, aren't you?"

Simon compromised by leaving the bathroom door half open. "Yes."

"How come you and your father are taking this trip?"

"Not my father." Simon pulled on his shirt and emerged.

"I didn't think he seemed terribly fatherly. At least not like our father. I get the feeling he's not used to children."

"I don't think he is." Simon sat on the edge of his bunk and pulled on navy-blue knee socks.

Charles, his hands behind his head, looked up at the ceiling of the cabin. "How do you happen to be traveling with him, then?"

Simon pulled the heavy sweater over his head. The rough wool felt comforting. He pulled Geraldo's cap over his still damp hair. His shoes were with his other wet things, so he took a pair of worn sneakers from the bottom of the wardrobe. "Cousin Forsyth offered me the trip, and Aunt Leonis thought it would be good experience for me, since I'm a country bumpkin. I guess you've done a lot of traveling."

"Oh, some, but mostly we've lived on Gaea—the island; the younger kids were born there. Last year we came back to America and moved to Benne Seed Island, but most of us still think of Portugal as home."

Poly appeared in the doorway, now dressed in a plaid skirt and a burnished-orange sweater which just managed not to conflict with her hair. "Daddy's a marine biologist, so islands are very good for his work. C'mon. Let's go brave the lions' den."

Charles rose from Cousin Forsyth's bunk and Simon smoothed the coverlet, almost as anxiously as Cousin Forsyth had supervised the loading of the crated portrait.

Poly helped him. "What would he do if he found Charles had sat on his bunk? Beat you or something?"

"No, oh no, he's very kind."

"It's okay." Charles glanced impatiently at the bunk. "You'd never know anybody'd even sat on it. Let's go. We're expected to meet everybody."

In the salon Geraldo was replacing one teapot with a fresh one. Poly led the way in; Charles slipped past her and sat on a sofa beside his father. Simon held back at the doorway, shyly looking at the people sitting on sofas and chairs around the tea table. Cousin Forsyth did not greet him; he seemed concentrated fully on the woman pouring tea, a dark, handsome woman, very Spanish-looking, though she turned out to have the incongruous name of Dr. Wordsworth. She and her traveling companion, Dr. Eisenstein, were professors on sabbatical leave from their university. Dr. Wordsworth taught Spanish—so she must be at least half Spanish, Simon thought.

Cousin Forsyth said, "It was indeed a pleasant surprise for me to find the lovely Inés Wordsworth on the *Orion*. We knew each other many years ago when we were both young in Caracas."

Dr. Wordsworth replied with distinct chilliness, "It was not that many years ago, and our acquaintance was slight. *Very* slight."

Cousin Forsyth raised his fine eyebrows, but made no comment, and Dr. Wordsworth went on to explain to the children that Dr. Eisenstein was an anthropologist, going to the Lago de los Dragones in Venezuela, to make what Dr. Wordsworth called an in-depth study of the Quiztano Indians, who lived at the far end of the lake.

Poly said with interest, "We're getting off at Puerto de los Dragones, too, and going on to the lake. Daddy's been asked to—" She caught a warning look from her father and hurried on. "I think it's lovely having a town and a lake be places of dragons. I'm very interested in dragons. Of course, one always thinks of St. George and the dragon, and he's my favorite, but did you know that Margaret of Antioch had a dragon, too?" As always when she came close to blundering, she talked too much about something else. "Fork lifts look a little like dragons, don't you think?"

After a slight pause among the company, Cousin Forsyth said dryly, "I hadn't noticed the resemblance."

"Maybe they don't spout fire," Poly said stubbornly,

"but they can be as dangerous as dragons. Right, Simon?"

Simon nodded, and continued to observe the pasengers and listen to the conversation. He learned that afternoon tea was not usually served on the *Orion;* this tea party was an impromptu affair; some of the passengers, seeing Geraldo brewing tea for Simon and Poly, had suggested that tea in the salon would be a pleasant and informal way for new and old passengers to meet.

Dr. Wordsworth did not offer tea to the children but began to refill the adult passengers' cups. Simon looked at her hands, which had long, scarlet nails. They were not young hands, and the flashing rings and bright nail polish accented rather than minimized their age. Aunt Leonis did not wear nail polish, and though her nails were horny with age, Simon compared Dr. Wordsworth's hands unfavorably with the old woman's.

Dr. Eisenstein appealed more to Simon—a brown mouse of a woman, brown all over, suit, eyes, the shadows below the eyes; there was considerable brown remaining in the greying hair, which she wore braided in a thin crown on top of her head. Her smile was friendly, Simon thought, and did not exclude the children.

He turned his regard to the three other passengers, two old men and one old woman—all three probably considerably younger than Aunt Leonis, but nevertheless old. Mr. and Mrs. Smith were both plump and beaming; they were from New Hampshire and were en route to visit their granddaughter and great-grandchildren in Costa Rica, and were obviously thrilled at the prospect. Mrs. Smith was knitting a blue baby's bootee, and with her pink cheeks and curly white hair she looked like a magazine illustration of the perfect grandmother.

The last passenger bore the formidable name of Emmanuele Theotocopoulos, and Simon was relieved when they were told to call him Mr. Theo. If Dr. Eisenstein looked like a friendly field mouse, Mr. Theo was small and frail as a sparrow, but he emanated enormous vitality, and he had lively dark eyes and a mop of yellowed white hair which stood out in a thick ruff around his head; he looked, Simon decided, not in the least like a bird, but rather like an aging lion.

Cousin Forsyth's words caught his attention. ". . . a portrait of Simon Bolivar which I am taking to Caracas as a gift to the Venezuelan government."

Simon's shyness was overcome by Cousin Forsyth's proprietary air about the painting. "The portrait has been in our family always. It is the greatest portrait ever painted of the General—and I'm named after him. Simon Bolivar Quentin Phair Renier. The portrait was given to my ancestor, Quentin Phair, by Bolivar himself, and it belongs to my Aunt Leonis—" He stopped short. Cousin Forsyth had bought the portrait from Aunt Leonis, the portrait which otherwise would one day have belonged to Simon. It was no longer Aunt Leonis's. It would never be Simon's.

The grownups had started playing the "Since it's a small world, do you know?" game. Cousin Forsyth and Dr. Wordsworth had once known each other, so it was likely there might be more connections between the passengers.

Mr. Theo asked Dr. O'Keefe, "I suppose this is a

very long shot, but one of my oldest friends was in Portugal a couple of years ago, and got involved with a marine biologist there. Could you be the one? Do you know Tom Tallis?"

Poly precipitated herself into the conversation. "He's my godfather! He's one of our favorite people in the world!"

Simon felt excluded from the excitement shared by the O'Keefes and the old Greek. Who was this man who was so important to them that Poly should be dancing with joy?

Dr. O'Keefe said, "I don't know what we'd have done without Tom. For a priest, he does get himself involved in some extraordinarily sticky situations."

Poly turned to Simon, drawing him in. "He knows everybody in Interpol and Scotland Yard and everything. He's not really a detective, but whenever there's big trouble he gets called in to help."

Dr. O'Keefe said wryly, "Let's hope there'll be no cause on this voyage to send for him. For once in his life he's living quietly as a canon of St. Paul's and being allowed to be a priest."

Mr. Theo nodded. "It would be splendid to have him along just for fun—but I've had my share of excitement—enough to last me for a long time. My doctor was very firm that this is to be a quiet voyage for me. My heart won't take much more wild adventuring."

Dr. Wordsworth came into the conversation. "That's exactly what freighter travel is for—peace and quiet. Ruth and I are exhausted. We slept the clock round last night and feel much the better for it. During the normal academic year I have precious little time for myself."

The tea party was breaking up. Mr. Smith tucked *The Wall Street Journal* under his arm, remarking that they would not see another newspaper until they reached Port of Dragons, and there would probably be only Spanish papers there; it was not a port which attracted many tourists.

Mrs. Smith held up a blue bootee to hide a yawn. "I think I'll have just a wee little rest before dinner. We were all so distressed at the accident. Coming, Odell?"

Mr. Smith helped her up. "I could do with some shuteye, too. You youngsters may have had the dunking, but it was quite something for us oldsters, too. What a mercy that no real harm was done. Patty and I'll see you later, folks." Arm in arm, walking with legs slightly apart so that they could balance themselves against the slight roll of the ship, Mr. and Mrs. Smith moved like storks out of the salon and into the first cabin on the starboard passage.

Forsyth Phair looked at Simon. "Have you unpacked?"

"Pretty much, sir."

Poly jumped up. "I haven't. Charles, have you?"

"Sort of. I was waiting to see which drawers Daddy wanted."

"Come along then, Charles," Dr. O'Keefe said, "and we'll get things sorted out."

Simon, again feeling somewhat lost, watched them leave.

Dr. Eisenstein rose. "I think I'll check my notes on the Quiztano Indians until time for drinks. We usually meet in here for drinks before dinner, Mr. Phair, and of course as soon as it's warm enough we'll sit on deck for our pre-prandial libation."

"That will be day after tomorrow," Dr. Wordsworth announced in her definite way.

"You are quite sure of that." Forsyth Phair smiled.

"Quite."

Dr. Eisenstein started out and turned toward the portside passage. "Coming, Inés?"

"Shortly, Ruth."

Mr. Theo retired to the farthest corner of the salon with a book. Simon went close enough so that he could see what it was: a complete Shakespeare, with print so small that he wondered that the old man could read it. But he had put on steel-rimmed spectacles and was smiling at what he was reading, totally engrossed.

Simon did not know what he was supposed to do. Cousin Forsyth was looking through some papers on one of the tables. Dr. Wordsworth was gathering books and embroidery into a needlepoint bag. He felt very young and inexperienced, standing uncomfortably in the middle of the salon. When Cousin Forsyth continued to read, Simon wandered across the room, bumping clumsily into a chair as the ship rolled, and returned to the cabin. It did not seem courteous to Cousin Forsyth to close the door, so he left it open and pulled flowered curtains across the opening; these, he assumed, were for use when the weather was hot and every available breeze was sought. Now they let in a draft which would have been unpleasant had he not been comfortably warm in Mynheer Boon's sweater.

He knelt on his bunk, his cheek to the porthole glass, and gazed out. The rain had stopped but the light was beginning to fade. Land was a dim purple shadow on the horizon. The ocean was dark and mysterious and speckled with white bursts of spume. The sound of water was all around him. The small ship creaked as it pressed through the waves. From somewhere below decks Simon could hear orders being shouted in a guttural Dutch voice; there was male laughter, solid and reassuring.

Outside the open cabin door he heard voices; he had been aware of them for some time without focusing on them.

". . . have nothing to hide." That was Cousin Forsyth, speaking in a warm and intimate way Simon had not heard before.

"Oh, do we not?" Simon recognized Dr. Wordsworth's strong, slightly harsh voice.

"Are you still dwelling on that, my dear? I had almost forgotten. No, I was not referring to that. But I was thinking that the fact that a young man should have fallen in love with a beautiful young girl is nothing that need be hidden. I am charmed that our cabins are adjoining."

"And I am not." Dr. Wordsworth's voice did not soften. "I waited because I wished to speak to you."

Simon cleared his throat, but evidently not loud enough to call attention to his presence, because Cousin Forsyth continued, "Lovely! I wish to speak to you, too."

"And I do not wish that. What I want to say to you is that I will not let you bring up the past. It is dead and buried and I want it to stay that way."

"Are you ashamed to claim acquaintance with me?"

"Acquaintance, F.P." She emphasized the initials. "Nothing more. And I would not speak of shame if I were you."

Simon felt acutely uncomfortable.

Dr. Wordsworth's voice shook with emotion. "I prayed that we might never meet again. I left Caracas and made a new life in a new world. I never should have come with Ruth—"

"Come, come, Inés. It's not so extraordinary that our paths should cross again. Can't this be an opportunity for a new understanding between us?"

She had difficulty keeping her voice low. "After what happened? I haven't forgotten."

"Can't I help you to forget? Can't you? After all this time?"

"I *had* forgotten, until I saw you. I will not allow you to presume on the past," Dr. Wordsworth said with icy control. "We are mere acquaintances. No more."

Phair's voice was tolerant. "How intense you still are, Inés. That has not changed. I hope that before the voyage is over, you may be willing to forget. Meanwhile, of course, I defer to your wishes, though I fail to understand."

"I gave up expecting you to understand anything a long time ago. The past is past. I'll kill you if you rake it up. Have I made this clear?"

Simon heard the door to the next cabin open. "Inés!" called Dr. Eisenstein. "I thought I heard your voice. Have you seen my green notebook?"

Dr. Wordsworth sighed. "Dear Ruth, you're always misplacing things. I'll go look in the salon."

Simon, too, sighed, and looked out to sea. At the horizon the light was soft and rosy, pulsing into green above, and then deepening to a blue almost as dark as the sea. It occurred to him that if he went down to the deck below and walked around or climbed over various pieces of cargo, he could get to the very prow of the ship and pretend to be his ancestor, Quentin Phair, who was indirectly the cause of Simon's being on the *Orion* now, sailing to Venezuela with the portrait of Bolivar.

He huddled into Mynheer Boon's heavy sweater and took courage. Quentin Phair may have been nineteen, a grownup, a man, when he left England to go to Venezuela to fight with Bolivar, but Simon had the same adventurous blood in his veins—he hoped. If Aunt Leonis had been with him, thirteen would have seemed a great deal older than it did when he was with Cousin Forsyth.

The tall radiators were too hot to touch. It seemed improbable that in just a few days the sun would be warm and they might even need to turn on the cabin fan.

"Hello, Simon." It was Cousin Forsyth. "What have you been up to?"

Simon got down from the bunk and stood politely before his cousin. "Looking at the ocean, sir."

"All settled in?"

"Yes, sir, thank you, sir. If you don't mind I think I'll go out on deck." He could not explain to Cousin Forsyth—he would not have needed to explain to Aunt Leonis—that he was going to take a journey into the past and pretend to be his own ancestor, Quentin Phair, setting out from England to the wild and glamorous new world of South America. Quentin was Simon's hero and model, and it was far more splendid to make believe that he was Quentin Phair, the white knight in shining armor, than Simon Bolivar Quentin Phair Renier, who was only a thirteen-year-old boy.

"Be careful," Cousin Forsyth warned, "and be sure that you're in time for dinner. Ship's meals are served promptly."

"Yes, sir. I'll be on time."

He left the cabin and as he walked along the passage he heard the cabin door shut behind him with a firm click. It was difficult suddenly to accept Cousin Forsyth as a man with the complete fabric of a past. Until a few minutes ago Cousin Forsyth had been for Simon only a month old. Before a month ago Simon had never heard of this tall, grave, suave man with whom he was traveling. It seemed unlikely that this close-mouthed, middle-aged person had once been young and in love.

He started down the steps, remembering that only a few hours ago Mynheer Boon had hustled him, blanketed and dripping, across the foredeck with a high sill over which he had tripped, past the crew's quarters and up these same steps which Mynheer Boon had told him were properly called a ladder, though they looked like an ordinary staircase.

From the crew's quarters came sound and smell, both delightful: someone was playing a guitar; someone else was rendering the melody on a flute or recorder. Through a partly open curtain he saw two young sailors lounging on a double-decker bunk. A delicious scent of baking wafted toward him as he passed the galley, and he could see the chef, a young man with round spectacles and a high white hat, taking a tray of steaming pastry out of the oven. The loveliness of the music and the comfortableness of the cooking cheered him. He remembered to step high over the sill and went out on deck into the clean raw wind. Most of the doorways on the *Orion* had sills far higher than those in a house, but the sill to the foredeck was even higher than the others, to keep out the waves in rough weather.

The boy stood on the gently rolling deck, breathing salt air, listening to the music coming sweetly from within the ship, punctuated by the sound of men's voices; he picked his way through the cargo, pausing in the clear evening light to look at the writing on the wooden crates. If it was Dutch he had trouble even in guessing; if it was Spanish he could usually decipher it; there was a lot of equipment for oil wells and refineries. He guessed that most of the bags of grain and seed he had seen being loaded were now stashed away down in the hold.

He moved through the narrow walkways left open between cargo, past the station wagon, two cars, and a large black hearse. He did not like the idea of having the hearse aboard. It was five years since the death of his parents, and he loved Aunt Leonis and was happy with her; nevertheless, the sleek dark hearse was a reminder of death, of grief, of the terrifying precariousness of all life. As he hurried past it he saw a rayed-out shattering in the windshield that looked as though it had been made by a bullet.

Simon shivered, only partly from the blustery wind, and hurried on until he came to the prow of the ship. By standing on one of the bales he could look out to sea. The cold wind blew through the heavy sweater. He pulled the cap down over his eyes and crouched so that he was protected from the wind. If he tried hard enough he could visualize the *Orion*'s great yellow masts holding billowing sails which slapped in the wind, as Quentin Phair must have heard them . . .

But he couldn't. Usually he was able to move deep into a daydream, the intense daydream world of an only child, so real that he heard nothing of what was actually going on around him. But the fact that the Bolivar portrait no longer belonged to Aunt Leonis, that it would never belong to Simon, that it had been bought by Cousin Forsyth, made it difficult for him to plunge deep into his favorite daydream of being the brave and heroic Quentin.

He felt lonely and lost. Poly and Charles were safe with their father; they had forgotten him. He closed his eyes tightly, forbidding tears, and withdrew inside himself, not onto a sailing vessel en route from England to Venezuela, but back to the known world of South Carolina and Aunt Leonis, back in time to the difficult decision to sell the portrait.

This time his concentration was deep. The sounds of the M.S. *Orion* no longer reached him. He was re-living a heavy, humid August evening at Pharaoh, the small cottage on an acre and a half which was all that was left of the once great plantation. Simon and Aunt Leonis sat on the tiny porch to their house—"shack" would have been a more realistic word, though it had once been a solid cottage—fanning themselves in slow, rhythmic movements with palm-leaf fans, rocking in quiet and companionable silence. Boz, the ancient pointer, snored contentedly at their feet. It was not yet dark, and Simon could see an expression of grief move across the old woman's face.

As though his awareness had been a blow, she put her hand up to her cheek. "Night soon," she said quietly. "There'll be a breeze later."

"Aunt Leonis, couldn't I get a job?"

"You're too young."

"But, ma'am, I could work as a field hand or something."

"No, Simon. Education is a tradition in our family, and I am going to see to it that you have yours."

"With you for a teacher, don't you think I'm educated enough?"

"No one is educated enough," Aunt Leonis said. "I am still learning. When I stop learning, you will bury me."

"That will be never, then."

"I'm an old woman, Simon, and ready to meet my Maker. I look forward to it with great anticipation. But I would prefer to be certain that you have mastered Latin, which you are not being taught at school. And next week I intend to start you on Spanish, a language I have forgotten, and which both of us surely should know."

Simon scowled. "I'm not apt to go to Spain."

"You have an ancestor who helped liberate the South American continent."

"And I'm not likely to go to South America."

"I realize that you are insular, child, but things will change, and meanwhile I will not permit you to be lazy."

"No, ma'am. But you've already taught me French."

"Next week we will start Spanish. I still have my old books."

"Buenas noches, señorita," Simon said. "¿Cómo está?"

"That is hardly adequate, and you are speaking with a French accent. And you are being ugly. Is something wrong?"

"No, ma'am."

They lapsed into silence, and darkness fell with the abruptness of the subtropics. Around them a light wind emerged from nowhere and stirred the Spanish moss in the live oaks. Aunt Leonis's fan moved more and more slowly until it stopped and rested lightly on the faded black of her dress. "Simon, I will have to sell the Bolivar portrait."

"But, ma'am, you can't! It's your most treasured thing." He was shocked and incredulous.

"It is only a thing, my son, and we must not be bound by material things."

"But, Aunt Leonis—"

"You think that I would let you go undernourished in order to hold on to some oil paint on an old, already decaying piece of wood?"

"Oh, Aunt Leonis, ma'am, let me get a job, please."

"Simon, you are not yet thirteen, and I made a promise to your parents."

"They wouldn't have wanted you to sell the portrait."

"When one nears a century, one surely should have learned not to depend on that which will rust or decay. You are the only person left in my life who has not crossed to the other side of time. I have survived much death, the loss of my only brother, of Pharaoh, of all the other things I used to believe made up the woman who is Leonis Phair. But we are not our possessions. That is one thing I have discovered. I am not sorry that I will be leaving you with no material goods. But I must leave you with enough education so that you will be able to choose the manner in which you will earn your living, and you are not getting that from the local school, particularly if you continue in your wish to be a doctor. You must be able to pass examinations and earn scholarships. I have to supplement your education. You are a good student, Simon."

"Yes, ma'am, but you're easy to learn from. You make it all fun."

Miss Leonis picked up her fan. "I will put a notice about the portrait in the Charleston papers and in *The New York Times*. I am not rushing into this unadvisedly. We have enough money to get us frugally through one more year, and by then we should have found an appropriate buyer." The summer dark was so thick that Simon could no longer see the old lady, but he reached over and took her hand in his. Her hand felt as thin and warm and dry as an old leaf. He knew full well that if she said they would start learning Spanish next week, start they would. He understood with a corner of his mind that Aunt Leonis was an extraordinary old lady, but she had always been part of his environment; now she was home, the rock on which he stood, and he could not look without flinching on another change of life which would be even more radical than the change that followed his parents' death. Without Aunt Leonis, where would he go? Who would he be?

As though following his thoughts, she said, "Quentin Phair's journals, his letters to Niniane, and to his mother in England, are in my jewel box. You might be able to sell them one day. When you are twenty-one they will be yours to read, even in the unlikely event that I am still alive, and who knows what you will learn? They are all that you will find in the box, but they will stand you in good stead. I have honored Quentin Phair's written request not to read letters or journals for six generations, which I consider a wise precaution. Even the most innocent of journals, if they are honest, contain pages which could hurt other people. It will be interesting for you to learn whether you are like him in spiritual as well as physical characteristics."

Simon demurred, "I'd rather read them with you."

"No. My memory stretches back a long way. There may be things in journals or letters which I'd rather not know."

Each month Aunt Leonis put the notice about the portrait in the papers. "We will not sell it to just anybody. It must be somebody who will appreciate and honor it."

On a cold evening in January, Cousin Forsyth Phair appeared.

Simon and Aunt Leonis were indoors, keeping warm by a lightwood fire. The resin-saturated wood burned so brightly that Simon was studying by it. He had finished his regular schoolwork and was doing the Spanish lesson Aunt Leonis had prepared for him. Together they could speak slowly but with moderate fluency, although she still deplored his French accent.

A knock on the door took them both by surprise. Aunt Leonis reached for her cane, and Boz growled deep in his throat. Simon went to the door.

They had learned to do without electricity, so he saw the man at the door only in the glow of the fire. Aunt Leonis rose rheumatically to her feet and turned on a lamp by the round table which served them as desk and dining table.

"Good evening," the man said. "Is Miss Leonis Phair in?"

"Yes, sir. Who is it, please?"

The man moved past Simon into the circle of lamplight. He was tall and thin and dark and elegant, despite stooped shoulders; his dark hair was greying at the temples and about the ears, and he held a dark hat in his gloved hands. "Miss Leonis Phair?"

She stood facing him, holding her cane as though it were a weapon. "Who are you, sir?"

"I am your cousin, Forsyth Phair. I saw your notice about the Bolivar portrait in *The New York Times,* and I have come to inquire about it."

"Hey, Simon!" It was Poly's voice.

Simon stood up, out of the protection of the lee of the ship. "Here!"

Poly and Charles were halfway across the foredeck and came hurrying toward him. Charles said, "We've been calling and calling."

"I didn't hear you. I'm sorry."

Poly asked, "What are you, deaf or something?"

"I guess I was concentrating."

Charles clambered over a bale and jumped to where Simon was standing in the *Orion*'s prow. "What a great place, Simon! How did you find it?"

"I came looking for a private place. Cousin Forsyth was in the cabin, and I thought people would be coming into the salon."

Poly put her hands on her slender hips and looked around. "You've found it, all right. We'd better check with the captain for protocol's sake, but this is it, Simon, this is absolutely it. I was wondering where we could go to escape the grownups. You're marvelous."

Simon felt himself flush with pleasure. "It's a little cold here unless you crouch down."

"It won't be cold in a couple of days. Hey, did you see that hearse with a bullet hole in the windshield?"

Simon spoke shortly. "Yes."

"Who would want to be driven in a hearse with a bullet hole in the windshield?"

"Who would want to be driven in a hearse, period?" Charles countered.

Simon did not laugh. Instead, he gave a small, involuntary shudder.

"Someone walk over your grave?" Poly asked.

Simon did not answer. He looked out at the foam breaking whitely about the prow.

Charles stuck his elbow into Poly's ribs, and she said quickly, "It's cold out here tonight, all right. Let's go in, Simon. I'm starved. How about you?"

"I'm pretty hungry, I guess."

"Charles and I looked in the galley and spoke to the cook. Dinner is going to be good. He's a super cook. I don't speak much Dutch, but enough to find out what we're eating. Come on."

"Poly thinks she speaks every language in the world," Charles said.

"I *like* languages!"

"Just stop bragging about them. Pride goeth before you know what."

Simon followed the amicably arguing brother and sister. As they approached the doorway they met the captain, dressed in a dark serge winter uniform, who greeted the children with paternal friendliness.

Poly pointed to the prow. "Captain van Leyden, is it all right if we go up there and sit sometimes? We'll be very careful, and we won't be in anybody's hair, and of course we'll stay out of the way when we're in port."

Simon added shyly, "And we can pretend we're setting out to help Bolivar free South America."

"It is all right," Captain van Leyden replied in his precise, guttural English, "as long as you disturb nothing. Do not climb into the cars, or try to open the crates."

"Oh, we won't, we promise, we'll be very careful."

The captain smiled down at them. "We do not often have children aboard."

"Why is that?" Charles asked.

"To be free to take a freighter trip means leisure, and for most people this leisure does not come until after the time of retirement. We usually have no one under sixty-five."

"Our father isn't anywhere near sixty-five," Charles said. "He isn't even fifty."

"No. We have a very young ship this time. There is not much for young peoples to do. I hope you will amuse yourselves."

"Of course we will," Poly assured him. "Everything's marvelous, Captain."

"It is cold now," the captain said, "and you and Master Simon were chilled this afternoon. You had best go in where it is warmer."

"We're just on our way. Thank you, Captain."

They stepped over the high sill and made their way along the passage and up the steps. Dr. O'Keefe, Dr. Eisenstein, Dr. Wordsworth, Mr. Theo, and the Smiths were in the salon, with Geraldo passing drinks and nuts. Simon did not see Cousin Forsyth.

"Let's go out on the aft deck," Poly suggested, "at least for a few minutes."

They walked down the port passage, past the professors' cabin, past Simon's and Cousin Forsyth's. At cabin 5, Simon paused. "This is where the Bolivar portrait is."

"Is it really famous, Simon?"

Simon pushed the fisherman's cap back on his head. "I never thought about it being famous before Cousin Forsyth came along."

"We have a portrait of our grandmother when she was young and beautiful, but it isn't famous. It's—" She stopped as a voice sounded loudly from cabin 5.

"I will not tolerate carelessness or curiosity." It was Cousin Forsyth's voice, followed by a low, indistinguishable murmur, then, "But you were trying to look at the portrait, don't deny that." The murmur came again, and Cousin Forsyth's voice was lowered, as it had been while he was talking with Dr. Wordsworth.

"Is there any reason people shouldn't look at the portrait?" Poly asked.

Simon shook his head. "Not that I know of. But it's all crated, so you can't see it."

"He certainly sounded mad at someone. Who do you s'pose?"

"I don't know."

"And wouldn't anyone have to pry open the crate to see the portrait?"

Simon shook his head again. "Beyond me."

"It's made me curious, at any rate," Poly said, but she moved on and rested her hand lightly on the handle of the fourth door. "For those like me who don't like showers, there's a bathtub in here. Geraldo says he'll unlock it for me tomorrow."

Simon asked, "Why is it kept locked?"

"Oh, things are always kept locked in ports, and he's

been so busy this afternoon, what with us falling in the drink and all, that he hasn't had time to do anything else." She started to open the door to the back deck, which was reserved for the passengers; there were lights strung up under the canvas awning, and it looked cheerful, if cold.

But just at that moment Dr. O'Keefe called from the head of the corridor, "Dinner's ready, kids. Come along."

The passengers sat at two tables: Cousin Forsyth, Simon, Mr. Theo, and the Smiths at one; the O'Keefes, Dr. Wordsworth, and Dr. Eisenstein at the other. At a third table sat Captain van Leyden; his first officer, Lyolf Boon; second officer Berend Ruimtje; and chief engineer Olaf Koster. The essential second language for these Dutchmen was Spanish, and their English tired easily, so it was simpler for the officers to sit apart from the passengers.

The captain's table was waited on by Jan ten Zwick, the chief steward; Geraldo tended the passengers. Poly was right: the food was plenteous and well prepared.

"I believe," Cousin Forsyth said in his lightly ponderous way—very unlike the way in which Simon had heard him speaking to Dr. Wordsworth—"that the chief reason freighters carry passengers is to afford a good chef for the officers. This is as good a rijstafel as I've ever tasted."

Whatever it was, thought Simon, it was delicious, and very unlike the nearly meatless diet he was accustomed to. He ate with appetite. He would have been happier at the table with Poly and Charles, where conversation was lively, with little bursts of laughter. Poly looked over and winked at him, and he winked back.

"What was that, Simon?" Cousin Forsyth asked.

Simon rubbed his eye. "Nothing, sir." He looked down at his empty plate, then across to the table where the officers were eating. Mynheer Lyolf Boon, the first officer, folded his napkin, said something in Dutch to the captain, and left.

Simon's table had finished dessert, a delectable mixture of apples and flaky pastry, well before the second table, and everyone had moved out of the dining room into the salon for coffee. Simon sat at the far end, on a long sofa under the fore windows. Mr. Theo settled himself in a chair not far off, with his volume of Shakespeare. Cousin Forsyth was talking to the Smiths, and pointing to a card table in the corner of the room near the door to the foyer. Simon closed his eyes, suddenly overwhelmed with sleep.

"Simon . . ." It was a whisper.

He jumped. Poly and Charles stood in front of him. "Oh. Hi. I was just sleepy for a minute."

Geraldo came up with a small tray of half-filled demitasses and a pitcher of hot milk, put it down on the table, and then bustled back to the other passengers.

Poly sat down beside Simon. "I'll pour. Have some, Simon?"

He nodded. "I've never had coffee before. Aunt Leonis and I drink tea."

"You may not like it, then. Put lots of sugar and milk in; then it tastes sort of like hot coffee ice cream."

Simon followed her instructions, tasted, and smiled.

"Oh, Simon," Poly said, her long legs in green tights stretching out under her plaid skirt, "I'm so glad you're you. Suppose you'd been some awful creep? Whatever would we have done, all cooped together like this?"

Simon nodded in solemn agreement. "I'm glad yawl are you, too." Now that he was relaxed, his voice was warm and rhythmic.

Poly flashed her brightest smile. "I like the way you talk, Simon. It isn't all nasal and whiny like some of the Southerners we've met."

"I was born in Charleston." It was a simple statement of fact.

Poly giggled. "Snob."

Simon blushed slightly. "I like the way you talk, too. It isn't British—"

"Of course not! We're American!"

"—It's just clean and clear. Aunt Leonis loves music more than anything in the world, so voices are very important to her. Her voice is beautiful, not a bit cracked and aged. Somebody compared her voice to Ethel Barrymore's—I guess she was some kind of famous actress in the olden days."

Poly poured Simon some more coffee and hot milk. "Hey, look at all the grownups over there, nosing each other out. And we knew about each other right away."

"Well, they didn't almost get drowned together," Simon said. "You saved my life, so that means—"

"It means we belong together forevermore," Poly said solemnly.

Charles was looking across the salon at the adults. "They've forgotten how to play Make Believe. That's a sure way to tell about somebody—the way they play, or don't play, Make Believe. Poly, you won't ever grow too old for it, will you?"

"I hope not." But she sounded dubious.

Simon pushed back a lock of fair hair from his face. "My Aunt Leonis is very good at it. Actually, she's my great-grandaunt, or something. When people get ancient they seem to remember how to play again—although I don't think Aunt Leonis ever forgot. She says you can tell about people—whether they're friend or foe—by your sense of smell, and that most people lose it."

"Fe fi fo fum," Charles intoned, "I smell the blood of an Englishman."

"It's probably our pheromones," Poly said.

"Our what?" Simon asked.

"Pheromones. They're really quite simple molecules, eight or ten carbon atoms in a chain, and what they do is send out—well, sort of a smell, but it's nothing we smell on a conscious level, we just react to it. For instance, a female moth sends out pheromones at mating time, and a male moth comes flying, but he doesn't know *why*, he just responds to the pheromones, and we're not any more conscious of it than moths. At least most of us aren't. Charles is, sometimes." She stopped, then said, "It's obvious that we're children of scientists. Maybe Aunt Leonis's sense of smell is simpler and just as good." She sniffed delicately and looked with quick affection at Simon. "You smell superb, Simon."

He sniffed in his turn. "You smell right lovely yourself. Maybe it's your red hair."

But Poly sighed. "I haven't worn a hat in years because I keep hoping that if I keep my hair uncovered and let the salt air and wind and sun work on it, maybe I'll bleach out and turn into a blonde. It hasn't shown any signs of happening yet, but I keep on hoping."

"You look right nice exactly the way you are," Simon said firmly.

He might be a year younger than she was, but Poly felt a warm glow. "Look, your Cousin Forsyth is playing bridge with the Smiths and Dr. Eisenstein. That's a funny combination."

Simon looked at the card table. Bridge was another unexpected facet in Cousin Forsyth, who was shuffling with great expertise.

"At any rate," Poly said, "we're certain about Mr. Theo."

"Certain?" Simon asked.

"That he's all right. He's a friend of Uncle Father's and that means he's okay."

"Uncle Father?" Simon asked.

"My godfather. Canon Tom Tallis. You remember, we were talking about him at tea."

"Why do you call him Uncle Father?"

Poly gave her infectious giggle. "Rosy, our baby sister, started it when she was just beginning to talk, and we all took it up. We see more of Uncle Father than we do of our own grandparents, because we live so many thousands of miles apart, but Uncle Father was in and out of Portugal for a while, so he's a sort of extra grandparent for us. And I guess I trust him more than I trust anybody in the world."

Charles said, "But he warns you about that, Pol. He says that no human being is a hundred percent trustworthy, and that he's no exception."

Poly shrugged. "I know, but I trust him anyhow.

Trust isn't a matter of reason. It's a matter of pheromones. I trust Simon."

Simon beamed with pleasure. "My Aunt Leonis
says that it isn't proper to ask personal questions. But
yawl can ask me anything you like."

Poly asked immediately, "How does it happen that
you have a portrait of Simon Bolivar in your family,
and why're you taking it to Venezuela with Cousin
Forsyth?"

Simon's eyes took on the pale grey stare which
meant that he was moving back into memory. Aunt
Leonis lived as much in the past as in the present, and
the games of Make Believe she played with Simon
were usually forays into time remembered. Simon, his
voice low and rhythmic, said, "My favorite ancestor is
Quentin Phair. He was the youngest son in a large
family in Kent. In England. In the olden days the eldest son got the title, then there was the army or the
navy or the law or the church, and after that the
younger sons had to fend for themselves. So when
Quentin Phair was nineteen and announced that he
was going to South America to help free the continent, his family didn't even try to stop him. He fought
with Bolivar, and became his good friend, and the
portrait is one painted at the time of the freeing of
Ecuador, when Bolivar was at the height of his great-
ness. Aunt Leonis said that in going to Venezuela the
way he did, Quentin really gave up his youth for
others."

"But how did you get the portrait?"

"Not me, and it won't ever be mine now. It came to
Aunt Leonis when her brother died, because he didn't
have children."

"Yes, but Quentin was English, wasn't he?" Poly asked. "How did the portrait get to South Carolina?"

"Well, when Quentin finally went home to England, his mother had just inherited a sizable hunk of property in the South of the United States, so he offered to come over and see about it for her, expecting to stay only a few weeks."

"But he took over his mother's property and stayed forever," Charles said, as though he were ending a fairy tale.

Simon smiled. "He met a young girl, Niniane St. Clair, and they fell in love and were married."

"What a pretty name," Poly said. "Niniane. She was beautiful, of course?"

"We have a miniature of her. It's very faded, but yes, she was beautiful. And when Aunt Leonis was young she looked just like her. Quentin built Pharaoh for Niniane, and all their children were born there. The landscape must have reminded him of Venezuela, especially in the spring and summer, with all the same kinds of flowers, bougainvillaea, oleander, cape jessamine, and the great, lush, jungly trees. It wasn't tamed and cultivated the way it is now."

"Pharaoh," Poly mused. "It's sort of a pun, isn't it?"

"I like it." Simon was slightly defensive.

"Well, so do I. And the portrait?"

"It's been handed down from generation to generation. It's a very special treasure. Since Aunt Leonis never married, it was to come to my mother as next of kin, and then to me. Only we had to sell it."

"But why on earth would you sell it?" Poly asked.

"We needed the money."

"Oh." Poly flushed slowly, as she had that afternoon when speaking Spanish to Geraldo over Simon's head.

"It was the last of the portraits. Aunt Leonis sold most of them when she had to sell Pharaoh—the big house and most of the furnishings and the silver and the grounds. Her father tried very hard to keep Pharaoh going, but he got into terrible debt, and when he died Aunt Leonis had to sell everything, even the portrait of Quentin Phair. But at least it stayed in the house, over the mantelpiece in the library where it's always hung. I look like him, my ancestor Quentin. I hope that when I grow up I'll be like him."

"If you had to sell Pharaoh, where do you live?" Poly asked.

"Aunt Leonis kept an acre and a bit, and we live in an old cottage. If there's a heavy rain from the northeast, the roof leaks in exactly eight places, which is a powerful lot for a small house. Aunt Leonis has various buckets and pots and pans which she puts out to catch the leaks, and she's managed to work it out so that as the rain hits each pot it plays a different note of the scale, and we have a mighty fine time listening to the different tunes the rain makes."

"Your Aunt Leonis," Charles said, "sounds like the kind of aunt everybody would like to have. Who else would have thought of making something magic about eight leaks in a roof?"

"I sometimes think Aunt Leonis doesn't enjoy it nearly as much as I do, but she never lets on that she'd really rather have the roof repaired. We have a purty little garden patch behind the house, and we have live oaks and water oaks all around to give us privacy—not that we need it; the Yankees who bought Pharaoh are only there a couple of months a year. Sometimes Aunt Leonis and I pretend that we're visiting our cottage, bringing turkey broth and custard to a sick child, and that we really live in Pharaoh, the way Aunt Leonis did when she was young. We have a right fine old time together."

Charles said slowly, "I think I love your Aunt Leonis."

"She's a great believer that all things work together for good. It's Cousin Forsyth who's come to the rescue now. And maybe that's good, but I didn't want her to sell the portrait."

Charles spoke quietly. "I'd guess that she sold it because she loves you more than she loves the portrait."

Simon nodded, and looked across the salon to where Cousin Forsyth was spreading out his cards with a flourish.

Poly's regard followed his. "How does your Cousin Forsyth come into it?"

"Out of the blue, you might say," Simon replied, and told them.

"So you really don't know him very well."

Simon looked across the salon, and thought of the conversation he had heard between Cousin Forsyth and Dr. Wordsworth. "I don't think I know him at all."

II

THE FIRST
NIGHT AT SEA

Charles and Dr. O'Keefe shared the second double cabin on the starboard corridor, and Poly had the first single cabin, next to theirs. She was in bed, reading, happy with her compact little nest, barely big enough for bunk, chest of drawers, washbasin. On the chest she had propped her favorite travel companion, an ancient icon of St. George battling the dragon, which she had taken from a calendar and mounted on a thin piece of wood. Wherever she had St. George she felt at home, and protected from all dragons, real or imaginary.

A brisk, rhythmic knock came on her door, the family knock, and Charles entered, wearing pajamas and bathrobe. "Hi. What are you reading?"

"*Wuthering Heights.*"

"Would I like it?"

"Not yet."

"I'm not that much younger than you are."

"You're a boy, and you wouldn't like it yet," she stated dogmatically.

Charles let it drop, looked around for a place to sit, and then climbed up onto the foot of her bunk and sat cross-legged, lotus position.

"I like it when you sit that way," Poly said.

"It's comfortable."

"And you didn't even know it was a special position, used by Eastern holy men when they meditate?"

"How would I know? It's a good position for thinking in."

"What do you think of Simon, then?"

Charles smiled his slow smile. "I've never met anybody before who wasn't in our century."

"What do you mean?"

"Aunt Leonis—he belongs to whenever it was she belonged to, and maybe it wasn't a whole century ago, but it certainly isn't now."

"We have to take care of him, then, don't we?"

Charles was silent for so long that Poly thought he was not going to answer. Then he said, "Someone has to. I don't think Cousin Forsyth is going to."

Poly looked interested. "What about Cousin Forsyth?"

"What Simon's Aunt Leonis calls sense of smell—"

"What about it?"

"I'm not sure. Maybe it's not Cousin Forsyth. But my sense of smell is giving me warnings."

"About what?"

"I'm not sure, Pol. I just get a sense of anger, and fear, and it's coming at me from all directions. Too many pheromones."

"Have you spoken to Daddy?"

"Not yet. It isn't definite enough."

Poly looked at her brother with absolute seriousness. "I don't like it when you get feelings."

"I like it if they're good ones."

"But this isn't?"

"It's strange. I've never felt anything like it before. It seems to come from almost everybody, and to have something to do with Cousin Forsyth, and that just doesn't make sense."

"I wish you'd speak to Daddy."

"I will, if anything begins to focus. It's all vague and fuzzy now."

"What about Simon?"

"Simon is our friend," Charles said.

Simon lay awake in his bunk. Cousin Forsyth snored. Simon had never slept in a room with anyone else before. In Pharaoh he and Aunt Leonis each had a private cubicle, his made out of what originally had been a small storeroom. He was afraid to move about lest he disturb Cousin Forsyth. He started to drift into sleep, and woke up with a jerk, dreaming that the fork lift was pursuing him, and the fork lift was alive and wild and hungry, with red eyes and smoke, like a dragon. Simon was prone to occasional nightmares, and at home he would go out to the kitchen and brew a cup of tea, and Aunt Leonis always heard him and came out to him, and they would sit and drink tea and talk until the nightmare had dissolved in the warm light of the kitchen, and he could go back to bed and sleep.

Cousin Forsyth's snoring was rhythmic and placid, but it was not a restful sound.

Then the *Orion* began to rock gently in the night swells of the ocean, and this living movement was as comforting as the lit candle in the kitchen at Pharaoh. Thoughts of fork lifts and dragons receded, and he went to sleep.

In the cottage at Pharaoh, Miss Leonis was reading by the bright light of a resiny fire. On the small table by her side lay her Bible, closed. She was not certain that consulting it had caused her to make her decision to open Quentin Phair's letters and journals, unread for so many generations, instead of waiting to leave them for Simon.

But ever since Mrs. O'Keefe had dropped her at Pharaoh, after an exhausting and stimulating afternoon, she had been restless and unable to settle down. Her sense of smell kept telling her that something was wrong, but not what that something was, except that it had to do with Simon, Simon who was miles away at sea in a small freighter heading into the Caribbean. Had she been right to accept Forsyth Phair's invitation to take his young cousin to Caracas with him? It would be a journey of less than two weeks; they would be returning by plane after leaving the portrait in Caracas. Surely this was an opportunity for Simon which should not be turned down?

—Something is wrong, something is wrong, an inner voice continued to nag. —Simon is in danger.

Had her concern over Simon's future dulled her sense of smell over Forsyth? He had come with documents tracing his descent from one of her great-uncles who had moved out West after the war. She knew that this shared ancestor had undoubtedly played politics with the carpetbaggers, but Forsyth Phair was not to be blamed for that, after all, and perhaps it was old-fashioned prejudice which made her hold this against him.

In any event, Forsyth was a Phair; his nose and chin told her that, the high-bridged, hawk-like nose— though Forsyth's eyes crowded close together, unlike the wide-spaced Phair eyes. But he had the strong chin softened by an unexpected dimple which usually turned into a formidable cleft by middle age. In Forsyth the cleft was almost a scar. Yes, he was a Phair, and hanky-panky with those who wanted to get rich on the troubles of the South was hardly to be blamed on him. His talk of his life in Caracas sounded serious, and surely it was commendable that he wanted to return the portrait to his adopted country rather than to keep it himself?

And then, Forsyth was the last of the Phairs. Simon was a Renier. The male line of Phairs had been prone to accident and sudden death.

Pride of name, she thought wryly. —Is that part of it?

Pride. Pride was always her downfall. When Simon's mother died she had concealed the fact of her poverty from the Renier relatives. They had wanted the boy to come to them, to his father's people. She had had to battle to keep him, and she respected the Reniers for letting Simon, in the end, make the choice. They would be ready to take him to their hearts when she died. They would see to it that he was properly educated, that he went to medical school. If she had asked them for money they would have given it to her. If she had asked them to buy the portrait they would have bought it—but then she might have lost Simon.

Pride. Forsyth Phair was Simon's one link with his mother's kin, with Miss Leonis, with Quentin Phair; indeed, with the very name of Phair. Not only pride was involved in her feelings here. The dying of a name was as real as the death of a person. If Simon kept in touch with Forsyth Phair it would keep the name alive a little longer.

—I am a foolish, proud old woman, she thought. —In eternity the end of the Phairs makes no never mind.

She was suddenly full of misgivings. Was Forsyth

really all that he appeared to be? Had pride of name made her too eager to accept this kind and considerate stranger who had appeared out of the blue?

She fed old Boz, and then walked slowly around the house with him. There had been sunshine in Charleston that afternoon and the air was warmer, but now the sun had set and she was glad to get back to the fire. She reached for her Bible. It opened to Nehemiah, and the first words she read were, "And Tobiah sent letters to put me in fear." This could hardly be construed as a suggestion that she open Quentin Phair's letters and journals; besides, she considered people who opened the Bible, put a pin on a word, and expected an answer to their problem, to be superstitious at the least, and idolatrous at the worst, and she wished to be neither.

"What do you think, old Boz?" She fondled the dog's ear.

The old hound sighed and put his chin heavily on her knee. Then he walked arthritically into her small bedroom, where she kept the carved wooden coffer which had once contained jewels and now held Quentin Phair's journals and letters. After a few moments she followed the dog. She took two of the journals and a few packets of letters from the coffer and returned to the fire.

She took one of the journals out of its oilskin casing and opened it at random. The ink was brown and faded, but the script was elegant and still completely legible. She read, ". . . when I returned from Dragonlake today Umara showed me our baby. It was an extraordinary feeling to take this tiny brown thing in my arms and to know that he is my seed, that his fair skin comes from me. Now 'I have shot my man and begot my man.' I am not the first, nor will I be the last, of the English regiment to leave my seed here on Venezuelan soil, but my Umara is not like the usual women we soldiers meet. Indeed, the Quiztanos seem a race apart as well as a world apart, a gentler world. I do not want to leave my son, my first son, here in this strange place, but I cannot send my Umara home to my mother and cold England. Why am I so unduly disturbed by what, after all, is nothing unusual?"

Miss Leonis closed her eyes. She sat, unmoving, until the fire died down and the room grew cold and the old dog began to whine.

In the cabin next to Cousin Forsyth and Simon the two professors prepared for bed. Dr. Wordsworth was brushing strong black tea through her luxuriant hair; Geraldo left her a pot of tea in the cabin each evening immediately after he had cleaned up demitasses and glasses. "I learned about brushing black tea into my hair at bedtime from an Armenian ballet dancer," she said, "and I don't have any grey, which at my age is not bad."

Dr. Eisenstein had heard about the black tea before. She looked at herself in the mirror, not pleased with what she saw. She reached for her toothbrush. At least she had all her teeth, which was more than Inés could say. The brownish circles under her eyes did not vanish when she had enough sleep. The study lines about her mouth and nose were graven deep; too much staring into books and not enough living. But when she could not see herself her inner mirror gave her a younger, more pleasing image. She did not feel nearly sixty. She brushed her teeth vigorously, and for a moment she was intensely irritated by Inés's glossy black tresses.

Dr. Wordsworth patted her cheeks with cotton soaked in astringent lotion. She sighed. "I wish Phair hadn't come aboard at Savannah. It's brought up a past I hoped I could forget."

"He seems very pleasant," Dr. Eisenstein said.

Dr. Wordsworth's voice was bitter. "If you will remember, my youth in Caracas was not exactly happy. I've deliberately tried to forget as much as possible."

"I know," Dr. Eisenstein murmured.

"You don't know. You didn't know Fernando."

"I know what you told me. I know he treated you abominably and made you very unhappy."

Dr. Wordsworth laughed harshly. "That's putting it mildly. I don't know why I let myself be talked into coming along with you on this trip."

"Inés, it's supposed to be a rest for both of us."

Dr. Wordsworth yawned elaborately, patting her wide-open mouth with her scarlet-tipped fingers. "I'm exhausted, all right. And I admit to being curious about your Quiztanos. Fernando was mostly Levantine, but he had a touch of Quiztano in him."

"You're still trying to understand him," Dr. Eisenstein said softly.

Dr. Wordsworth finished wiping off her face cream and threw out the astringent-soaked cotton. "No, Ruth. I'm trying to understand myself."

"Then why are you so upset about meeting an old acquaintance?"

"I don't feel logical about my past, and he reminds me of it."

"He appears to be very much of a gentleman, and he plays an excellent game of bridge."

"As long as he doesn't presume on mere acquaintance—"

"I'm sure he won't," Dr. Eisenstein reassured. "Anyhow, it's only a few more days before we debark at Port of Dragons and he goes on to Caracas."

Dr. Wordsworth got under the covers. "I look forward to your Quiztanos, Ruth. Twentieth-century civilization has lost its appeal for me."

Dr. Eisenstein put her notebooks away. She felt a stirring of envy. Fernando may have caused Inés great pain, but at least she had known life and love. There had never been a Fernando in Dr. Eisenstein's life, and she felt the poorer for it.

Simon was awakened by his cousin's stertorous breathing. It was so loud that Simon smiled into the darkness because it seemed a strange and primitive sound to be coming from Cousin Forsyth. He thought of the two professors in the next cabin and wondered if they could hear it through the walls, and what kind of conversation two such different people as Dr. Eisenstein and Dr. Wordsworth would have with each other.

Aft of Simon and Cousin Forsyth was cabin 5, the cabin with the portrait, the Bolivar portrait which was the reason for this journey. The thought that once they left Caracas he would never see the portrait again gave him a sharp pang of regret.

—Pride of possession, he thought. —Aunt Leonis told me to beware of that.

Cousin Forsyth gave an extra-loud snort which evidently woke him up. Simon could hear him turn over in his bunk and start to breathe quietly.

He lay in a strange bed on his way to a strange land. Now that the snoring had stopped he could hear again the soothing sound of wind and wave. He remembered that he had new friends on board. He tried to feel adventurous and brave like Quentin Phair. He tried to feel that one day he, too, might be a hero. The ship rocked like a cradle. He closed his eyes, turned over, and returned to sleep.

III

THE WORD *UMAR*

Captain van Leyden had teenage children of his own at home in Amsterdam, and he enjoyed the presence of the three young ones on his ship. After breakfast the next day, which pleased and astonished Simon by consisting of platters of sliced Gouda cheese, sausage, salt herring, freshly baked rolls, honey, jam, peanut butter, and boiled eggs, the captain gave them a grand tour of the *Orion*, introducing them to the crew, and then took them up on the bridge. "You may come up whenever you wish," he told them, "except when the pilot is coming aboard. Consider this to be your ship. I can see that you are careful young persons." He instructed them in detail on the use of each of the vast array of instruments, and then showed them his radar machine, of which he was obviously proud. "You see," he explained, "it not only blips around at various distances—ten miles from shore, five miles from shore, and so forth—but look: now you see a photographic representation of sea and shore at various distances— not now, of course; all we see is water. But after lunch you will be able to see Cuba, from the starboard side, and if you wish to come and look at it through the radar machine, you may."

"Oh, we do wish," Poly said. "Thank you, Captain."

"Tomorrow I will have the chief engineer, Olaf Koster, take you all over the engine room. It will be hot and dirty, so please dress accordingly."

"We will."

"You are amused?" he asked them several times.

"We're having a marvelous time," Poly assured him.

"You are not bored?"

She stretched with enjoyment. "I've never been bored in my life. And certainly I couldn't be bored on the *Orion*. Where is the hearse going?"

"To Caracas."

"What about the bullet hole in the windshield?"

"It was sold at what you would call bargain price."

"And all the big boxes and cases?"

"They contain mostly equipment for oil fields, refineries."

"The *Orion* carries almost everything, doesn't she, Captain?"

"We are an all-purpose ship."

"You know that list of cargo on the table in the salon?"

"For the information of the passengers. Jan ten Zwick made the translation."

"Maybe sometimes his English is a little peculiar."

"Peculiar?"

"Well, it says 5 *boxes reefers*. What are the reefers, Captain?" Poly was simply curious. She did not think for a moment that the little ship was carrying marijuana.

The captain looked at her in surprise. "Reeferigerators, Miss Poly. They are expensive in Caracas, and not as large as American reeferigerators. If one is successful, one has an American car, or a Mercedes, and one has an American reeferigerator."

Simon and Charles were looking at each other with laughter in their eyes, but all three of them kept polite and straight faces. Poly said, "I see. Thank you. And all the grain down in the hold?"

"That goes to various places. Port of Dragons, for one. We should see the coasts of Colombia and Venezuela by Friday evening—three more days."

Poly looked across the vast expanse of water. "That'll be exciting. But it's even more exciting to be in a small ship in the middle of the ocean and to see no land at all—almost as though we were like Noah."

The captain said dryly, "Noah, I assure you, was very happy to see land."

After lunch the three children went to Simon's place in the prow of the ship. The adult passengers had retired to their cabins for a siesta. On the promenade level two young sailors were swabbing down the deck. Others were running up and down the ladders, carrying ropes, buckets. On the boat deck a young sailor was painting the white rail, while another was polishing the brasses. The sailors smiled or waved at the children while continuing about their business.

In the prow the wind was still chill, and they were well bundled up. Ahead of them, and to starboard, was a shadow of land.

"Cuba," Poly said, "but I don't think we're going to get anywhere near enough to get an idea of what Cuba's like. I wish we could see it better. Geraldo says we'll be close enough to see something on the radar by mid-afternoon."

Simon looked at Cuba, which revealed nothing, and then down at the water, which was a deep dark blue, streaked with white caps. He braced his feet against the gentle rolling of the ship. Around the prow the water looked like fluid marble and he thought it was one of the most beautiful things he had ever seen. "Hey, look, yawl. Liquid marble, sort of the way rock must have been when the earth was being formed, only that was boiling hot, and this is cold." He shivered. Geraldo had given him an extra blanket in place of a coat, and he pulled it more tightly around him and sat on a crate of oil-well machinery in the lee of the wind. "It occurs to me," he said in his old-fashioned way, "that I answered a lot of questions last night, and there are some questions I would like to ask you."

Charles perched in his favorite position on another crate. "Ask ahead."

Poly sat on the deck between the two boys. "We ought to have a name for our place."

Simon's face lit up. "So we should! What?"

"Let's each think about it till after dinner, and then tell each other what we've come up with, and we can decide which name is best. What did you want to ask us, Simon?"

"How come you two're going to Venezuela with your father, and leaving your mother and everybody else behind?"

Charles stared up at the sky, watching the movement of the clouds, and left Poly to answer.

"Well, you know Daddy's a marine biologist, and we used to live on Gaea Island off the south coast of Portugal, and now we're living on Benne Seed Island . . ."

"Yes."

"Well, this isn't for general information, Simon. As a

matter of fact, you might call it classified. But Charles and I decided last night that we could trust you."

"Thank you." Simon bowed with grave formality.

"The Venezuelan government asked Daddy if he would come spend a few weeks at Dragonlake and study what's happening to the lake. It's a big source of oil, and you know how important oil is right now."

"Well, no, I didn't."

"What do you and Aunt Leonis heat your house by?"

"Firewood."

"Oh. Well, oil *is* important. People thought it would sort of keep spouting out of the earth forever and ever, and suddenly there's not enough, and Americans are used to having more than enough. So places that have oil are important. But at Dragonlake the oil wells are *in* the lake, they way they are in Lake Maracaibo, and in Dragonlake the fish and other marine life are dying, and if they can't find out what's causing it, Dragonlake is going to be a dead sea. Some people are saying that the dragon has been angered by the oil wells, and is drinking the oil. And maybe that's just a way of saying that if we don't take care of the earth, the earth is going to rebel. Anyhow, when the Venezuelan government asked Daddy, he decided he'd go, and take Charles and me out of school for a month and bring us with him. The reason that it's all top secret is that the oil companies might get upset, so you won't say anything?"

"Of course not."

"Daddy's purportedly going to get some unusual specimens of marine life, and of course he'll do that, too, and Charles and I can help him there. He and

Mother say that the trip and working with Daddy that way is an education in itself for Charles and me, and fortunately the principal of our school agreed. And Charles and I are due a proper vacation, aren't we, Charles?"

"Definitely."

"You two are the eldest?"

Charlies's face lit up with his slow smile which began with a quirk at the corners of his lips and spread all over his face, focusing in the deep blue of his eyes, the same gentian color as his father's. "We have five brothers and sisters—well, you saw them in Savannah—all younger than we are. If you're used to being with Aunt Leonis, we're usually surrounded by infants, and because we're the eldest, we do try to help out."

Poly added, "It would be impossible for Mother, otherwise, though she was the one who thought of having us go along with Daddy. Say, Simon, what about your Cousin Forsyth, and why didn't you think maybe he was an impostor?"

Charles looked sharply at Poly, but she was looking at Simon.

Simon answered, "He had all kinds of credentials, but I don't think Aunt Leonis would just have accepted them if he didn't have the Phair nose and chin. If you had looked at him, and then at some of the old daguerreotypes Aunt Leonis kept because they weren't salable, you'd know he was kin. He has a swarthy complexion, but otherwise he looks like the Phairs."

"You don't look like him, not one bit. You're blond as Jan ten Zwick."

"My hair comes from the Reniers. My father's family."

"Did Aunt Leonis open her arms and embrace Cousin Forsyth, like the long-lost son, and so forth?"

"Not exactly. She wasn't entirely happy about Cousin Forsyth because he comes from the branch of the family which collaborated after The War."

"Way back with the Nazis?"

"No, no, with the carpetbaggers."

"Simon, what war are you talking about?"

"The War between the States." Simon looked surprised.

Charles and Poly exchanged glances. Poly said gently, "Simon, there have been several wars since then. When you said 'The War' you sounded as though it were the only war."

"Maybe its effects are still felt more at Pharaoh than the other wars . . ."

"But slavery was bad."

"Sure it was bad. But mostly that wasn't what the war was about. Anyhow, we didn't have slaves at Pharaoh."

"You sound as though you'd been there. Why didn't you have slaves?"

"Quentin Phair. After all, he spent a long time with Bolivar fighting for freedom. He could hardly have slaves on his own plantation. It was what might be called a commune today. Everybody worked together, black and white. All the slaves were given their freedom by Quentin Phair when he built Pharaoh, and then they could choose whether to stay as part of the family, or to go. And it was the same way in my father's family, the Reniers. Their plantation was called Nyssa, and there weren't any slaves there, either."

"You're not telling us that this was typical, Simon?"

"I know it wasn't typical. But it's the way it was for

the Phairs and the Reniers, and that's where I come
from. And after the war everybody was poor, poor
unto starvation."

Poly continued to probe. "If you didn't have any
slaves, and everybody worked together, why was everybody so poor?"

"You forget we were an—an occupied country. Like
Israel at the time of Christ, or Norway with the Nazis.
Pharaoh wasn't burned the way Nyssa was. The Yan-
kee officers took it over for their headquarters, so the
house was saved. But they burned the fields and then
they salted them. It took years before the land would
yield any crops. If you've lived off the land, by dint of
very hard work on everybody's part, and the land is
destroyed, then things aren't easy for anybody."

"Oh," Poly said in a chastened way. "That's something I hadn't realized. Every time I think I know it
all I get taken down a peg, and I guess that's a good
thing. What about Cousin Forsyth's family?"

"They had money and food and clothes and luxu-
ries, and people didn't unless they collaborated with
the carpetbaggers. So you see why Aunt Leonis wasn't
entirely happy about him. Maybe it *was* like collabo-
rating with the Nazis."

"But the carpetbaggers weren't Nazis. They were
us." Poly stopped, then said, "Maybe that's the point.
Oh, dear. So what happened with Cousin Forsyth's
family?"

"They moved up North, and then out West, and we
lost track of them until the evening Cousin Forsyth
knocked on our door."

"And it was only a month ago that he came?"

"Yes. He stayed in Charleston at Fort Sumter
while all the arrangements were being made—calls to

Caracas, and our booking on the *Orion,* and every-thing. And all that month Aunt Leonis tried to make me speak only Spanish."

"Have you lived with her all your life?" Poly asked.

Simon's face hardened, and he looked older than thirteen, but his voice was calm. "I've known her all my life and been in and out of Pharaoh, but I've only lived with her all the time for five years—since my parents died."

"Oh, Simon!" Poly reached out to touch him gently on the arm. "I'm so sorry!"

Simon nodded gravely.

"Was it an accident?"

"Well, it seemed to me it was a sort of cosmic one. My mother was dying of cancer, and six months be-fore she died my father—my father had a heart attack. He died. So Mother and I moved in with Aunt Leonis, and she nursed Mother until she died." His voice was stiff and dry.

Poly's chest tightened in sudden panic. She thought she would not be able to bear it if anything happened to her parents. Charleston and Benne Seed Island seemed more than a day away by sea, and suddenly she missed her mother and her younger brothers and sisters so badly that it hurt. If only she could run to a telephone and hear their voices, be reassured of their being—but the telephone was one of the aspects of civilization that Dr. O'Keefe had said he would be pleased to do without for a while.

—No emergency, please, Poly pleaded silently. —Don't let there be any emergency.

Simon's color came back to his cheeks. "Not every-body would have an Aunt Leonis to take over. I'm lucky."

Poly shook herself, shedding ugly thoughts like water. "Let's go to the promenade deck and see what the grownups are doing."

She led the way, and as they passed the door to the cabin with the portrait, she tried the handle. It did not move under the pressure of her hand. "Oh, well, I suppose it would be locked—but if it's so heavily crated and all . . ."

"It's a nice portrait." Simon, too, tried the door. "Bolivar looks handsome, and you can actually see energy in his expression, and a sort of excitement. He looks the way a great hero ought to look."

Poly pushed the handle of the bathroom door, which opened under her pressure to reveal a long, deep tub, almost the size of her bunk. "Oh, wonderful, wonderful, I'll have a gorgeous soak this evening. I don't care if I never see a shower. I love to wallow in a hot tub. In Gaea we had the whole ocean for a tub most of the year round, but it's been much too cold at Benne Seed Island for swimming."

On the promenade deck Geraldo had put out some games for the passengers—a set of rings to toss, and pucks for shuffleboard. Dr. Wordsworth and Dr. Eisenstein, wrapped in blankets, their heads swathed in scarves, occupied two of the deck chairs. Poly led the way out the door, across the back of the deck, and then in the door to the starboard passage. "I have a hunch our two professors don't care much for the companionship of children. You can't have secrets very easily on freighters, and I heard them talking about us after breakfast." She assumed Dr. Wordsworth's voice—strong, pedantic, and with a faint trace of accent. " 'What do you make of those three children?" Her voice changed to Dr. Eisenstein's, gentler than Dr. Wordsworth's, with a touch of Boston. " 'They're moderately polite, which is a refreshing change. And they do not have the usual moronic lack of vocabulary and the mumbling speech of the affluent American young.' And Dr. Wordsworth said, 'At least they are keeping out of our hair.' And Dr. Eisenstein said, 'I wish you'd stop reminding me how gorgeous your hair is,' and changed the subject."

Simon and Charles laughed at her accurate mimicry of the two women. They passed Mr. Theo's single cabin, and came to Poly's. She ushered them in.

"I'm hardly affluent," Simon said.

Charles climbed up onto the foot of the bunk. "I know you must be poor as far as money goes. But you're not like most poor people in any other way."

"Most poor people aren't like Aunt Leonis. We're rich in education, and we're rich in tradition. We're very lucky."

Charles nodded. "I don't think we're affluent, either. We're not poor or anything, but marine biologists aren't apt to make millions, and Daddy's always having to buy expensive equipment. The Smiths like us, by the way. Mrs. Smith keeps trying to pat me on the head and tell me what a nice little boy I am, and that they have a great-grandson in San José who's very much like me. She told me, 'You're so courteous and considerate. Not like a little American boy at all.' "

"I hate that!" Poly said vehemently. "We're completely American. And anyhow it implies that all American kids are rich slobs and that's not true."

Simon, leaning against the chest of drawers, agreed gravely. "There are quite a few of us poor slobs, too."

Poly sat on the small space of floor between bed and chest, leaning against the bed. "Tell us more about you and Aunt Leonis. Why are you so poor, as far as money goes?"

"I'm not exactly sure. When my parents were alive I guess we were sort of like you—not rich, not poor. But my father had a newspaper and his business was all in his head, and when he died there just wasn't anything left over, because Mother's illness had already cost so much. Aunt Leonis says that only the very rich and the very poor can afford to be ill. I guess being poor is a lot harder on her than it is on me, because she grew up in the big house at Pharaoh, and she's the one who's gone from riches to rags." He pushed the fisherman's cap up on his head. "Everybody's so nice on this ship," he said, changing the subject, "the captain letting us watch him up on the bridge, and Geraldo giving me this cap, and all. It's almost worth having to sell the Bolivar portrait. Not quite, but almost." He swung around and saw Poly's icon. "What's that?"

"It's St. George and the dragon. I take it with me wherever I go. St. George looks so kind, even while he's being fierce with the dragon."

"Aunt Leonis and I have a dragon—a make-believe one, but he's a good dragon, and protects Pharaoh and our garden. Hey, yawl, that's what we can call our place—the Dragon's Lair!"

He looked so delighted that Poly and Charles immediately agreed that the Dragon's Lair was the perfect name.

"Because there *are* good dragons, like Aunt Leonis's and mine. He eats nothing but Spanish moss, and he sleeps curled around one of the live-oak trees, and whenever there's danger he spouts fire."

Charles asked unexpectedly, "Did he spout fire when Cousin Forsyth came?"

Simon looked uncomfortable. "Why would Cousin Forsyth be dangerous?"

"I don't know," Charles said flatly.

"Even the dragon couldn't keep Aunt Leonis from having to sell the portrait. If it hadn't been Cousin Forsyth it would have been someone else. And Aunt Leonis says that if it had to go, she's glad it's going back to Venezuela where it came from. She says that things know where they belong, and maybe the time had come for the portrait to return to its native land."

Poly scrambled up from the floor. "We've got St. George with us on the *Orion*, and he'll take care of us if we encounter any dragons that aren't as nice as yours." She stretched and yawned. "I think I'll take my bath now, before dinner. Come along and talk to me while it runs. And maybe the cabin with the portrait will be unlocked. I'd like at least to see the case."

"Who'd have unlocked the cabin door in the last fifteen minutes?" Charles asked.

The boys trailed after her, out the door to the aft deck, behind the deck chairs of the two professors, and in through the door to the port passage. Poly opened the door to the bathroom, and leaned over the tub to turn on the taps, then raised her finger to her lips. Simon started to speak, but Poly turned on him. "Shush."

There were voices coming from the cabin next to the tub room, the cabin with the portrait. A heavily accented voice said, ". . . saw the word *Umar*."

"Nonsense. You are mistaken." It was Cousin Forsyth's voice. "And you are spying again."

"I do not spy. But the word *Umar* I saw."

"Impossible."

"You remember—when we were bringing the portrait into the cabin—there was a loose board which I hammered back into place. That is when I saw it—*Umar.*"

"So? A random grouping of letters. It means nothing."

"You think that?"

"Of course. Totally unimportant."

The voices stopped. Poly bent back over the tub and turned on both taps, full force.

"We eavesdropped," Simon said.

"We listened."

"Aunt Leonis says—"

Poly held her hands under the flow of water, adjusting the taps until the water suited her. "Your Aunt Leonis is absolutely right for her world. But this isn't Aunt Leonis's world."

"What do you mean?"

"Simon, this is the end of the twentieth century. Things are falling apart. The center doesn't hold. We don't have time for courtliness and the finer niceties of courtesy—and I've learned that the hard way. Does *Umar* mean anything to you?"

"No."

"Is there something written on the back of the portrait?"

"I don't know. I never looked. Only at the portrait itself. There was never any reason to turn it around."

"That was Cousin Forsyth we heard."

"Yes."

"And the man with him had a Dutch accent. Who helped him with the portrait yesterday?"

"I don't know. It was while we were getting dry after the fork lift—"

Charles sat down on the small white stool which was the only piece of furniture in the tiny tub room. "Don't make too big a thing of it, Pol."

"Am I?" She looked fiercely at her brother.

"I don't know," Charles said.

Darkness fell more quickly at Pharaoh for Aunt Leonis than it did for Simon at sea. In the last of the light she sat on her small, sagging front porch (Simon had kept it from tumbling down altogether) and read her ancestor's journals. Her heart was heavy, and she was not sure why. His was not an unusual story. A virile young man expending his energies in fighting for the freedom of a beleaguered, overtaxed country could hardly be expected to be celibate. Wherever foreigners fight in a strange land they leave their foreign seed, and leave it probably more casually than did Quentin Phair.

"My son grows apace," wrote Quentin. "Each time I manage to get to Dragonlake he seems to have doubled in size. Already he is walking, falling, picking himself up and walking again. Like his Indian cousins he is learning to swim almost more quickly than he is learning to walk. I cannot pretend that he is not mine. I cannot forget Umara and our child. The Quiztanos are not like any of the other natives I have met in my five years here, not like the other Indians, not like the white Creoles, certainly not like the tragic, imported Africans; they are not like anybody. Dragonlake is another world. If I cannot bring my Umara and my son to England—and I cannot; Umara would not be welcomed; she would be insulted, and I will not have that—then it seems to me that when my work is done I must stay here, though I doubt if this battling the royalists will be over before several more years. What is there to take me home to England? I have become used to this country and these people and even this malaria, with which I have been bedridden for the past week. I will go back to Kent briefly—I owe my dearest mama that much. And then I will set sail for the last time and make my home at Dragonlake—if the Quiztanos will have me, and Umara says they will. My fellow officers already think me mad—Simón is the only one who understands, and he only because he is my friend—and so, then, this will be my final madness and I feel cold and strange even while my heart rejoices." Miss Leonis, too, felt cold and strange and there was no rejoicing in her heart. When Quentin wrote those words he had not yet met Niniane; the future toward which he looked with fear and joy was not the future which was to come. He did not know, as Leonis did, the end of the story—or was it the end? Did such stories end with the death of the protagonist? Or were there further scenes to be acted out before the curtain could fall?

It was too dark to read, and with the setting of the sun the shadows moved in coldly; in her warm coat the old woman shivered, and went indoors to light the fire, followed by Boz, who nudged at her hand. She moved heavily, unable to throw off the thought that Quentin Phair's drama was being continued through Simon Bolivar Quentin Phair Renier, and that Simon was in danger.

* * *

Simon, who had accustomed himself to Cousin Forsyth's snoring, slept. He dreamed that he and Dr. Eisenstein were carrying the Bolivar portrait along the edge of a deep lake; they were running, stumbling over hummocks and tussocks, because a dragon was after the portrait. Dr. Eisenstein turned into Mr. Theo, who put the portrait down, put two fingers in his mouth, and whistled loudly. The dragon came hurrying to him, puffing and panting in eagerness, and then Simon and Mr. Theo climbed onto the dragon, who soared into the sky.

It was a nice dream. It had started out to be a nightmare, and then it turned into fun.

In his sleep Simon sighed peacefully.

He woke up shortly after dawn, the memory of his dragon ride fading at the edges of his mind. Cousin Forsyth was still snoring. It would be another hour before Jan ten Zwick or Geraldo would ring the breakfast bell.

He was wide awake. For a while he tried to get back into the dream, but he could not. The dragon who had carried him aloft had vanished with daylight. The dragon had had a name. Mr. Theo had whistled, and when the dragon had come, he had called him by name. What was it? Then he remembered: *Umar.*

That was the word they had heard from cabin 5, and *Umar* meant nothing to him, although it seemed to have considerable import to whoever was talking with Cousin Forsyth. Why was something written on the back of the Bolivar portrait? Did Aunt Leonis know about it? and if she did, why hadn't she said anything?

—Probably because it doesn't mean anything. Probably because it's unimportant, just as Cousin Forsyth said.

But Poly and Charles had not thought it was unimportant.

He dressed quietly, without waking Cousin Forsyth, slipped out of the cabin, and went to the aft deck.

The air was fresh but no longer cold; the sky was soft with spring. Mr. Theo was out on deck ahead of him, leaning on the rail and looking out to sea.

Shyly, Simon went and stood beside him. Next to the O'Keefes, who were a revelation and a joy to him, he was most drawn to Mr. Theo, who sat next to him at table; and the dream had made Mr. Theo even more of a friend.

"Look, Simon," the old man said, and pointed down at the water. "Flying fish. There. Like little flashes of silver."

"Oh—oh—beautiful!" Simon exclaimed.

They stood in companionable silence, watching the brilliant brief flashings until the school of fish was left behind them. Then Mr. Theo went and sat on one of the cane chairs under the canvas awning, motioning Simon to sit by him. "We are the two early birds today. I wonder if there will be a mouse to catch."

"It's nice enough, just being here with you, Mr. Theo. And I had a dream about you last night."

"Was I an ogre?"

"No. You whistled for your dragon, and we both went for a ride on it."

The old man seemed pleased. "I have always wanted to ride a dragon. I'm sorry I didn't dream it, too."

Simon smiled at him. "You remind me of my Aunt Leonis, and I've been homesick for her."

"It's hardly a compliment to her that I remind you of her. I'm nearing eighty."

"Aunt Leonis is ninety."

"Is she!" He sounded pleased. "And how do I remind you of her, then, since I am such a young chicken in comparison?"

"She likes Shakespeare, too, especially *King Lear* and *The Tempest*. And she loves music. Dr. O'Keefe says that you're an organist, a famous one."

"Not that famous. But I am only part of a person when I am separated from an organ. Does your Aunt Leonis play an instrument?"

"She used to play the harp, until we had to sell it. And sometimes in the very early morning or in the evening she still plays the flute, though she says she doesn't have the lips or the lungs for it anymore. Are you going to read all of Shakespeare while you're on the *Orion?*"

"If I get through half a dozen plays I'll be doing well. I, too, love *King Lear* and *The Tempest*, but right now I'm reading *Romeo and Juliet*. He is like a great organ, that Will, and gives me much solace from being separated from mine. So your Aunt Leonis is ninety, eh?"

"In chronology only. Ninety and not quite a month."

Mr. Theo fumbled in his pocket and pulled out dark glasses which clipped on over his regular spectacles. "I once heard someone say that the job of the very old is to teach the rest of us how to die, and I still feel young enough so that I'm looking for someone older than I to teach me."

"Aunt Leonis does that. I'm the only person she has

who hasn't died. She was with my mother when she
died, and if someone has to die, it's good to be with
Aunt Leonis."

"Methinks she's teaching you how to live," Mr. Theo
said, "but of course they're part of each other."

They lapsed into silence, but it was a good silence.
After that brief exchange he felt completely comfortable with Mr. Theo. He could, he thought, tell the old
man things that he couldn't tell anybody else, the way
he could with Aunt Leonis. Aunt Leonis was, he supposed, teaching him about both life and death; she
had taught him how to be at least a little less enraged
at the thought of death in a world created by a loving
God.

After his mother's death the local minister, Dr.
Curds, had come to call, and had immediately alien-
ated Simon by talking of this premature death as the
will of God.

Aunt Leonis looked down her long, aristocratic nose
at the middle-aged man in his dark suit. "I wonder
how it is, Dr. Curds, that you are so certain that you
understand the will of God?"

Dr. Curds looked at her with patient gentleness.
"You must not fight the Lord, my dear Miss Phair.
Trust in his will, and he will send you the Comforter."

"Thank you. I believe that he has already done so. I
also believe that my niece's illness and death were not
God's will. I doubt very much if he looks with approval on such suffering. It seems to me more likely
that it has something to do with man's arrogance and
error. However, being mortal and finite, I do not presume to understand God's will, so I am not certain."

Dr. Curds murmured something about it being part
of God's plan.

Aunt Leonis replied, "It may be part of God's plan that a young woman should suffer and die, or it may be the work of the enemy."

"The enemy?"

"Don't you believe in the devil, Dr. Curds? I do."

Dr. Curds murmured again, "The Church in these more enlightened times . . . the devil seems a little old-fashioned."

Aunt Leonis raised her left eyebrow. "I haven't noticed many signs of enlightenment. And I am undoubtedly old-fashioned. But I do believe that God can come into the evil of this world, and redeem it, and make it an indispensable part of the pattern which includes every star and every speck of hydrogen dust in the universe—and even you, Dr. Curds."

Despite his grief, Simon nearly laughed.

"Hello there, young Simon. Where were you?"

"Oh—Mr. Theo—I'm sorry. I was remembering."

"You go deep into your memories."

"Too deep, Aunt Leonis says."

"Was that a good one?"

"No. It was bad, except for Aunt Leonis. It was about when a minister came to call on us after my mother died, and he was horrible, and Aunt Leonis put him in his place. Do you believe in God, Mr. Theo?"

"I do. It would be difficult to have lived as long as I have and to think that one can get along without God."

"Well, I'm glad you and Aunt Leonis believe in God."

"Don't you?"

"I'm not as old as either of you, and he let my parents die."

Mr. Theo apparently changed the subject. "Do you know why I'm on the *Orion*, Simon?"

"For a vacation?"

"Partly. My doctor ordered me to go by sea rather than air. But mostly I'm on the *Orion* because I'm going to Caracas to hear the first concerts of the pupil who is dearest to my heart. When she was ten years old she was blinded in a vicious accident. But she didn't moan and groan about God's allowing such a cruel thing to happen. She just went on with her music."

"Am I moaning and groaning?" Simon asked.

"You're not far from it, are you?"

Simon closed his eyes and clenched his fists. Then he relaxed and smiled. "You really and truly are like Aunt Leonis. I'm going to get on with it, Mr. Theo. I really haven't moaned and groaned for a long time. It just isn't possible to do much moaning and groaning around Aunt Leonis. This is the first time I've been away from home, and I guess I've regressed. Mr. Theo, does the word *Umar* mean anything to you?"

"Umar?" Mr. Theo repeated. "No, I don't think it does. Should it?"

"It was the name you called the dragon. Don't say anything about it, if you don't mind."

"Very well, *Umar* shall be between the two of us. There goes the breakfast bell. Are you hungry?"

"Starving."

* * *

Cousin Forsyth had made it clear that in the morning after breakfast he wished to have the cabin to himself while he shaved, so Simon wandered out to the promenade deck. The wind was brisk but the sun was warm. Dr. Eisenstein was settling herself in a deck chair with a plaid steamer rug to wrap round her legs, and a straw basket stuffed with academic-looking magazines and several spiral notebooks. Simon took the ring toss and moved to the far end of the deck, but after he had tossed several rings, missing the post with most of them, he realized that she was looking at him. She smiled at him welcomingly and he crossed the deck to her and bowed politely.

"It must be very dull for you young ones traveling with us old folk."

"Oh, no, ma'am, not in the least dull. We're having a lovely time."

"Self-sufficient, eh? Don't need to be amused? What about television?"

"We don't have one, Aunt Leonis and I."

"Most unusual for your generation. What are your interests?"

"Well, ma'am, I'd like to hear about the Indians you're going to visit."

Dr. Eisenstein's eyes gleamed. "The Quiztanos?"

"Yes, ma'am."

"They are of particular interest to the anthropologist because they are one of the very few tribes to remain virtually unchanged in numbers and culture—you see, usually when a country is taken over by a higher civilization, the native strains diminish radically in number, or change from their old ways. Most of the other Indian tribes in this section of South

America have either dwindled in number while their culture has deteriorated, or, on the other hand, they have adapted to the ways of the invaders. Los Dragones peninsula was one of the first places on the South American continent to be visited by Spanish explorers in the sixteenth century, but neither the land, which is thick jungle, nor the comparatively small number of Indians invited conquest. And they were not welcoming. According to Dr. Wordsworth's old Guajiro Indian nurse, the legend that the Quiztanos are waiting for a young white savior from across the sea evidently postdates the sixteenth century, possibly even the seventeenth. I'm not boring you?"

"No, ma'am." —But Aunt Leonis makes learning more fun.

"I'm not used to talking to young children."

"I'm not that young, ma'am. I'm thirteen."

"Thirteen, eh? I'll try not to be too dry. But I find it fascinating that long after the Spaniards came, long after the Quiztanos knew white men, and what white men did to the Aztecs, they should acquire a legend about a young white man who will come to them from far away."

"Yes, ma'am. That's right interesting."

"The source of this legend is one of the things I hope to discover when I go to the Quiztano settlement, though I may need a Guajiro contact. Evidently the Quiztanos and the Guajiros have been involved in smuggling together for many generations, and the smuggling trade today is less innocent than it was when the colonists were oppressed by Spain."

Out of the corner of his eye Simon saw Poly and Charles emerge from the starboard passage and stand waiting for him. His mind was more on them than on the Quiztanos, but he maintained his expression of courteous interest.

"Los Dragones peninsula, with its almost unpopulated coastline, has been easily accessible to small smugglers' boats, especially since the Dutch occupied Aruba and Curaçao in the early years of the seventeenth century."

"Yes, ma'am."

"After the wars of independence, when the border between Venezuela and Colombia cut across the southern side of both the Dragones and Guajiran peninsulas, smuggling became even more active." Suddenly she realized that she did not have Simon's full attention. She turned slightly and saw Poly and Charles in the background. "Your friends are waiting for you. And here comes Inés—Dr. Wordsworth—looking for me."

"Yes, ma'am. Thank you. That was very interesting. I'd like to hear more."

"Would you, honestly?"

"Yes, ma'am. Really and truly."

"We'll get together again, then, shall we?"

"Yes, thank you, ma'am." He left Dr. Eisenstein and he and Poly and Charles repaired immediately to the Dragon's Lair.

Dr. Wordsworth pulled a deck chair beside Dr. Eisenstein. "I see you've found your proper level."

"That's a highly intelligent boy."

"Because he was listening to you ride your hobbyhorse?"

Dr. Eisenstein raised her eyebrows. "You're in a fine mood this morning."

"That blasted Phair. I dreamed about Fernando last night. I haven't dreamed about Fernando for years."

"Try to forget him," Dr. Eisenstein urged. "Anybody who'd let you take the rap for his smuggling activities isn't worth dreaming about."

"Not only his smuggling." Dr. Wordsworth's voice shook with irritability. "Mine, too. You don't seem to understand that smuggling is as natural a part of my background as juggling income tax is with some of our reputable colleagues. My father was a highly successful dealer in jewels, and so was his father before him, and a good part of their business involved smuggling." She looked at a chip on one of her nails. "Poor Ruth. Have I shocked you?"

Dr. Eisenstein spoke with sympathy. "It must have been horrid for you when you found out."

"I didn't 'find out,' as you so kindly put it. I always knew. Our family, like many other early colonials, was forced by the Spanish throne into smuggling as a way of life long before I was born."

The tenseness in her voice made her friend look at her sharply, but all Dr. Eisenstein said was, "It seems somewhat like the problems my own ancestors in New England had to cope with—such as the Boston Tea Party."

"Something like. But for us in South America it was even more intolerable."

"But why so much smuggling?"

"Dear Ruth. You know a great deal about primitive tribes and very little else. Colonists were not allowed to export any products except to Spain. The ships belonged to Spain. All prices were fixed in Madrid—Madrid, mind you—by people who knew nothing of the supply or demand in Venezuela." Her voice was bitter.

—But at least she's not thinking about Fernando. "I do see how unfair it was," Dr. Eisenstein said.

"You know how excellent our wines are, and our olive oil?"

"Superb."

"They were superb in the early days, too, but the colonists were stopped from planting vines and olive trees because they were forced to buy wine and oil from Spain, at high prices. And any interprovincial trade tried by my forebears was exorbitantly taxed. So do you see how smuggling of wine and oil and spices and all the things we ourselves could grow became inevitable?"

"I suppose I do," Dr. Eisenstein said.

"It was not the kind of criminal activity I can see you think of all smuggling as being—unless it's your precious Quiztanos."

"No, no—"

"We never went in for blackmail or extortion. We were not like Fernando, who blackmailed as he breathed. And he was willing to sell anything to anyone—jewels, oil-well parts, wine, drugs, women. He almost sold me, but I preferred jail."

"Oh, Inés." Dr. Eisenstein leaned forward in her deck chair and clasped her small hands about her knees. "Don't keep at yourself this way."

"I want a drink," Dr. Wordsworth said.

"This early?"

"Coffee."

"All right," Dr. Eisenstein said. "I'll ring for Geraldo. How about a game of gin rummy?"

"You're very kind, Ruth," Dr. Wordsworth said. "Sometimes I wonder why you put up with my bad temper. Yes, by all means let's play gin."

* * *

It was warm and comfortable in the Dragon's Lair.
The breeze had summer in it, and Simon took off his
fisherman's cap and let the wind ruffle his hair.

"What were you and the professor talking about?"
Poly asked curiously.

"She was telling me about the Quiztano Indians.
She's a very nice person. She doesn't know much
about children, but once I'd persuaded her I was thirteen and not three she treated me like a human
being."

"Look at that sort of olive mist of mountains on the
horizon." Poly leaned out to sea and pointed. "That's
Haiti. Geraldo the Herald Angel says we're still tech-
nically in the Windward Passage, but once we get to
Haiti we'll be in the Caribbean. I'm sort of sorry we
aren't stopping in Haiti."

"How about being Norsemen today for a change,
Simon," Charles suggested. "There *is* a theory that
they actually got to South America."

"They got almost everywhere," Simon said. "May I
be Leif Ericson?"

They moved only halfheartedly into their game of
Make Believe, and Charles broke out of it to say, "Simon, I went to Pharaoh last night."

Simon raised his left eyebrow in a commendable
imitation of Aunt Leonis.

"In a dream."

Poly asked with interest, "Was it a regular dream, or
a special dream?"

"A special dream."

Simon asked, "What's a special dream?"

Charles leaned on the rail and gazed down at the churning marble water. "It's hard to describe. It's much more vivid than a regular dream, because it's much more vivid than real life—I mean, when I go to a place in a special dream I see it much more clearly, I'm much more aware than I am most of the time in everyday life."

"Do you have special dreams?" Simon asked Poly.

"No. Charles is the only one. The rest of us just dream common garden-variety dreams."

"Me, too. Except that last night I dreamed that Dr. Eisenstein and I were trying to save the portrait from a horrible dragon, and then Mr. Theo whistled and the dragon turned out to be friendly, like the one at Pharaoh, and Mr. Theo and I rode him up into the sky, and Mr. Theo called him Umar. Charles, please tell me your dream about Pharaoh."

"It was just the way you described it. In the dream it was very early morning, barely dawn, and Aunt Leonis went into the kitchen to make tea in a dented copper kettle."

"Did I tell you about the kettle?" Simon demanded.

"I'm not sure. Maybe. Do you remember?"

"No."

"Anyhow, I'm sure you didn't describe everything in the kitchen, and I could tell you where each cup and saucer is, each pot and pan. And the way Aunt Leonis was dressed, in an old-fashioned long cotton dress, white, with little blue flowers. Does she have a dress like that?"

"Yes." Simon nodded uncomfortably.

"You see, Simon, when we were on the wharf in Savannah, waiting to board the *Orion*, Poly and I saw Aunt Leonis, remember?"

"Yes."

"And what we see gets recorded in our memory, and most of the time we draw on our memory only in bits and pieces. But when I have a special dream it's all more complete than I could possibly remember."

"She didn't have on the blue and white dress that day."

Charles sighed. "I know. Well. I saw Aunt Leonis going out to the kitchen. You were still asleep. And she said good morning to the kettle, as though it were an old friend, and she talked to it while she filled it with water and put it on to heat; and she talked to the fire while she built it in the stove—paper and wood and then a couple of chunks of coal."

"Yes," Simon corroborated.

"Then, while the water was heating, she went outdoors and spoke to an old tin watering can in the same way, and filled it from an old hose, and then she watered her plants, her camellias and gardenias, only she didn't call them gardenias—"

"Cape jessamine," Simon supplied.

"That's right. And then"—Charles continued to look down at the water, away from Simon and Poly—"then she talked to your mother."

"You mean in the dream it was before my mother died?"

"No. Your mother was dead. But Aunt Leonis was talking to her."

Simon did not speak for a long moment. Then he said, "Yes. I know. She does that. I wish I could. Aunt

Leonis says she's so old she's already partly on the other side, and that's why she can talk to things, like the kettle, and to people who aren't here anymore, people even longer dead than my mother. She sometimes talks to Niniane."

"Not to Quentin?"

"I think only Niniane, because they're somehow specially close. She doesn't speak about it often, even to me, because she says she knows it makes me uncomfortable, and she's afraid if anybody else hears about it they'll think she's gone dotty from old age. And, she says, maybe she has."

"Do you think she has?" Poly asked.

"She's the most sane person I've ever met."

Charles turned from his contemplation of the sea. "Does it make you uncomfortable, my having dreamed about her that way?"

"Yes. But I'm getting used to being uncomfortable." He tried to laugh.

"Do you mind?"

"No. I don't understand it, but I don't mind. And I want you to come to Pharaoh in real life."

"It couldn't be any more real. But I want to come."

"When we all get back from Venezuela, maybe your parents will bring yawl to visit us?"

"Of course they will," Poly said. "Wild horses couldn't keep us away. We belong together, Simon. You and I almost drowned together, and now Charles has been to Pharaoh, and that makes us family."

"I'm glad," Simon said. "It's very nice to have a family."

* * *

After lunch Jan ten Zwick, the chief steward, invited them into his cabin, which was at the starboard end of the foyer, between the salon and the starboard cabins. It was not much bigger than Poly's cabin, but the bunk was higher, and the space underneath was filled with drawers with recessed brass pulls. There was a desk with a portable typewriter, and pictures of Jan's parents and his younger brothers and sisters. The photograph of the father was much as Jan might look in another twenty years—square-featured, a little heavy, with straw-colored hair, and completely Dutch. The mother, on the other hand, was dark and exotic-looking, though overweight. The children were a mixture of dark and fair.

Poly examined the picture of the children assembled about their mother with interest. "Your mother doesn't look Dutch."

"She isn't."

"You look Dutch. You look like your father. But your mother looks—well, not Oriental, maybe Indian."

"She is half Quiztano Indian. Her mother was a Quiztana, my grandmother."

"From Dragonlake?"

"Yes. They are nowhere else, the Quiztanos."

Charles said, "That ought to please Dr. Eisenstein. Isn't she doing an in-depth study of the Quiztanos? You ought to be able to give her a lot of input and feedback and help her finalize her foci."

Jan looked baffled and Poly giggled, explaining, "He's just using educationese jargon. Don't pay any attention. But Dr. Eisenstein probably will want to ask you all kinds of questions."

"Oh, please, please—" Jan spread out his hands imploringly. "I did not think. I would much rather that Dr. Eisenstein does not ask questions. It is a matter of time. I have much work to do. And I think she does not understand my people."

Poly said wryly, "A particularly primitive and savage tribe, didn't she say? Or was it Dr. Wordsworth?"

"It has to be Dr. Wordsworth," Simon said. "I'm sure it wasn't Dr. Eisenstein, not after the way she talked this morning."

"We won't say a word, Jan," Poly promised. "We don't want anybody bloodsucking you."

"She does not understand. We are a very old civilization. We have forgotten more than the New World remembers."

Simon said, "We won't say anything, we promise. But don't you want to set her right about things? Dr. Eisenstein is really interested, she really is."

"There is no point. To people like Dr. Eisenstein and Dr. Wordsworth, different is the same thing as savage."

"I really don't think that's true of Dr. Eisenstein," Simon started, and gave up.

Jan smiled. "It is all right. I am proud of my Quiztano blood."

Poly asked, "Have you been to Dragonlake?"

"Many times, now."

"Jan, we're going to Dragonlake, you know. Would it be possible for us to meet any of your relatives? Am I asking something awful?"

"No, Miss Poly. I know that you are not like the professors. Geraldo tells me how simpático he finds you. If we are at Port of Dragons long enough I will take you to see my many-times-grandfather, Umar Xanai."

Poly dug her elbow into Simon's ribs. "What did you say your grandfather's name is, Jan?"

"Umar Xanai."

"It's an—an interesting name."

"It is part of my name," Jan said. "I am Jan Umar Xanai ten Zwick. My mother is Umara, after her mother and grandmother. There are many Umars and Umaras among the Quiztanos, Polyheemnia."

"Poly," she corrected automatically.

"But it is a beautiful name, Poly-heem-nia." He sounded the syllables lovingly.

"Maybe I'll like it one day. I don't like it now. Do you like your name?"

"It is important to me. Jan is the name also of my father and of my grandfather, both seafaring men. As you know, Umar is the name of my grandfather."

"Jan, do you speak Quiztano?" she asked.

"A little. A few phrases. It is a deep language."

"How many languages do you speak?"

Charles grinned at Simon. "Here we go again. She's off."

Jan answered Poly. "I speak Dutch, Spanish, which of course is necessary in my work, and a reasonable amount of French, German, and English. It is a constant astonishment to me that well-educated Americans, such as travel with us, should be so unproficient in languages, and show no interest in learning them. I understand from Geraldo that you speak excellent Spanish."

"Well, we lived in Portugal. Simon speaks quite well, too."

"I speak French better, though," Simon said.

Jan pointed to his typewriter, on which he was typing out the menu for the following day.

"Why do you do the menus in French?" Poly asked.

"Because the French have the great cuisines. And for my own amusement." He pointed to the word *rognons* on the menu for lunch, and gave them a very young grin. "I heard Dr. Eisenstein say that she cannot abide kidneys. Our chef cooks *rognons* superbly. I wonder if she will know she has eaten kidneys?"

Poly giggled. "Jan, you're a snob."

Charles said, "So are you."

"Okay, probably I am." —It had to be Jan who was in the cabin with the portrait the day before, she thought. Again she nudged Simon.

Uncomfortably he turned to Jan. "Did you help Cousin Forsyth with the portrait? Getting it into the cabin next to ours and all?"

"Yes. He seems very concerned for it."

"It's valuable, I guess."

"That I quite understand. But it is completely safe on the *Orion*. No one would trouble it."

"Well—of course," Simon said. "I know that. Thank you for letting us come see your room, Jan."

"*Es su casa,*" Jan said.

Poly led the way swiftly to the promenade deck. The Smiths and Mr. Theo were stretched out on deck chairs, wrapped in blankets. "I would have thought it would be too windy for them," Poly muttered, and climbed the steep stairs to the small upper deck with the lifeboats. The captain had showed them how the lifeboats worked, and warned them never to stand in the space between the deck rail and the lifeboats. 'You could slip and fall into the ocean,' he cautioned. 'Always stand by the rail.'

Now Drs. Wordsworth and Eisenstein were briskly walking the small span of deck. Dr. Eisenstein smiled at the children. "This appears to be our only way to exercise, and we have to be careful not to walk into the captain's laundry." She indicated a small line on which flapped several snowy handkerchiefs, undershirts, and underpants.

Dr. Wordsworth added, "Fifteen paces each length, and forty paces the full walk from starboard to aft to port. We are trying to walk at least three miles a day."

"We like to exercise, too," Poly said politely.

Simon and Charles followed her back down the stairs, through passage and foyer, downstairs again, past the galley, where they waved at the chef, and out onto the deck.

Charles asked, "Why didn't you come here in the first place?"

"I called my shots all wrong. I thought everybody'd be in the salon or in their cabins. Now we know who was in the cabin with Cousin Forsyth yesterday. It was Jan. And no wonder he was interested when he saw his name on the back of the portrait."

"But it doesn't make any sense," Simon cried. "Why would one of Jan's names be on the back of the Bolivar portrait?"

"We have to find out."

"Should I ask Cousin Forsyth?"

"No." Charles spoke quickly. "If Cousin Forsyth knows, he certainly wasn't telling Jan yesterday. And he didn't want Jan poking around the portrait, that's certain. I wouldn't ask him if I were you. It's more than just yesterday, and what we heard. I just—well, don't say anything to Cousin Forsyth, Simon. I'm not sure exactly why, but I just know you shouldn't."

Poly said, "Simon, when Charles knows something—

I mean, knows it with his pheromones, sort of, not with his thinking mind, then you have to take whatever it is that Charles knows seriously."

"I think I would always take Charles seriously anyhow."

"Simon, you're so nice." Poly took his hand in a swift gesture of affection. "You're too nice for the end of the twentieth century. I worry about you."

"I'm all right, and I'm not very nice."

"Umar," Poly repeated. "Just keep your eyes and ears open. And if there's anything to report . . ."

"Oh, I'll tell you," Simon said. "The portrait has always been a treasure, a happy treasure, and now I feel kind of funny about it and I don't like feeling that way. Why on earth should it have one of Jan's names on it? That makes me feel very peculiar. I wish I could ask Aunt Leonis."

"Daddy says if there's an emergency we could use the radio room," Charles said.

Poly scowled in thought. "This isn't an emergency. Yet."

"Anyhow," Simon said, "we don't have a telephone. That's why Cousin Forsyth just arrived instead of calling. The nearest phone is at the filling station a mile down the road. Is it all right if we don't think about it for a while? Can we be Quentin Phair and Bolivar and his sister again?"

IV

A STRANGE GAME
OF BRIDGE

By the third day at sea the blankets were put away and the Caribbean sun was warm on winter-white skin. The captain and the officers had changed from winter serge to summer whites, and Jan told the children that in the afternoon the sailors would fill the pool. The 'pool' was a large wooden box at the end of the promenade deck; it had a lining of heavy plastic, and would be filled with ocean water by a large hose which lay coiled like a boa constrictor aft of the deck. The pool was hardly big enough for swimming, but Jan said the crew enjoyed splashing about in it when the weather was hot, and the passengers were welcome to use it, too.

The breeze was warm and moist. Dr. Eisenstein and Mrs. Smith still carried sweaters, but Simon, Poly, and Charles went to the Dragon's Lair dressed for summer. It seemed as though they had been at sea for weeks. They found it no trouble to keep to themselves, mostly in the Dragon's Lair, leaving the promenade deck for the adults.

"Which I think they actually appreciate," Poly decided.

"It's not that I don't like old people," Simon replied, "but these aren't like Aunt Leonis. But then I don't suppose anybody is like Aunt Leonis."

Poly leaned against a box of oil-well equipment.

"It's a wonder we aren't sick and tired of Aunt Leonis. But we aren't—we love her," she added swiftly.

Reassured, Simon nodded. The sun was warming and comforting him. He pulled Geraldo's fisherman's cap forward to keep the sun off his nose. "What do you want to be when you grow up?" he asked the two O'Keefes.

Charles countered, "What do *you* want to be?"

"A doctor. I haven't decided yet whether or not to be a people doctor, or to go into research, to stop heart attacks or cancer from ever happening."

"Then there'd be something else," Poly said. "People do die. We have a life span, just like every other organism."

"It's supposed to be threescore years and ten," Simon said.

"Yes. Okay. I understand. You'll be a good doctor, Simon. I'll come to you."

Charles said, "I want to be a kind of people doctor myself."

"What kind?"

"Well, I don't want to do research, or to be a psychiatrist, and I don't think I want to be a philosopher or a priest—"

"Although my godfather is a priest, remember," Poly said.

Charles continued thoughtfully, as though she hadn't interrupted. "I want to take care of all of a person—body, mind, and spirit. It will probably mean getting several kinds of degrees, a medical one, and maybe a theological one."

"I don't think much of church." Simon looked dour.

Poly said, "That's a lovely dream, Charles, but may I remind you how many years of school are involved?"

Charles smiled his slow, bright smile. "Sometimes I'm glad I haven't inherited Mother's talent for math. If I counted I might never begin. But it's what I want to do and I plan to do it." He spoke with quiet conviction.

Simon nodded, then looked at Poly. "What about you, Pol?"

"I don't know yet. Not that I haven't thought about it. Our grandmother—Mother's mother—is a bacteriologist and a biologist with two earned doctorates; she won the Nobel prize when she isolated farandolae within a mitochondrion."

"You expect me to understand what you're talking about?" Simon asked.

"Not before you study cellular biology. I don't understand it very well myself. Anyhow, I don't think I want to be a cellular biologist or a chemist or anything. Mother's a whiz at math; Daddy says she could get a doctorate with both hands tied behind her back, but she just laughs and says she can't be bothered, it's only a piece of paper. I'm not sure what I want to be. You and Charles are lucky. I think you'll be a marvelous doctor, Simon."

But Simon scowled ferociously. "What's the point of being a doctor if people die anyhow? If we find the cure for cancer and then people die of something else?"

"Of course there's a point. You can care about people, and about their lives. And you can help take away pain, and stop people from being frightened. Of course there's a point. You have to be a doctor."

"If I can get scholarships."

"You'll get scholarships," Poly promised grandly. "If

you want something badly enough and aren't afraid to work you can usually get it."

"I'll hold on to that thought." He sounded grave. "I wish you were right."

"I'm always right," Poly said, and before the boys could pounce on her she jumped up and ran across the deck.

"She's off to talk to Geraldo," Charles told Simon. Simon raised his left eyebrow.

"Geraldo is teaching her Dutch."

Simon grinned. "With a Spanish accent?"

"His Dutch is probably pretty good. He's been on a Dutch ship since he was twelve."

Simon's smile vanished. "He's not twelve now."

"No. But he's only seventeen and Poly's fourteen, and Geraldo is the first male friend she's ever had who wasn't lots older. Why do you think she calls him Herald Angel?"

"Because the *G* in Spanish sounds like an *H*."

"You don't think maybe she thinks he looks like an angel? He is extremely handsome."

"I hadn't noticed."

"Oh, come on, Simon. He has beautiful classic features, and beautiful black hair and huge eyes with lashes so long they'd look funny on anybody except a Latin."

"I know Geraldo's nice-looking," Simon said. "And he's our friend, too, not just Poly's."

"True, but it's different."

"Well, it shouldn't be."

"Why shouldn't it be? Come on into this century, Simon."

"I'm not at all sure I like this century. Does your father feel the same way that you do?"

"About what? This century?"

"Poly and Geraldo."

"We haven't exactly discussed it. But Daddy has sharp eyes and ears, and his pheromones work as well as mine."

Simon sighed. "I suppose we could be Quentin Phair and Bolivar for a while, but I don't feel much like that right now. Let's go see if the pool is filled."

In the evenings it was already looked upon as established procedure that after dinner Forsyth Phair would play bridge with old Mr. and Mrs. Smith and Dr. Eisenstein. The first officer, Mynheer Lyolf Boon, often stood behind one of them, kibitzing, though he refused to take a hand.

Simon, Poly, and Charles were sitting quietly in the background, finishing their sweet coffee, and in a pause in their conversation they heard Cousin Forsyth saying in his calm, reasonable way, "I'm not suggesting that we play for enormous stakes, after all. I doubt if any of us has either the money or the gambling instinct. But it's more fun if we play for a penny or two a point—gives a fillip to the game."

Mr. Smith's old voice was slightly quavery. "I'm sorry, Mr. Phair. I do not play for money."

Dr. Eisenstein said, "But for only a penny—"

"Not even for a penny. I enjoy the game, but if you want to gamble, then ask one of the others." He cleared his throat and his dewlap quivered and he mumbled something about his religion forbidding any form of gambling.

Mr. Phair looked pointedly at Mr. Smith's after-dinner drink of whiskey and soda.

Dr. Eisenstein looked toward Dr. Wordsworth, who said sharply, "Sorry, I don't play bridge."

Dr. Eisenstein looked at her in surprise, but did not pursue the matter.

Dr. O'Keefe smiled. "Afraid I don't, either. Never had time for it."

Mr. Theo, when questioned by Dr. Eisenstein, looked up from his book, shaking back his yellowish hair, which had a habit of falling across his face. "You would not want to play with me. I ace my partner's deuce, or whatever you call it. I am better off to stick with *Romeo and Juliet*."

"One of Shakespeare's more inept plays," Forsyth Phair said. "He does not understand the Latin temperament. The deaths of the young lovers would have increased the enmity between Capulet and Montague rather than making peace."

Mr. Theo made no comment but returned to his reading.

Mr. Phair turned to the first officer, who was leaning against the door frame between salon and foyer. "Mynheer Boon?"

"No, no, thank you, no. I'm on duty in a few minutes."

Old Mrs. Smith looked anxiously at her husband. "Odell, dear . . . couldn't you . . ." Her gnarled hands fluttered over the green felt of the card table.

Mr. Phair shuffled the cards with an expert riffling. "No sweat, as the kids would say." (Poly, Simon, and Charles exchanged glances.) "We'll play as we have been doing, for points. No money. I'd never want to disturb anybody's religious scruples. Now let's see, Dr. Eisenstein, you and I were five hundred points ahead of the Smiths last night. Let's see if we can't give them an even bigger trouncing tonight."

Mr. Smith wiped the back of his neck with his handkerchief, as though the room were extremely warm. As a matter of fact, the evening was breezy and quite cool. Jan ten Zwick, coming into the salon to see if more drinks were needed, noted the curtains blowing straight out from the prow windows, and lowered them.

"Let's go." Simon put down his cup.

"I think I'll go on the upper deck and take a walk," Dr. Wordsworth announced in her penetrating voice. "I find that the Dutch food, delicious though it is, weighs heavily on me, especially that superb pastry. This afternoon I walked a hundred and seventy-five laps, and I doubt if it was two miles."

The children rose, and Dr. Wordsworth preceded them to the foyer, then turned down the starboard passage to the aft deck, from which she climbed up to the boat deck.

Poly whispered, "I wonder if the captain's warned her about not standing between the rail and the boats?"

Charles said, "I like to sit there sometimes, with nothing between me and the ocean. But I'm very careful."

"You'd better be." Poly looked around. Dr. Wordsworth had vanished. Geraldo was in the galley washing out the coffeepot, waiting until he could clear the after-dinner coffee cups, and the glasses, and wash up and go to bed. He smiled and waved at them as they turned to go downstairs.

"He's hardly any older than I am," Poly said.

Simon said, "He's a *lot* older than you are."

"Only three years."

"I'm twelve. Do you think Mother and Daddy would let me go to sea?" Charles said. "I'm the same age Geraldo was when he started."

"No."

"Why not?"

"Such things are beyond logic." She led the way down the stairs.

Charles said, "What about Geraldo's parents?"

"We're affluent compared to Geraldo's family. He has a whole lot of brothers and sisters and his parents were relieved when he got a job and they had one less mouth to feed. Listen, what was all that about?"

"All what?" Simon asked crossly, still concentrating on the unwelcome thought of Geraldo being more important to Poly than Simon.

"Around the card table."

"It was about bridge," Charles said reasonably, jumping over the high sill between passage and deck.

"It wasn't just about bridge. They were all trying to pretend that it didn't really matter whether or not they played for money—but it did matter."

"Especially to Mr. Smith." Charles picked his way carefully through the dark shadows between cargo, heading for the prow.

"And Cousin Forsyth," Simon said. He did not understand Cousin Forsyth.

Poly detoured around the hearse. "Adults are strange. And they seem stranger as I start to become one of them."

Simon seated himself on a keg. "I think it's stupid to play games for money, even if you have money to

spare. But Cousin Forsyth wasn't suggesting high—
watchamacallem—high stakes."

"It was all more important than it was." Poly leaned
over the rail and looked at the slightly phosphorescent
spume breaking about the prow of the *Orion.* "Which
is what's so peculiar about it. Dr. Eisenstein would
have liked Dr. Wordsworth to play, and Dr. Wordsworth wasn't having any of it—as though Cousin Forsyth had suggested they play for a thousand dollars a
point or something."

Simon thought he knew why Dr. Wordsworth didn't
want to play with Cousin Forsyth, and he wished he
felt he could tell Poly and Charles about the conversation he had overheard.

Poly continued, "And Mynheer Boon wasn't about
to play, either. He sounded almost frightened at the
idea, and I don't see why it would be that out of line
for an officer to play cards with the passengers for a
few minutes. Now, Daddy and Mr. Theo were casual
about saying no; it really was just because they aren't
much for card games."

Charles leaned back against the rough paint of the
rail. "I like Mr. Theo—and thank heavens he said to
call him Mr. Theo. I can never remember Theoto—
whatever it is."

"Theotocopoulos," Poly said. "I can remember it because it was El Greco's real name, and El Greco's my
favorite painter in the world."

"You're a walking encyclopedia," Charles started
automatically, then said, "Sorry, Pol, I know you love
El Greco." He stared up at the stars, at constellations
in completely different positions from those in the sky
above Benne Seed Island or Gaea. "Those two profes-

sors are a funny combination. Dr. Wordsworth looks like a Spanish opera diva, and Dr. Eisenstein has sort of Norwegian hair, what with those brown-grey braids around the top of her head."

"She's got a very big nose for a Norwegian," Poly said.

"How do you know Norwegians don't have big noses?"

Poly settled herself in a more comfortable position. "As we said, adults are peculiar."

A voice called from the gangway. "Simon! Simon!"

Simon sighed. "Cousin Forsyth. Every time his hand is dummy at bridge he decides he'd better be cousinly about me and send me to bed." He called, "We'll be right in, sir. Don't worry. We won't be more than five minutes."

"I'd prefer you to come now." Mr. Phair moved around boxes and bales, disappeared in the shadow of the hearse.

"All right." Simon rose.

"We'll come, too." Poly stood up, shaking out the pleats of her skirt. "I've got a book I want to finish. Here we are, Mr. Phair. You can go back to your game. *Umar!*"

Mr. Phair's dark form stiffened. "What was that you said?"

"What was what?" Poly sounded over-innocent.

"What you said just now, that word."

"All I said was that we were coming and you could go back to your game and then I yawned." But she grabbed Simon's wrist in a steel-strong clamp. "See you at breakfast, Simon."

V

NOCTURNE

The passengers of the *Orion* usually retired early. Occasionally Dr. Wordsworth and Dr. Eisenstein lay out on the small back deck for half an hour or so, their deck chairs pulled out from under the shading canvas, so that they could study the stars. They were very serious about this, and it seemed to Simon that they forgot to notice the beauty of the night sky.

But this night they were in their cabin early, Dr. Wordsworth brushing her black tresses with the ritual tea. Dr. Eisenstein, in brown cotton bathrobe, looked up from her notebook. "Inés, what on earth did you mean by saying that you don't play bridge? You know you play a far better game than I do."

Inés Wordsworth did not deny this. "I just didn't want to play with that bunch."

"Why? What's wrong with them?"

"Oh, Ruth, the Smiths are thousands of years old. I got a peek at her passport—she's eighty-one, and he's obviously older. They're sweet and all that, but they're dull old fuddy-duddies."

"What about Phair?"

Dr. Wordsworth knew how to swear picturesquely in a good many languages. She brought all of them into use, while Dr. Eisenstein put down pen and notebook in amazement.

A slow tear trickled down Inés Wordsworth's cheek

and she wiped it away furiously. "My God, to think that I was once in love with that desiccated fop!"

"Oh, my dear!" Dr. Eisenstein cried. "I'm so sorry—how dreadful for you."

"Forsyth, forsooth," Dr. Wordsworth said, and blew her nose furiously. "At least it does begin with an *F*."

"You don't mean—you can't mean—Mr. Phair is Fernando?"

"Aren't you being a trifle slow? Fernando Propice: Forsyth Phair: F.P. both, and Propice does mean *fair* in English. And for him I went to jail. Is it so surprising that I tried to put the past behind me?"

"My dear," Ruth Eisenstein said slowly, "of course it is behind you. But it is not good to bury things. They will always erupt and in that way they may even destroy you. I hate to see you in pain, but I think that it may be a very good thing for you to come to terms with the past. It will always be part of you, and until it is acknowledged and put in its proper perspective it will always be able to hurt you."

Dr. Wordsworth lay still in her bunk, looking away from her friend.

Dr. Eisenstein put away her notebook and pen and got into bed.

Still looking away, Dr. Wordsworth said, "You may be right. Thank God he's going on to La Guaira. I'll be better when we get to Lago de los Dragones and your Quiztanos. Perhaps it will do me good to talk about the past. I know you want to help me. I'm very grateful."

"Nonsense." Dr. Eisenstein turned out her light. The curtains were drawn across the portholes and the room was dark and stuffy. That morning Geraldo had folded their blankets and put them on top of the wardrobe. Dr. Eisenstein thought of turning on the fan and decided it was not quite warm enough for her thin blood.

Through the darkness came Dr. Wordsworth's voice, back in control. "Thank God my father was English. My temperament is basically far more Anglo-Saxon than Latin."

Dr. Eisenstein barely stopped herself from laughing. "We have been colleagues for nearly twenty years and I have yet to find an Anglo-Saxon trait in you."

"You've always been deceived by looks. I meet a situation with reason. That is an Anglo-Saxon trait. The Latin crashes into everything with emotion."

"And that," said Dr. Eisenstein, "is a generality."

Jan ten Zwick, still in his white uniform, sat at his desk and finished tallying the day's accounts. His cabin was hot and the fan did little to cool it. His blood, unlike Dr. Eisenstein's, was not thin. And he was disturbed. He decided that he would go up on the boat deck, where Dr. Wordsworth walked laps, and that he would stand in the breeze for a few minutes before going to bed. He locked the drawer where he kept money and records, and left his cabin, crossing the foyer and walking down the port passageway so that he would pass the cabin with the Bolivar portrait.

As he went by he put his hand against the handle, but the door, as usual, was locked, and the handle did not move to his touch. He had keys to all the cabins, but he did not go in. No use risking further unpleasantness.

—Umar, he thought. —Umar. Why should a Quiztano

name be written on the back of the portrait? What
else is written there? If that one board had not come
loose as we were carrying the case into the cabin, I
would never have seen that much. What possible reason could there be for a Quiztano name to be written
on the back of a portrait of Bolivar that was given to
an American? Umar. Umar. It is very strange. Perhaps
I will talk about it to Mynheer Boon.

In his tiny cabin next to Poly's, Emmanuele Theotocopoulos prepared for the night. He read an act of
Romeo and Juliet—an inept play!—then turned out the
light. Within easy reach of his hand—and the cabin
was so compact that anything he might need was in
easy reach—was a worn music manuscript of Bach organ preludes and fugues. He knew them so well that
it was unlikely that he would need to refer to the music. He lay on his back, his mane spread out on the
pillow, and let the music fill the cabin. He heard it as
he himself had played it during his many years as Cathedral organist; the small cabin grew and expanded
until harmony and counterpoint overflowed the ship
and spread out into the ocean. He felt relaxed and at
peace. He looked forward with joy to Emily Gregory's
first public concerts; he felt little anxiety; she was a
superb musician, with the depth and power of suffering behind her technique, a musical wisdom far beyond her age. He looked forward to taking her to
some of the great restaurants, to being proud of her.

The girl, Poly O'Keefe, just growing out of gawki-
ness, reminded him of his pupil, despite Emily's black
hair and Poly's flame. But they were more or less of
an age, moving into adulthood with a kind of steel-

spring stubbornness and an otherworldly innocence almost as acute as that old-fashioned boy's, Simon's.

He was both surprised and annoyed to have the great strands of the fugue broken thus by thought: thoughts of the girl he was sailing across an ocean to hear; of the three children on the ship. He was, for no logical reason, worried about his three young traveling companions, and since Mr. Theo was both a Greek and a musician he paid attention to such illogical notions.

He sat up in his bunk. —I am too old to be bothered with children. And there is nothing wrong. They are all quite safe. Dr. O'Keefe is as loving a father as I've ever come across, and Mr. Phair treats young Simon as though he were a piece of Venetian glass. Phair: harrumph: there was something odd going on around that bridge table.

He pushed the unwelcome thoughts away, went back several phrases in the music to pick up the theme, lost it again. It was not only the niggling, irrational worry about the children, or a sense that there had been unexplained tension at the bridge table that was interfering with the music: it was the heat. He realized that they had moved into sultry weather and he was damp with perspiration. He had always disliked hot weather; why hadn't he had sense enough to get on a ship with air-conditioning? He hated airconditioning, that's why.

The cabin was too small. Even with the door open, the drawn curtains kept out the breeze. The little fan did no more than recirculate warm air. He decided to go out on deck. Dr. Wordsworth was right; they were eating too much and exercising too little. He would make several laps around the deck. It would not be as good exercise as playing a great organ, but it would have to suffice.

Charles sat on his bunk, lotus position, and watched his father getting ready for bed. After Dr. O'Keefe had finished brushing his teeth, and would therefore be able to respond, Charles said, "Are you missing Mother?"

"Very much."

"Poly and I miss her, too."

"I know you do, Charles, but you're enjoying the trip, aren't you?"

"We're having a fabulous time. But you can have two very different feelings simultaneously. You miss her differently from Poly and me, don't you?"

"Yes." Dr. O'Keefe pulled on his pajama bottoms.

"And the kids—Poly and I miss them, but that's different, too."

"I suppose it is, Charles." Dr. O'Keefe turned on the fan over the washbasin.

"And I guess they miss us. But it's really a good kind of missing, because we know it's only for a month, and then we'll all be together again, and maybe we'll love each other more because of not having seen each other all that time."

Dr. O'Keefe stretched out on his bunk. "Maybe we'll appreciate each other more, but I doubt if I could love your mother or any of you kids more than I already do."

"But love always has to grow, doesn't it?"

"Yes, Charles. You're quite right." Dr. O'Keefe had an idea that his son was leading up to something, so he lay back and waited.

"When Aunt Leonis dies, what will happen to Simon?"

"I suppose his Cousin Forsyth would take care of him."

Charles was silent for so long that his father decided the conversation was over, without really having gone anywhere. But Charles said, "There's something wrong about Cousin Forsyth."

"Why do you say that?"

"I don't know. I just know it. The way I know things sometimes."

Dr. O'Keefe did not contradict his son. It was quite true that occasionally Charles knew something in a way not consistent with reasonable fact. It was odd, and it was disturbing, but there was no denying that it happened. "What do you want me to do, Charles?"

"I don't know. It's all vague and foggy. There's something wrong, and I don't know what it is. I wish we weren't getting off at Port of Dragons day after tomorrow and leaving Simon alone with Cousin Forsyth. I'm afraid, Daddy."

Dr. O'Keefe did not scoff. "It's not till day after tomorrow, and I'll keep a close eye on both Simon and his cousin in the meantime."

"Thank you, Daddy. If the worst comes to the worst, could we stay on the ship till La Guaira?"

"I doubt it, Charles. Let's hope there's no reason to."

"All right. I'm not sleepy. I think I'll go talk to Poly for a few minutes."

"Please don't worry her about this, Charles."

"I wasn't going to. But it's hot tonight."

When the boy had left the cabin, his father stared at the ceiling for some time, thinking. Charles's intuitions were too often right for comfort, and he found himself wishing, along with his son, that they were not leaving Simon with Cousin Forsyth when they docked at Port of Dragons. There was something unpleasant about Forsyth Phair, despite his rather Latin courteousness. That bridge game, for instance. It had seemed to Dr. O'Keefe that Phair was baiting old Smith, and enjoying his discomfiture. But why? It also seemed to Dr. O'Keefe that Phair had taken uncommon trouble to learn about his fellow passengers.

—I know that I am well known in my field, he thought, —but Phair knows more about my experiments with starfish than I would expect a layman to know. And I think he suspects that I am going to Dragonlake for more than my own personal interest in marine biology.

But Phair, he hoped, did not know that in one section of Dragonlake starfish were no longer able to regenerate when they lost an arm. Or that on shore there had been reports of death as a result of industrial effluents poured into the lake. Or that there were rich and ruthless industrialists who would resent interference.

He picked up an article on mercury poisoning and tried to read, but he could not concentrate. Had he been foolish to bring Poly and Charles with him on this journey? Was he bringing them into danger? Had he, in his single-minded devotion to science, underestimated the greed and brutality of those to whom money and power are more important than human life?

He must warn Poly and Charles again not to mention that he was going to Dragonlake at the urgent request of Venezuela.

* * *

Mrs. Smith was preparing for bed, brushing her soft, sparse white hair. She took out her dentures and placed them carefully in a dish of water in which she had dropped a cleansing tablet.

Mr. Smith came through the curtains in the doorway.

Mrs. Smith, toothless, lisped, "Thay, Odell, where have you been?"

"Up on deck, having a cigar." He began to undress, folding his clothes carefully.

Mrs. Smith hurriedly cleaned her dentures and fitted them back in her mouth. When she spoke, her speech was clear but her voice was tremulous. "Odell, you made too much of it."

"Too much of what?" He folded down the top sheet and lay on his bunk, reaching for a paperback novel set in Costa Rica.

"Playing for a penny a point. It sounded as though—"

"As though what?"

"We lost last night. It sounded as though you didn't want to pay if you lost . . ."

His mouth set in a rigid line. His voice was tight. "I can't, Patty. Not even . . ."

She sat on the side of her bunk and looked at him across the narrow width of cabin. "Everybody thought it was strange."

"You mean Forsyth Phair thought it was strange."

"All right. But he did."

"I'm sorry, Patty, but I'm like an alcoholic. You know that. I cannot and I will not start gambling again."

"But you're cured. It's been over fifty years since—"

He looked at her over the book. "Patty, you know it cannot be cured. That you of all people should want to tempt me . . ."

Her soft lips trembled and quick tears rushed to her eyes, which were magnified by heavy cataract lenses. "I'm sorry, Odell, I didn't mean—but I'd thought the past was over, that we could forget it—and one fear got the better of the other. If Mr. Phair should make the connection—"

Mr. Smith snapped, "I had been gone from the bank and back in the United States for ten years before Forsyth Phair came to work in Caracas. Everybody on the ship knows we are going to Costa Rica to visit our granddaughter and her family. It's a pleasure trip for us, and we've been looking forward to it for months. There's no reason anybody should think of Caracas in connection with me at all, or even know that we ever lived there. You're just imagining things. Mr. Phair will get off at La Guaira with his precious portrait of Bolívar, and we can forget it as though it was all a bad dream."

Mrs. Smith got into her bunk and picked up the baby's bootee, now almost finished. "Oh, Odell, I hope so. I hope so. You paid back every cent of the debt; you've had a good name all these years. Oh, Odell, why does it have to come back to hurt us all over again?"

Captain Pieter van Leyden was on the bridge, but ready to turn the helm over to Lyolf Boon. The sea was calm; he expected no difficult weather conditions, and the report for Port of Dragons was clear.

The radar was void of disturbance. Not even a fishing boat marred its serenity.

Lyolf Boon looked at his captain; Van Leyden's face was frequently stern; he ran a tight, albeit happy ship. Even though he permitted the guitar and flute and the sound of singing as long as the work was done, and well and promptly done, he seldom smiled or sang himself. At this moment he was frowning, not in an angry way, but as though he was worried about something; and he did not immediately hand the vessel over to his subordinate.

Boon checked the radar, found no cause in sea or sky for anxiety. He had learned early that it was not wise to ask questions of the Master of the *Orion*, so he continued to look at the ship's instruments, finally saying, "An interesting group of passengers this voyage."

"They are a pleasant change from our usual elderly types. I like children. They are happy, not spoiled or noisy."

Boon agreed. "The girl isn't much now, but give her a few years and she'll have every sailor looking at her."

"A few years and a few pounds." The captain nodded. "Geraldo seems to find her already attractive. Perhaps we should have Jan speak to him—though I do not think Geraldo will overstep."

"Geraldo is a Latin." Boon grinned. "Latins always overstep."

Van Leyden turned away from wheel and instruments, paused at the doorsill, and moved back toward his second-in-command. "There is one passenger—"

Boon waited.

It seemed that Van Leyden would leave without completing his sentence, but at last he said, "I will be glad when we reach La Guaira. Not that I have anything to fear personally, but I have met Mr. Forsyth Phair once before—though I think he did not have the same name. It was on my first voyage." He paused. He did not see the sudden look of surprise in Boon's eyes. "He made life extremely difficult for the Master of the ship."

There was another long silence, which Boon broke at last. "He does not seem unusually demanding. Quite the contrary."

Van Leyden shrugged. "On my first voyage—I was only a seaman but I had eyes and ears—Mr. Phair went to the authorities when we docked at La Guaira and made accusations about carelessness in accounting for cargo. In the end it was impossible to prove that my captain had tried to pocket money for oil-well machinery, but it was also impossible for him to prove that he had not. However, I knew my captain. He would never have been caught in any kind of petty thievery or smuggling. The matter was dropped, but my captain wrote out his resignation as Master of his ship, and I will never forget the look in his eyes as he said goodbye to us all in Amsterdam and we knew he would not be going to sea again."

Silence once more. The *Orion* slid quietly through the night.

Van Leyden went on, "The young man made a public apology. 'If I was mistaken in this matter I am truly sorry. But we all know that there is considerable dishonesty over cargo.' I did not feel that this was an adequate apology. I loved and honored my captain."

Boon asked, "How on earth did you recognize him after all these years, particularly if the name is not the same? Are you sure?"

"I would take my oath on it. One does not easily forget one's first voyage, especially such a voyage. The moustache is the same, and the nose and jaw, with that deep cleft. There is the same look to the eyes. The moment I saw him in Savannah, that first voyage of mine flashed before my eyes. I do not think I am mistaken."

"Only a few days more," Boon said, "and he will be gone. But why would he have a different name?"

"Many men find occasion when a change of name is helpful."

"True," Boon agreed. "I can think of one or two myself. Perhaps I should tell you a rather strange thing. Jan ten Zwick came to me just a few minutes ago with an odd story of a Quiztano name painted on the back of Mr. Phair's portrait of Bolivar—not just any Quiztano name, one of Jan's names. He seemed very concerned over this. I told him that it was probably no more than a coincidence, and asked him if he was absolutely certain of what he had seen. Apparently a board came loose on the crate as they were carrying it into the cabin, and he saw *Umar* written there. He said he went back later to verify this, and Mr. Phair came into the cabin and was extremely angry and disagreeable. I thought the whole business totally unimportant, but under the circumstances perhaps it is wise to mention it."

The captain sighed. "Are there still rumors that the Quiztano treasure is somewhere around the Lake of Dragons?"

"There are always rumors. The treasure of Dragon-

lake is in the lake itself: the oil. But that is not colorful enough for some imaginations. It had not occurred
to me that Jan might be wondering about the treasure, but that is possible. He told me once that the
Quiztanos are awaiting the return of some Englishman who fought with Bolivar, fell in love with a beautiful Quiztano girl, and disappeared. They've apparently learned nothing from the Aztecs. But I don't pay
too much attention to his Quiztano fairy tales."

The captain turned to leave. His face moved in one
of his rare smiles. "I am just as happy that we are not
carrying an Englishman with us." He looked out to
the horizon where sea met sky and no land was to be
seen dividing water and air. "In any event, I will be
glad when Mr. Phair leaves the ship at La Guaira and
takes his portrait to Caracas. I would like to know how
he got hold of such a portrait, and what he is being
paid for it."

"I understand that he is giving it to the Bolivar Museum in Caracas."

"People like Mr. Phair do not give away valuable
things for nothing."

Simon undressed and brushed his teeth and drank a
glass of ice water from one of the two thermoses
which Geraldo filled morning and night. Cousin Forsyth had not yet come to bed.

Simon knelt on his bunk and looked out his porthole
into the warm dark of sea and sky. The ocean was
calm, and he could see starlight reflected in the water.
They would be at Port of Dragons too soon for comfort, and Poly and Charles would be leaving, and he

was homesick for them in advance, which, in turn, made him homesick for Aunt Leonis, for his small cupboard of a room, for the wind stirring the Spanish moss in the live oaks, for old Boz, and for the dragon who was a vegetarian and ate only Spanish moss.

He sighed, pressing his cheek against the porthole frame, and looked out to the horizon where sky and water mingled. The light breeze was wet and salty.

He thought of being on the *Orion* without Poly and Charles and unaccountably shivered. —Am I moaning and groaning again? he asked himself, shook himself slightly, and then sang softly:

> *I met her in Venezuela*
> *With a basket on her head.*
> *If she loved others she did not say*
> *But I knew she'd do to pass away*
> *To pass away the time in Venezuela,*
> *To pass away the time in Venezuela.*

His mother had sung that song to him. Aunt Leonis had given him back the song by singing it, too. At first he had not wanted to hear it, but she had said, "Don't put away the things that remind you of your mother because they hurt, Simon. It will hurt much worse later on if you try to wipe out such memories now."

> *I gave her a beautiful sash of blue,*
> *A beautiful sash of blue,*
> *Because I knew that she could do*
> *With all the things I knew she knew*
> *To pass away the time in Venezuela,*
> *To pass away the time in Venezuela.*

It still hurt, but it was a bearable pain, and it was, at this moment, more nostalgia than anything else; the song was Aunt Leonis's song even more than his mother's, because it was Aunt Leonis, long before Simon was born, who had taught it to his mother.

He lay down on his bunk on top of the sheet. Cousin Forsyth still did not come, and he felt that it would be discourteous to turn out the overhead light and let Cousin Forsyth fumble in the dark. It was hot. Almost as hot as in the summer at Pharaoh. A sadness surrounded him like the breeze, a sadness which had nothing to do with reason.

He thought of going to Poly's cabin and knocking and asking if he could come in and talk for a few minutes, but she had said she wanted to finish a book. Nevertheless, he stood up and pulled on his worn seersucker bathrobe. He left the cabin and went past the galley, through the foyer, and down the starboard passage. He paused at Poly's cabin; the door was open and he could see the light through the flowered curtains, but somehow he hesitated to go in uninvited. He went on, past Mr. Theo's cabin, out onto the back deck, and up the steps to the upper deck. Here he stood between the rail and one of the lifeboats. He remembered the captain's warning, and stepped back slightly, but the sea was calm and was moving with very little roll, and as long as he kept one hand lightly on the rail he would be perfectly safe.

The old song kept going around in his head.

> *When the moon was out to sea,*
> *The moon was out to sea,*
> *And she was taking leave of me*

I said, Cheer up, there'll always be
Sailors ashore in Venezuela,
Sailors ashore in Venezuela.

The melody was minor and haunting and reminded him not of Venezuela, which he still had never seen, but of South Carolina. All those generations ago the land around Pharaoh reminded Quentin Phair of Venezuela, and perhaps Simon would feel a flash of recognition when he stepped on Venezuelan soil, but now he imaged only a small, comfortable shack protected by oak trees hung with moss.

He looked up into the sky and the stars were so close and warm he could almost feel their flame. The stars at home were clear, too, because they were not near any city lights.

He moved, within himself, back in time, as he and Aunt Leonis had so often done together. Now, standing on the *Orion,* on the way from one world to another, he remembered the first days after his mother's death—days he had not thought of since that first year. But his pre-breakfast conversation with Mr. Theo had for no explainable reason brought it all back. Neither Mr. Theo nor Aunt Leonis would want him to moan and groan, and he didn't intend to. But when a memory flickered at the corners of his mind he had learned that it was best to bring it out into the open; and rather than making him sorry for himself, it helped him to get rid of self-pity.

The time of his mother's dying had been a time of limbo; it was not until they left the cemetery that he realized completely that both his parents were dead and that he was starting an entirely new life with Aunt Leonis. After the numbness of shock had worn off, a strange irritation had set in; it was worse than moaning and groaning. The smallest trifle sent him into a rage. Soap slipped out of his fingers onto the floor. His socks wouldn't go on straight. Aunt Leonis overcooked the rice. He was furious with the soap, the socks, the rice, furious with Aunt Leonis.

She remained patient and unperturbed.

The humid South Carolina heat thickened and deepened, and although he was used to the heat and it had never bothered him before, now it added to his anger. 'There's no use going to bed. It's too hot. My head's as wet as though I've been swimming.'

Aunt Leonis looked at him quietly over her half-moon spectacles, then put down her knitting—she was making him a sweater. 'Let's go for a walk. If there's any breeze around, we'll find it.'

But no breath of air was moving. The night shadows seemed a deepening of the heat. The stars were blurred. The Spanish moss hung limp and motionless from the trees. The old woman and the boy moved under the thick shade until they had left the trees and stood under the wet stars.

'Look at them.' Aunt Leonis pointed skyward. 'They're all suns, sun after sun, in galaxy after galaxy, beyond our seeing, beyond our wildest conceiving. Many thousands of those suns must have planets, and it's surely arrogant of us to think of our earth as being the only planet in creation with life on it. Look at the sky, Simon. It's riddled with creation. How does God keep track of it all?'

'Maybe he doesn't,' Simon had said.

'You're thinking, perhaps, that he didn't keep very good track of your mother and father.'

Simon made no answer.

Aunt Leonis continued to look up at the stars. 'I don't know about you, Simon, but I get very angry with God for not ordering things as I would like them ordered. And I'm very angry with your parents for dying young. It is extremely unfair to you.'

'They didn't do it on purpose,' Simon defended hotly. 'They didn't mean to die. They didn't want to die.'

He was so deep in the reliving of that evening that he did not sense the dark presence moving slowly toward him.

He heard only the old woman's voice. 'I am aware of that. But it doesn't keep me from being angry. Nor you. You've been angry all week, Simon, but you're taking it out on the wrong things. It's better to take it out on God. He can cope with all our angers. That's one thing my long span of chronology has taught me. If I take all my anger, if I take all my bitterness over the unfairness of this mortal life and throw it all to God, he can take it all and transform it into love before he gives it back to me.'

Simon dug his hands into his pockets. 'If he has all of these galaxies and all of these stars and all of these planets, I wouldn't think he'd have much time left over for people.'

The dark figure moved slowly, silently, closer to Simon.

* * *

Unaware, Simon continued to look out to sea. He heard Aunt Leonis, her voice as clear in his memory's ear as though she were present.

'I somehow think he does. Because he isn't bound by time or quantity the way we are. I think that he does know what happens to people, and that he does care.'

'Why did he let my father and mother die, then?'

'We all die to this life, Simon, and in eternity *sooner* or *later* doesn't make much never mind.'

'I don't want you to die,' Simon said.

The dark figure was nearly on him. Hands were stretched out toward him. One quick push would be all that was needed. Simon was standing exactly where the captain had warned them not to stand.

From the shadow of the deck came another figure who grabbed the arm of the first. The first figure jerked away and turned with incredible speed to streak down the steps and disappear into the shadows.

His pursuer, equally swift, leaped after him.

Simon had heard nothing. He reached across the ocean to the woman who had given him life as much as if she had borne him.

'I'm a very old woman, Simon, and in the nature of things I don't have a great deal longer to live. But I've already so far outlived normal life expectancy, and I'm so fascinated by the extraordinary behavior of the world around me and the more ordered behavior of the heavens above, that I don't dwell overmuch on death. And I'm still part of a simpler world than yours, a world in which it was easier to believe in God.'

'Why was it easier?'

'Despite Darwin and the later prophets of science, I grew up in a world in which my elders taught me that the planet Earth was the chief purpose of the Creator, and that all the stars in the heavens were put there entirely for our benefit, and that humankind is God's only real interest in the universe. It didn't take as much imagination and courage then as it does now to believe that God has time to be present at a deathbed, to believe that human suffering does concern him, to believe that he loves every atom of his creation, no matter how insignificant.'

Simon leaned against the guardrail. He whispered, "O God, I wish I believed in you." So even at a distance the old woman's influence worked in him. He sighed deeply, at the same time that he felt strangely relaxed, as though Aunt Leonis had actually been with him there on the deck.

The breeze lifted, lightened, cooling him. He was ready to go back to the cabin. And he felt no need whatsoever for any more moaning and groaning.

Poly lay propped up on the pillows in her bunk. She liked the tidiness and snugness of her little cabin; it gave her a sense of protection and peace. She was finishing the last few pages of *Wuthering Heights* and it was good to be in a warm place while she was feeling the chill wildness of Emily Brontë's Yorkshire.

The O'Keefe rhythmic knock sounded on her doorframe.

"Come in, Charles," she called, and he pushed through the curtains. "Sit on the foot of the bed and wait a sec. I've just got two more pages."

Charles sat, lotus-like, at the foot of the bed, but his face held none of the tolerant merriness of a Buddha. When Poly closed the book with a long-drawn sigh, he said, "Pol, do you think Cousin Forsyth likes Simon?"

"He certainly overprotects him."

"But does he *like* him?"

Poly hesitated. Then she looked directly at her brother. "No. I don't think he does. Does Simon feel it? Has he said anything?"

"No. But Simon is not an idiot. If Cousin Forsyth doesn't like him, he's had lots more chance to sense it than we have."

"I don't think Cousin Forsyth likes children. Period. As a matter of fact, I think he's a xenophobe. But how could anybody not like Simon?"

"You like him because he likes you. Liking someone isn't a reasonable thing. It's a sense, like seeing and hearing and feeling."

Poly nodded. "Yah. Okay. Pheromones. But I still think Cousin Forsyth doesn't much like anybody. Now that you've brought it up, Charles, I've had the feeling since the first night that he wishes we weren't on the ship, taking Simon away from his watchful eye."

"You'd think he'd be grateful to us for getting Simon out of his way."

"He isn't."

"I know he isn't. What I want to know is why."

A timid knock came on the doorframe. Poly called out, "Who is it?"

"Simon."

"Oh, come in, come in."

Simon pushed through the curtains. "I saw your light was still on and I heard you talking so I thought maybe you wouldn't mind if I came in."

"Of course we don't mind, Simon. Have some bed."

Simon perched on the edge of the bunk. "This is the first hot night, and it's not really hot. Not the way it gets in the summer at home."

"It was cold when we left Savannah," Poly said. "That must be why we feel it. Benne Seed Island gets hotter than this, too, and so did Gaea."

Charles asked, "Simon, is anything wrong?"

Simon looked down at his bare feet—Cousin Forsyth would not approve—and said, "Nothing wrong. I was just going back into the past."

Poly put her hand lightly on Simon's knee. "We're going to miss you when we get off the ship day after tomorrow."

"I don't even like to think about it," Simon said.

"Let's not, then. Let's just remember we have all day tomorrow to be together. Hey, Simon, do you like your Cousin Forsyth?"

Simon did not answer.

"I probably shouldn't have asked."

"Oh, that's okay. I didn't answer because I don't really know. He keeps telling me that I'm like a son to him, and how happy he is that we can be together. But I don't think of him as a father, or even an uncle-ly sort of person, and I don't think he really feels fatherly about me. So that's why I didn't answer. Aunt Leonis has never said that she feels like a mother to me, but I know she loves me. And I don't love her like a mother. I love her because she's Aunt Leonis. And I

guess maybe I don't much like Cousin Forsyth. I feel
that I ought to, but there's something—I don't know,
but I don't think I like him. There."

Charles said, changing the subject in his own calm
way, "Speaking of special dreams, I had one last
night."

Simon turned and looked at him.

"It was a good one," Charles said reassuringly. "It
was one of those brilliant pictures, with all the colors
more alive than they ever are when we just see them
with the awake eye. I think it must have been Dragonlake—I'm going to check it out with Dr. Eisenstein
sometime. I was looking at a great, beautiful lake,
with small grass-roofed cabins up on stilts out in the
water, and a forest behind. And I saw a dugout canoe
with two people in it. One was an Indian, a girl, with
huge velvet eyes and delicate features and skin that
lovely rosy-bronze color. The other was a young man,
not an Indian. In fact, he looked very much like you,
Simon, except that he had dark hair and he was grown
up. When I woke up I thought, —That was Quentin
Phair. It was a beautiful picture. Just one lovely flash
and then I woke up."

"It couldn't have been Quentin Phair," Simon said.

"Why not?" Poly asked. "After all, he was in Venezuela for a long time. He could perfectly well have
gone to Dragonlake at least once."

But Simon shook his head stubbornly.

"There is a theory," Charles said dreamily, "that
somewhere in the universe every possibility is being
played out."

"I'm not sure that's a comforting thought," Poly
said.

At that moment there came a firm knock, and Dr.

O'Keefe came through the curtains. "Here you are, Simon. Your Cousin Forsyth is worried about you."

"I'm sorry, Dr. O'Keefe. I was hot, and I went up on deck for a few minutes, and when I came down I saw that Poly had her light on—"

"That's quite all right, Simon, but maybe you should have told him."

"He wasn't in the cabin, sir, or I would have."

Dr. O'Keefe looked at his watch. "It's nearly midnight. Did you three know that?"

"Heavens, no, Daddy! Go to bed, Charles. Good night, Simon."

Charles untwined his legs. "I've been thrown out of better places than this. Come on, Simon."

Dr. O'Keefe and the two boys left. Poly lay back on her pillows for a few minutes, relaxing, thinking. Then she turned out the light.

Cousin Forsyth was holding out his pocket watch when Simon came into the cabin. The boy let the scolding slide off him, murmured courteous apologies, got into his bunk, and turned off the light. But somehow Cousin Forsyth had turned the evening sour.

Miss Leonis sat in front of the dying embers of the fire. Her hand dangled loosely. It should have been fondling Boz's ear, but she had buried Boz that afternoon, managing with extreme difficulty to dig a shallow hole. She could not lift the old dog to carry him to the grave (despite the gauntness of age he was still too heavy for her), so she dragged him, apologizing for the indignity, until she could push him into the waiting rectangle, barely big enough, and cover his ancient bones with the loose dirt.

Now she was exhausted. She had been too tired to eat. She was too tired to make the effort of taking off her clothes and preparing for bed. A thought fleetingly passed across her mind: —If Simon should need me I am free to go to him without worrying about finding someone to take care of old Boz.

She tried to shake the thought away, but it would not go.

Her empty hand reached for a letter of Quentin's which she had read earlier in the day:

"I am anguished, dearest Mama, at the plight of the poor and ill in this beleaguered country. And our wounded soldiers die of infection or exposure because there is no way to care for them. Manuela—and I do have an eye for beautiful women, Mama—is giving me jewels with which to buy ointments and bandages, but we must depend on generosity from the Continent and England for a great deal. Could you turn your kind heart to our predicament? You will know what we most need—quinine, of course, but you will know what else. And I have a flair for tending wounded men. Had I not been your youngest son I might have been a physician."

This was the Quentin Miss Leonis knew and loved and understood—even the reference to the unknown Manuela was, in this context, understandable; this was the Quentin she had taught Simon to revere.

And she had been wrong.

The next letter held cold comfort:

"Forgive me, dearest Mama, for the long delay in writing, and if my script is somewhat shaky. I have had an adventure which nearly proved fatal. Some-

what over a month ago I was out in the jungle hunting. I had strayed slightly from my companions, and
suddenly I heard a horrid rattling and my horse
bolted. He is a spirited but nervy creature and it was
some time before I could calm him, and by then I was
thoroughly lost. I tried to guide myself by shadows
and sun, but evidently misjudged most woefully, and
by nightfall I had to admit to myself that I was indeed in a plight. I will spare you details, but I survived in solitude and mounting distress for several
days, eating roots and berries and drinking water from
various streams. Whether from water, or from insect
bites, I do not know, but I fell violently ill of an ague.
The time came when I knew that I was dying, and I
could do naught but welcome death, though I felt
sore alone and near to weeping. Then in my delirium
I felt that you were with me, your cool hand on my
fevered brow. You held my head up and put water to
my lips and I opened my eyes and looked into eyes of
black flame instead of cool grey water like yours.
Somehow or other I had been transported to a small
round dwelling smelling sweetly of fresh grass and
flowers. I learned when I was stronger that I had
been found by a small party of hunters from the Quiztano village—found just in time."

The next letter contained detailed descriptions of
the Quiztano village, and then Quentin wrote, "Oh,
Mama, what a gift for caring the Quiztanos have in
their hands. I was brought back from the very doors
of death. Umara says that healing is the Gift of the
tribe."

The letter which followed dealt impersonally with
politics and battles and had only a parenthesis men-

tioning a few days spent resting with the Quiztanos because of a brief return of the fever. Then, "Oh, my mother, how I am torn. I never would have believed that my heart could thus be rent in twain. Manuela is ever dear to me, and her father, it seems, begins to look on me kindly; it would be an alliance most suitable and you and Papa would approve. And yet my little Quiztana is deep within my heart. We have a dream of making a place where the wounded can be brought and nursed by these gentle people, who in no way deserve the name of savage."

And then, "Am I fickle by nature? I would never have believed so. I love Manuela not one whit less. I never believed it possible to love two people simultaneously, but I find that it is so. I adore my little Umara, who brings healing in her small and beautiful hands."

Wearily Miss Leonis let the letters fall from her hands, but her tired mind kept worrying (like old Boz with a bone) over what she had learned. The Quiztano gift for healing was widely known throughout the peninsula. Indians of other tribes, and even some Creoles, brought their injured or desperately ill people to Dragonlake for healing.

The young Englishman was deeply impressed by this vocation, and promised, in his gratitude, to provide the Indians with money if any of them wished to be trained as physicians. This was a promise he was quite capable of fulfilling, for he received jewels not only from Manuela. As Bolivar's victorious forces moved triumphantly through the liberated towns and villages, the general and his officers were greeted not only with flowers, speeches, and songs of welcome, but with jewels, with gold; and Quentin Phair happily received his full share, that being the way of the world. As the liberation of the continent continued he amassed considerable treasure.

Manuela—whoever she was—became betrothed to a fellow officer, and Quentin's conscience was relieved. By now his infatuation with the Indian princess outweighed all else. It became his intention to leave his treasure with his—he called Umara his wife, but as far as Miss Leonis could gather they were not married, at least not in any way that would be considered binding in an English court.

Not long after this there was a bitter entry in his journal. "Why do I tend to idealize, and then get disenchanted? Idolize might be the better word for me to use against myself. It is not my Umara. She is still as lovely and as pure and as good as when I first was brought back to life by her tender hands. But I tried to believe that all the Quiztanos were like my Umara, that they were indeed the Noble Savage—and that is true of some of them, perhaps the majority, but of this I am no longer sure. Others—and Umara's favorite brother is one—have little patience with the gift of healing, and are deeply involved in smuggling—not that I blame them; they have no reason whatsoever to be loyal to Spain, and they have every reason to ignore Spanish prohibitions against foreign trade. So it is natural for them to be an important link in the chain of smuggling luxury goods which would be prohibitive otherwise. All this I understand. But they do have cause for some loyalty to those of us who have been risking life and limb to set their country free, and they appear to care about us no whit more than they love Spain. I begin to doubt if they will really accept me when I come back from England, but I see no alternative. I wonder if I could take Umara and the child and live in Caracas, perhaps?"

But Umara did not want to leave Dragonlake, and when Quentin left Venezuela for Kent he expected to return in a few months, and then to remain with the Quiztanos for the rest of his life. The bulk of his considerable accumulation of treasure would then be used for the education of his son, and though Quentin had decided, despite reservations, to cast in his lot with Umara's people, he planned an English education for his son, and the contradiction implicit in this either had not occurred to him or did not disturb him.

—I thought I knew that all people were a mixture of good and bad, even the best, but I did not expect quite this amount of complication, Miss Leonis thought. —Oh, Niniane, what was it like for you?

The discovery of the young Indian girl in Venezuela must have been a ghastly shock for the young bride in South Carolina, pregnant with her first child. Quentin had told her only that he had lived the typical life of a soldier of fortune, and that he was ready now to settle down and live like an ordinary citizen.

Niniane must have known that her husband's experience was as great as her own innocence, and he quickly made her sure and secure in his love. Few people in the pioneer South of those days would have thought twice about the rights of some South American Indian girl, even had they known about Umara. Stories like Quentin's were casually accepted and soon forgotten, Miss Leonis thought bitterly, and he must have had no suspicion that the past would have any effect on the present. Pharaoh was built, and they were happy and their affairs prospered. If Umara had

anything to do with Quentin's decision to free his
slaves, he told no one. And if he had played free and
easy with his loves in Venezuela, there was no indication in letters or journals that his love for Niniane was
anything but faithful and true.

—And it was, wasn't it, Niniane? Miss Leonis
asked. —It was. But fidelity built on broken promises
has a shaky foundation.

One week when the mail was delivered, Quentin
was in Charleston. Niniane sorted the mail and was
mildly curious when she came to an envelope ad-
dressed to Sra. Niniane St. Clair de Phair, an envelope
mailed from Venezuela. It must be something to do
with the portrait of Bolivar which he was having sent
from Caracas.

So she opened the letter, suspecting nothing.

But the letter was from one of Umara's brothers and
Niniane's safe world of home and husband was shat-
tered.

With white face and cold hands and heart she
learned of Umara and of Quentin's promise to return
to Dragonlake. She learned that the Indian girl had
died giving birth to a still-born child conceived just
before he left Venezuela and his Quiztano wife and
little son.

"This is to warn you," Umara's brother continued,
"you who took Umara from the heart of her husband,
that we will not forget and that we will be avenged.
When your so-called husband sent for his portrait of
Bolivar—a portrait which rightfully belongs to his son—
we made our plans. Know that you are much hated. It
was you who made Quentin Phair betray his wife. We
will not kill him—that would be too easy, and small
satisfaction to us. We understand that in your religion

you are told that the sins of the fathers are visited on the children, even for seven generations. Beware. You will find to your sorrow that for you this will be true. This letter has been put into English by Sean O'Connell of the Irish regiment."

Miss Leonis could feel within her own body the storm of sobs which racked Niniane. Her love for Quentin, and his for her, must have been real indeed, that it had survived such an opening of the past, and that it continued despite horrible proof that Umara's brother had meant his threat. Quentin's and Niniane's first-born son was thrown from his horse and died of a broken neck. He had been alone. There was no reason for anybody, other than Niniane and Quentin, to suspect anything other than accident. They must have lived in terror, and there was nobody with whom they could share their fears. Of their five sons, only the two youngest survived. If Quentin had thought, when he left Venezuela, that a small fortune in jewels would satisfy Umara and her brothers he learned that he was wrong. He had lived by the standards of another age, standards, Miss Leonis thought, still acceptable by far too many people today, and those standards became a boomerang for his undoing. He died of a heart attack before he was fifty. Niniane lived to be nearly ninety-nine.

They must have warned their surviving children, and surely the warning must have been passed from one generation of Phairs to the next. Perhaps at the time of the War between the States, fear of the revenge of the Quiztanos had faded in view of what was going on at home. And then it seemed to have been forgotten; perhaps those who were to carry the warning had been killed in battle. Certainly Miss Leonis's parents had not mentioned it, nor had there been any questioning when her only brother was killed while hunting, by a gun accidentally set off. And perhaps she was overreacting, imagining things in her senility.

No. There had been too many unexplained accidents; the family tree showed the untimely death of a young man in every generation.

She began to pray.

VI

THE BOLIVAR PORTRAIT

The sun was brilliant and fierce the next morning. Charles was awake before his father; he dressed and went out into the passage, where he bumped into Poly, also up early and wearing her lightest cotton dress. She asked, "Where are you going?"

Charles sighed in his tired, adult manner, and Poly knew that he was concerned. "I'm going to talk to Dr. Eisenstein."

"Dr. Eisenstein!" she exclaimed. Then, "Oh, I see, to ask her about the Quiztanos."

He nodded.

She said, "Well, then, I think I'll go talk to Geraldo."

"What about Simon?"

"He's probably already up in the prow, pretending to be Quentin Phair. He really has a *thing* about that ancestor."

Charles paused at the door to the promenade deck. "He says that it's a Southern trait, particularly among the gentry, or whatever you call them, who don't have any money. After the Civil War they didn't have anything left except their family trees. And Quentin Phair sounds like a good person to live up to."

Now it was Poly's turn to look old for her age. A shadow moved across her face. "Nobody's that good."

They parted, Poly going to the galley, Charles to the deck, where he was pleased but not surprised to see Dr. Eisenstein in her usual deck chair under the canvas awning. She was writing busily in one of her notebooks, but looked up and smiled at him.

"It has been an unexpectedly pleasant part of this voyage to be with you three young ones, nicer for us than for you, I daresay."

"We've liked it very much," Charles said. "We're all used to being with grownups, and we enjoy lots of grownup conversation. May I ask you something?"

She closed her notebook, marking her place with her pen. "Fire ahead."

"The Quiztano village—is it the only one, or are there others?"

"There are, I believe, a few scattered groups in the jungle related to the Quiztanos, but the tribe keeps to the settlement at the lake."

"Are their houses sort of airy grass huts built upon stilts right out into the lake? Do you have any pictures, maybe?"

Dr. Eisenstein reached into her straw carry-all and pulled out a *National Geographic* which opened automatically to a double-spread color photograph.

Charles studied it carefully. It showed a sizable greensward on which were two long screened houses raised slightly from the ground, and a few small round huts on higher stilts. Behind these the darker green of jungle and the shadow of mountain pressed closely. The greater part of the village stretched out into the lake, and consisted of round, airy straw houses with peaked roofs and movable straw screens like those in the long houses. The huts stood stork-like on long thin legs: under most of them, small dugout canoes were tethered. Charles studied it and nodded. "Yes. That's it."

Dr. Eisenstein looked at him questioningly.

But Charles gave no explanation. "There's the breakfast bell. I'm hungry. Aren't you?"

Everybody came to the dinner room in summer cottons. The heat seemed to put a damper on conversation. Simon helped himself to cheese and herring and decided that right after breakfast he'd go out to the Dragon's Lair and snooze. If it hadn't been for Cousin Forsyth he'd have slept through breakfast, but Cousin Forsyth was a regular riser and made it clear that he expected Simon to be, too.

But his feeling of heaviness was not only because he was sleepy. After the O'Keefes debarked, would Geraldo talk with him as he did with Poly? Or would Simon feel lost and isolated? He felt lonely and unsure.

Mr. Theo pulled him from his thoughts, speaking softly, only to the boy. "Tell me, young Simon. Would you like to go to a concert with me in Caracas?"

"Oh, sir! That would be marvelous."

At the other table Poly yawned and turned away from one of Dr. Wordsworth's dissertations, this time on the virtues of the Spanish language, and tuned her ear to the officers' table, trying to see how much Dutch she could understand. The men spoke rapidly, so that sometimes she could barely get the gist of the conversation; occasionally she was able to understand entire phrases, and this always pleased her.

Geraldo brought in a platter of ham and eggs.

"Port of Dragons tomorrow," Dr. Eisenstein said. "Hard to believe the days have gone by so quickly.

But I feel rested and ready for work. You, too, debark tomorrow, don't you, Dr. O'Keefe?"

"Yes, we do."

Mr. Phair turned in his chair so that he could speak to the other table. "Simon will miss Poly and Charles, will you not, Simon?"

Simon speared a piece of herring. "Yes."

Poly tried to catch Simon's eye, but he continued to look at his plate. She said, "We'll see each other when we get back. That's a promise."

Mr. Phair said, "That is a pleasant thought, Miss Poly, although shipboard romances seldom continue once the voyage is over."

Simon raised his left eyebrow but continued to concentrate on his breakfast.

Charles was firm. "Our friendship will. Simon is our friend forever."

Mr. Phair looked at the Smiths, sitting side by side, eating the toast and cheese. "When Simon and I—and Mr. Theotocopoulos, too—debark at La Guaira, Mr. and Mrs. Smith will be the only passengers."

—He'd never deign to call anybody by a nickname, Poly thought. —I'm glad he doesn't know my name is Polyhymnia.

Then a phrase from the officers' table caught her attention.

Lyolf Boon was speaking. ". . . a strange tale brought me by Jan, who had it from Geraldo." She missed the next words, then was sure she understood ". . . tried to push Simon overboard. Jan said that Geraldo swears he was not mistaken. He grabbed the man . . ."

Dr. Eisenstein's voice covered the next words. ". . .

and thanks to Inés's perfect Spanish I expect to have fewer problems than if I were traveling alone."

Poly scowled in her effort to hear Boon.

". . . a man in winter uniform, but he slipped out of Geraldo's grasp and disappeared into the ship before the lad could see who it was."

"The Quiztano language is extremely difficult, as . . ."

Poly leaned toward the captain's table.

". . . my winter uniform is missing. That would seem to support Geraldo's tale."

Poly felt a cold chill run up and down her spine. She began to spread jam on a roll in order to conceal her shudder.

She had not heard enough.

She *had* heard enough.

Captain Pieter van Leyden said, "But this is incredible."

Boon said, "That girl is listening."

The captain looked over at the next table, but Poly was talking with Dr. Eisenstein about the Quiztano vowels. Nevertheless, he spoke in a low voice. "If Jan gives it credence I cannot dismiss it offhand. And if your winter uniform has disappeared—when did you notice this?"

"Not until after Jan had come to me. I had no reason to think about it before. Then, since Geraldo had said the man who attempted to push the boy overboard was wearing a winter uniform, I automatically checked my own, partly to prove that the whole thing was a wild tale. If you will remember, it is the second time in a few hours that Jan has come to me with great worry."

Berend Ruimtje, the second officer, was thoughtful. "Jan may look more Dutch than we, but he is part Quiztano. All Quiztanos are superstitious."

Olaf Koster, the engineer, asked, "How does superstition come into this? Geraldo told Jan that the man's arms were outstretched, ready to push, and if he had not been there the boy surely would have gone overboard. A pity Geraldo couldn't identify the man."

The captain spoke slowly and thoughtfully. "Just in case there is a grain of truth in this—which I doubt— we will keep a careful watch on the boy until he debarks at La Guaira. And I would like to see Jan and Geraldo at nine-thirty, sharp."

Immediately after breakfast Charles sought out Jan and firmly closed the door to the compact office/ bedroom. The steward was at his desk, typing out the next day's menus. He had a worried look and the furrows between his eyes were deep. Charles began without preamble. "One time when I was talking to Dr. Eisenstein she said something about the Quiztanos expecting a young white man to come to them from over the sea. I didn't think much about it then, but now . . ."

Jan looked at his watch. It was barely nine. "It is a folk story. Why does such ancient folklore interest you?"

"I'm interested in old stories, and in different kinds of peoples. Poly and I told you about our friends, the Gaeans. Lots of people thought they were primitive, too. But . . ." He paused, appeared to move into a brown study. Jan looked at him expectantly. Finally Charles continued. "I dreamed about it."

"It?"

"The Quiztano village at Dragonlake. I dreamed I was there. I saw a picture of Dr. Eisenstein's this morning, and it's exactly the way it was in my dream. And I've been dreaming about Quentin Phair. Do you know about him? He's Simon's ancestor who was given the Bolivar portrait. I'm sure it's Quentin because he looks like Simon, only older, and with dark brown hair. Maybe it's just because Simon talks so much about his ancestor, and because Poly and I were reading about the Aztecs last year . . ."

Jan asked, "But you think it's more than that?"

Charles looked questioningly at Jan. "These dreams—they aren't regular dreams. They seem to break through barriers of—"

Jan was listening intently.

Charles sighed. "Barriers of time and space. It's as though a window opened and I could see through, see things people don't ordinarily see."

"I am a quarter Quiztano," Jan said. "Dreams are to be taken seriously. What have you dreamed about Simon's ancestor?"

"I thought I saw him in the Quiztano village. He was dressed the way people used to dress in olden days—velvet and silk and lots more color than nowadays. He was saying goodbye, and all the village had turned out to wish him Godspeed. He was going across the ocean to England, and he stood next to the young Quiztano woman I saw him with in another dream. He promised, in front of everybody, that he would return. Then the dream faded." Charles stopped.

Jan picked up a paper knife and looked at it intently. He said, "We are speaking in private?"

Charles indicated the closed door.

"What we say will not leave this cabin?"

"I promise."

"You are still only a child—but it did happen as in your dream. The Quiztanos are still waiting. When I first came to Venezuela from Holland I made my first pilgrimage to the Quiztano village at Dragonlake, to see my grandfather, and to try to understand that part of me which is not Dutch. Umar Xanai—my grandfather—came to meet me. And so did the Old One."

"The Old One?"

"The Umara."

"Umara?"

With much questioning, Charles learned that the Umara presides over the religious ritual of the Quiztanos. She is trained from birth to hold the Memory of the Tribe, and this Memory, Jan emphasized, is the chief treasure of the tribe—"the Memory and the Gift."

"Greater than the jewels and things Dr. Wordsworth told Dr. Eisenstein about?"

"Without a memory a race has no future. This is what my grandfather told me."

On the day when Jan went first to the Quiztano village, the Umara had come with Umar Xanai to greet him. She was older than anyone Jan had ever seen before. She was so old that it was said she had spoken to Bolivar himself, although Umar Xanai made it clear that the chronological age of the Umara was not important; it was the extent of her memory which gave the ancient woman her authority.

She had walked slowly to Jan, helped and supported on either side by two young women, one of whom was being trained by her in the Memory, to be the future Umara. When she was close to Jan she stared at him in silence for a long time. Then she shook her head. 'He is not the One. He is not the Fair.'

"So they are still waiting," Jan told Charles. "Whenever a young white man comes to the village the Umara is brought out to see if he is the one."

"Will this happen to me when we go there—if we're allowed to go?"

"She'll come and look at you—the Umara."

"Umara," Charles said. "That's both a name and an office?"

"Yes."

"She's a princess?"

"We do not call it that. You might. You might also say priestess, though that would not be accurate, either. As I told you, the Umara is the Keeper of the Memory of the Tribe, and of the Gift."

"Do you mean treasure?"

Jan shook his head scornfully. "No no, what treasure there was is long gone. The gift for healing. People from other tribes bring their ill to us, and the people from the barrio, and even people who could afford doctors but who value our gift."

"Do all the Quiztanos have it?"

"Only a handful in each generation. But we watch for it, and when we see it, we help it to blossom."

"We—" Charles mused. "You sound as though you think of yourself as Quiztano."

"When I am in Holland I am as Dutch as anyone. But as we draw near to Venezuela I begin to think Quiztano."

"Can you tell me anything more about the Englishman and the Umara?"

"They had a child, as is the way with such things.

When the boy was still very young, the Fair—for that is what the Englishman was called—sailed for England and promised to return. After he left, the Umara learned that she was to have another child. And there was not a word from the Fair, not a word. She knew he would not return and she died, and the babe with her. And then—my grandfather tells me—the next Umara saw a vision and she said that the Englishman *would* return, and she is still waiting for him. She is very old—we do not even know how old—and very wise, and she says that she will not die until the Fair returns."

Charles looked unhappy. "Is there anything more?"

Jan spread out his hands and stretched his fingers apart. "It is all history, and my grandfather and the Umara are very old and sometimes they get confused and their stories are not always the same. After the Fair did not return and the Umara died—young, young, for the Umaras usually live to be very old— there was talk of revenge, undying revenge, unless the Fair should return. From his son—the one who was a little boy when he left, remember—there have been many descendants. Some have had the Gift, and some have not, and some have left the tribe, strong with other blood. The Umara—she has dreams, too, Charles, dreams like yours. And she says that there is still anger and hate and lust for revenge, and it will not stop until the return of the Fair."

There was a long silence. Jan looked at his watch. Ten more minutes before it was time to go to the captain.

Then Charles asked, "Jan—my dreams—the Umara's —do you think Simon could be the One?"

* * *

The morning sun blazed as brilliantly in Pharaoh as on the *Orion*. Miss Leonis moved slowly and sadly through her morning ritual. The kettle did not gleam as brightly as usual. The flowers did not fill the air with their scent. There was an emptiness to the world.

—And all because of one old hound dog, she thought.

She walked the mile to the mailbox slowly. It was not her habit to collect the mail daily, because there was little mail. Simon's Renier relatives wrote him regularly, newsy but undemanding letters. But she had apprised them of Simon's trip to Caracas. The box would undoubtedly be empty. But the walk would mitigate her loneliness.

Usually Boz walked with her. In his youth he had circled about her happily; in his old age he had creaked arthritically along beside her. She could almost feel his presence. She opened the mailbox absently and pulled out a white envelope without realizing that she had expected no mail. Then she came back into herself and looked at the envelope in surprise. It was from her bank, the bank where she had been known all her life, although for most of that life she had had little or no money in it. Whenever she sold a piece of silver or a bit of jewelry, she had deposited the money. The check Forsyth Phair had given her was one of the largest deposits she had ever made.

She opened the letter from the bank. The check, they informed her regretfully, was not good.

She reached out to steady herself on the mailbox.

Forsyth Phair's check dishonored? It had—she searched for the phrase—it had *bounced*.

There must be some mistake.

But her heart told her with dull certainty that there was no mistake.

And she had allowed Simon to go off with this—this scoundrel.

Instead of going to her cabin or out on deck after breakfast, Poly sat at the foot of Charles's unmade bunk. Geraldo usually did the cabins fore to aft, and would come to her father's and Charles's cabin before he came to hers. Even if she could not speak to him in front of anybody, she could give him some kind of signal that it was imperative that she talk with him alone, at once.

Charles was not in the cabin, but her father was sitting in the chair and adding to the journal which he expected to send home to Benne Seed Island as soon as they got to Port of Dragons and a post office. Without looking up he asked, "What's wrong?"

"I am in a high state of perturbation."

"That's obvious. What about?"

"If I knew, I mightn't be so perturbed. I don't have intuitions and intimations and revelations like Charles, but I do have sharp eyes and ears, and there's something wrong on this ship."

"What's wrong, Poly?"

"Mr. Smith is afraid of Mr. Phair. Dr. Wordsworth can't stand him. Charles and I don't think he likes Simon. But it's more than that. Do you think the fork lift going after Simon was an accident?"

Dr. O'Keefe spoke in his most reasonable voice. "Why wouldn't it have been an accident?"

"Fork lifts aren't likely to go out of control."

"It is quite possible for an accelerator to jam."

"I suppose so. But I'm worried about Simon."

Dr. O'Keefe sighed. "I was glad to find that Simon was on the *Orion* and that you and Charles would have a young companion, but I think that possibly all three of you are letting your imaginations run riot."

"Charles doesn't imagine things." At that moment Poly decided not to tell her father the fragments of conversation she had overheard until she talked with Geraldo himself. "You know that, Daddy. And what about the portrait? Mr. Phair treats it as though it were far more valuable than I'd think any portrait could be, even a great portrait of Bolivar. He goes in to check it at least three times a day, as though anybody could move it with all that heavy wooden packing case around it."

Dr. O'Keefe smiled. "You do sound in a high state of perturbation, Pol."

"Well, I am. The ship has been marvelous. I've loved every minute of it. But I keep having this funny feeling about getting off at Port of Dragons tomorrow. I'm sorry I'm showing my perturbation so visibly. I'll get along to my cabin now. I was sort of waiting for Geraldo."

"Oh?"

"I need to talk to him. And then maybe I'll need to talk to you." Without further explanation she departed, leaving her father to think that he was glad she would not be on the ship much longer.

* * *

When she pushed through the curtains to her cabin, Geraldo was already there. Her bed was made, and the cabin cleaned, and he was just standing there.

He said, "I've been waiting for you. There is something I have to talk about."

After breakfast Simon followed Mr. Theo into the salon. The old man had a music manuscript spread out on one of the tables. He looked up, his attention quickly focusing on Simon.

"Mr. Theo," Simon asked, "do you believe in dreams?"

"Believe, how? That they can predict the future?"

"Not so much the future. The past. I don't mean that they *predict* the past, but that they can pick things up, things that have happened a little while ago, and even a long time ago."

Mr. Theo asked with interest, "What have you been dreaming?"

"I haven't. Charles has."

Mr. Theo raised his bushy brows in question.

"He dreamed that he went to Pharaoh, and he described things I'm sure I never told him, like the dented copper kettle and the way Aunt Leonis talks to it. And then he dreamed about Dragonlake, and he said that he checked it with Dr. Eisenstein and she showed him a picture that was exactly like what he dreamed. What do you think, Mr. Theo?"

The old man threw back his mane. "Charles is not, in my opinion, a romanticizer. I take dreams seriously, young Simon, possibly because in my dreams I am always young and I play the organ as Bach might have played it."

"Is that dreaming about the past?"

"Not in the way you're implying Charles dreams. That sounds to me more like the ripples you see spreading out and out when you throw a pebble in a pond, or the way sound waves continue in much the same fashion. So it seems quite likely to me that there are other similar waves. Strong emotion, I would guess, either very good or very bad, would leave an impression on the air. And what about radio?"

"That picks up sound."

"And television?"

"Sight."

"And a good radio or television set will give you brilliant sound or a clear picture, and a bad set will be fuzzy and full of static."

Simon pondered this. "You mean, Charles may be like a very, very good set, and in his dreams he picks up things?"

"I don't discount the possibility."

"Okay, then," Simon said. "Neither do I. I'm sleepy this morning. Charles and Poly and I talked till midnight. I think I'll go have a nap."

He left Mr. Theo and went out into the heat of the sun, stretched out in the shadow of a large crate, and went to sleep. He was deep in slumber when he felt a hand on his shoulder, and somebody shaking him. He rolled over and saw Poly, not with Charles, but with Geraldo.

"Wake up, Simon," she said. "Geraldo and I have to talk to you."

The intensity in her voice woke him completely and he sat up.

Geraldo, too, looked solemn and anxious.

"Simon," Poly said, "while you were up on the boat deck last night, did anything happen?"

"Happen? No. Why?"

"Nothing? Are you sure?"

"Yes. I was feeling homesick, and I went up and daydreamed about Aunt Leonis."

"Were you very deep in your daydream?"

"I guess I was. She was almost as real as though we were talking face to face."

"Did you know that Geraldo was up on deck, too?"

"No."

"Well, he was, and he saw a man come toward you, very softly, so you mightn't have heard if you were concentrating. Geraldo said the man crept toward you, and then he put out his arms and he was going to push you overboard; you were standing right between the lifeboat and the rail, weren't you? right where the captain told us not to?"

"Yes, but I had my hand on the rail and the ship wasn't rolling. I was perfectly safe."

"You were right where someone could give you one shove and send you overboard."

"Who would want to do that?"

"I wish I knew," Poly said. "You really didn't hear anything?"

"No. I told you. Who was the man, then?"

"Geraldo saw only his back. He had on a uniform hat, so he couldn't even see his hair. Geraldo ran across the deck and grabbed his arm, and the man was slippery as an eel and ran down to the promenade deck and into the ship and vanished."

"That doesn't make sense. Nobody would want to push me overboard. Geraldo, are you sure you didn't dream it?"

"Geraldo knows the difference between being awake and asleep," Poly said indignantly.

"Then why didn't I notice anything?"

"You do go awfully deep into your dreams, Simon. Both Charles and I have noticed that."

"They're not proper daydreams unless you go deep."

"So you might not have noticed, if you were in the middle of an important part."

"That's true," Simon acknowledged. "But I don't like it. It scares me."

"Simon, do you think maybe the fork lift wasn't an accident?"

Simon put his hands over his ears in an instinctive gesture of rejection. "Stop! Don't talk like that!"

Poly's voice was low and intense. "But if somebody's trying to kill you—"

"No! Why would anybody want to kill me? There's no reason! I'm not important—no, Poly, no!"

Geraldo spoke. "The portrait of Bolivar—Jan told me he saw *Umar* painted on the back."

Simon scrambled to his feet, lifted his arms heavenward, and then flung them down to his sides. "What I think we should do is go and look at the portrait and see exactly what is written on the back, even if we have to get a hammer and chisel to take the crate apart."

"That's a good idea," Poly said, "but do you have a key to that cabin?"

"No."

"I have all the keys," Geraldo reminded them.

"Good." Simon nodded. Now that he had made a decision to act he was brusque and business-like. "Let's go, then."

They went quickly to the galley. Geraldo opened the small cupboard where he kept the keys, each on its own labeled peg. He lifted his hand to the pegs in bewilderment: the key to cabin 5, the cabin with the portrait, was not in its place. "The key—it is gone."

"But who would take it?" Simon asked. "Cousin Forsyth has his own key—"

"Come," Geraldo cried, and ran down the port passage, Simon and Poly at his heels. The passage was empty. Geraldo tried the door handle. It moved under the pressure of his hand. "It is open."

"But it's always locked—" Simon said.

"Like Bluebeard's closet—" Poly started, then closed her mouth as Geraldo opened the door wide.

They looked into the cabin, and then at each other, in utter consternation.

On the floor of the cabin lay the boards from the face of the case, tidily stacked. The back of the case was still in one piece. It was empty.

"The .portrait!" Simon croaked incredulously. "It's gone!" He looked wildly about the cabin for the great gold frame, for the familiar face of the general, dark and stern and noble.

For a moment they hovered on the threshold. As Simon started in to look for the portrait, Poly stopped him. "Don't touch anything. There may be fingerprints. Let's go tell Daddy, quickly."

They ran back up the passage, stopped short at the galley.

Jan was hanging the key to cabin 5 on its peg.

"Where did you get the key?" Poly demanded.

Jan turned around, looking surprised. "Mynheer Boon found it in the salon. He said Mr. Phair had left it lying on his crossword puzzle."

"But this isn't his key, it's Geraldo's."

"I know," Jan said, still looking surprised. "I saw Mr. Phair and he told me he had his key. So I came and looked on the board and saw that the key was missing. What is wrong?"

Poly said swiftly, "Later, Jan, I have to talk to Daddy."

Jan stood by the keyboard, looking after them in puzzlement as they raced through the foyer and down the starboard passage. "Geraldo, I need you to set up for lunch," he called, but Geraldo had disappeared.

VII

THE HEARSE

Dr. O'Keefe and Charles hurried to the cabin and stood on the threshold, silently looking at the empty packing case.

Dr. O'Keefe said, "You were quite right not to touch anything. We must tell Mr. Phair at once."

He strode along the passage, the others hurrying behind him, to Mr. Phair's cabin. It was empty. "We'll try the salon."

Mr. Theo smiled at them as they came in. He touched his music manuscript. "It's quite warm in here this morning, but I'm afraid that these loose pages might blow overboard."

"Best not to run the risk," Dr. O'Keefe agreed. "Seen Mr. Phair?"

"No. But he's seldom sociable in the morning." Mr. Theo turned back to his music.

"The promenade deck, then," Dr. O'Keefe said. As they left the salon they met Mynheer Boon in the foyer. Dr. O'Keefe asked him, "Have you seen Mr. Phair recently?"

"Not since breakfast."

"But you found the key to the portrait cabin on his crossword puzzle," Poly said.

"What are you talking about, Miss Poly? I found no key."

Poly looked at Simon and Geraldo in consternation.

"Come," Dr. O'Keefe said, and led them to the promenade deck. "Seen Mr. Phair anywhere around?" he asked casually of the Smiths, who were sunning in deck chairs.

"Not since breakfast," Mr. Smith said. "How 'bout you, Patty?"

"I haven't seen him since breakfast, either. Maybe he's checking on his portrait."

"Quite possibly," Dr. O'Keefe said dryly, and turned to climb the steps to the boat deck, where Dr. Wordsworth and Dr. Eisenstein were briskly taking their morning constitutional. In a calm, unemphatic voice he asked, "We're wondering if you've seen Mr. Phair?"

Hardly interrupting their stride, the two professors assured him that they had not.

Dr. O'Keefe said, "We've tried all the likely places. I'd better go to the captain and tell him about the portrait. Wait for me in the cabin."

"I have work to do, please, sir," Geraldo said. "It is time for me to set up for lunch. Jan will need me."

"I would prefer you to stay with my children and Simon, Geraldo. Jan can do without you for once. I'll explain to him."

"Please, Daddy," Poly asked, "do we have to wait in the cabin? It's so terribly hot. Couldn't we wait for you in the Dragon's Lair? We can stay in the shade and we'll get the breeze."

It was indeed hot. Dr. O'Keefe wiped the back of his hand across his brow. "All right. But go there directly and immediately. And do not leave until I come for you. I want to know exactly where you are."

—He's worried, Poly thought, —more worried than he wants us to know.

"Sir," Simon asked, "who would steal the portrait?"

"And on a small ship," Poly said, "with no place to hide it—and it's a big portrait. It's absolutely mad, isn't it, Daddy?"

"It's very strange. Please go to the Dragon's Lair now and wait for me."

Simon looked white and strained. As they started down the stairs to the lower deck he said, "I'm afraid."

Geraldo spoke reassuringly. "We are with you, and we will not leave you. We know that you love the portrait of Bolivar, that you love it much more than Mr. Phair does."

Poly took Simon's ice-cold hand. "Daddy'll get it back, Simon. After all, it's got to be on the ship." Her grip was firm. "I wish you didn't have to sleep in the cabin with Cousin Forsyth, but I don't think anybody can hurt you there, unless . . ."

"What?"

"You don't think Cousin Forsyth—you don't think he had anything to do with the fork lift?"

"It was an accident. Anyhow, wasn't he on the *Orion* taking care of the portrait?"

"Or last night?" Poly continued.

Charles said, "If only we could begin to guess who the man was."

Geraldo frowned. "It is more difficult because there are many men on the ship who might have been on the boat deck, from your father and the captain to Mynheer Boon and Olaf Koster. If he had been heavy, like Berend Ruimtje, or very short, like the radio officer, or a string bean like the cook. . . . I keep trying to recall exactly what he looked like, and all I can see is a shadowy form in a dark winter uniform who might have been one of many people. The only thing which has come to my mind—and about this I am only guessing—is that he was slow in his movements until I caught his arm, and then he moved like lightning. The slowness makes me think that perhaps he was reluctant, that perhaps he was glad to be caught. But this is only a guess."

Simon's heart was pounding with panic. He tripped over the high sill.

"Careful," Poly warned, leading him through the blazing sunlight, strong and life-giving. The breeze kept the heat from being oppressive, and the beauty of the day gave her a sense of reassurance. There had to be some kind of rational explanation for all the irrational events of the last few days.

They walked silently around kegs and boxes, around the station wagon, and approached the hearse with the bullet hole in the windshield. Suddenly Poly stopped.

"What's the matter?" Simon asked nervously.

"The hearse—" she whispered. "The doors are open—in the back—look. They've never been open before."

No. The hearse had always been sealed tight as a tomb. But now the double back doors were slightly ajar.

"Geraldo—" Poly whispered. Her hand was as cold as Simon's, and she clutched to get comfort as much as to give it.

Geraldo, followed by Charles, went up to the hearse and opened the doors wide.

Walking slowly, pulling back, but somehow managing to go forward, Poly and Simon followed them. The sunlight was so brilliant that it was difficult to see into the shadows within the hearse.

"Simon—" Poly whispered. It seemed that her voice had vanished.

There was something—someone—in the hearse.

Something—someone—lying there.

Cousin Forsyth.

VIII

MURDER

For Simon the next minutes were a haze of terror.

Poly pulled him roughly away. "We have to get Daddy—"

"Why is he in the hearse?" Simon asked stupidly. "What is Cousin Forsyth doing in the hearse?"

Charles said, "Cousin Forsyth is dead, Simon. There's a dagger in his chest."

Chronology got all upset. Simon could not remember in which order things happened. Geraldo, trained to obey orders, reminded them that Dr. O'Keefe had told them to stay in the prow of the ship.

"But he doesn't know!" Poly cried. "He doesn't know about Cousin Forsyth! We have to tell him!"

Simon was not sure how he and Poly and Charles got to the O'Keefes' double cabin, who had gone for Dr. O'Keefe, where he had been found. Had he brought them to the cabin? Certainly he had told them to stay there until he came for them. They were to lock the door from the inside, and under no circumstances to open it to anybody else.

"It's sort of locking the stable door after the horse has gone," Poly said.

Charles sat cross-legged on his bunk. "Is it? There's a murderer at large on this ship. Someone has already tried twice to kill Simon."

"But I thought it was Cousin Forsyth!" Poly exclaimed. "I thought he wanted Simon out of the way."

"Somebody obviously wanted Cousin Forsyth out of the way." Charles looked at Simon, who was sitting, still and upright, in the small chair.

They all stiffened as they heard a key turn in the lock. They did not know who had access to the key to the cabin besides Dr. O'Keefe and the two stewards. And although they trusted Jan, either the chief steward or the first officer was lying about the key. Simon realized that everybody on the *Orion* was under suspicion, even those he thought of as incorruptible and his friends.

Dr. O'Keefe came in, his face markedly pale under his tan; even the red of his hair seemed more muted by grey than usual.

"Daddy!" Poly jumped up. "Please, please send for Canon Tallis!"

He replied, "I have thought about it, Poly. But I'm not sure that it's fair to ask Tom to come running whenever anything difficult happens."

"But, Daddy, this isn't just something difficult. This is murder. And Simon is in danger."

"Poly, we'll have to wait."

"But you'll go on thinking about sending for him?"

"I'll think about it, Poly, but I doubt if I'll do more than that. Now. The captain wants us all in the salon."

"Just us?"

"All the passengers, plus Jan and Geraldo."

"Jan and Geraldo haven't done anything wrong!"

"I doubt if they have, though Jan's story about the key is not very convincing. In any case, we must all be questioned. The captain will speak to the crew and officers separately. Jan and Geraldo are the ones in

closest contact with the passengers. Simon—" Dr.
O'Keefe held out his hand.

Simon put his hand into Dr. O'Keefe's.

The passengers were all sitting in the salon much as
they had been when Simon, Poly, and Charles were
first introduced to them. Dr. Wordsworth was presid-
ing over the teapot; it seemed that disasters produced
tea parties. But on that first day it had been cold,
with steam noisily pushing through the radiators. Now
it was hot. And Cousin Forsyth was not there.

It was stifling. The fans did not seem to stir the air.

Geraldo stood by the door nearest his galley; the
tidy arrangements of cups and saucers, cream pitchers, tea- and coffeepots seemed to give him a sense of
order and reassurance. Jan ten Zwick stood at the fore
windows, his hands clasped tightly behind his back,
which was turned to the passengers.

Charles sat on the sofa beside his father.

Simon and Poly stood.

The captain sat, looking somberly at his passengers.
Mr. Theo, the Smiths, the two professors looked at
him questioningly.

Dr. Wordsworth broke the silence. "Captain van
Leyden, why have you brought us here?"

"There has been an unfortunate—a deplorable oc-
currence." He shook his head at the inadequacy of his
own words. "There has been a tragedy." He paused.

Dr. Wordsworth whispered to Dr. Eisenstein,
though they could all hear her. "Where's Phair? I
thought we were all summoned to the salon."

"Mr. Phair is dead," the captain said harshly.

Dr. Wordsworth dropped the teapot. Tea flooded

over the tea tray, onto Dr. Wordsworth, onto the floor.

Mrs. Smith let out a breathy shriek.

Geraldo and Jan began mopping up the floor.

"But he can't be dead," Dr. Eisenstein said. "He was perfectly all right at breakfast."

Dr. Wordsworth patted her orange shorts with her napkin. "How clumsy of me! I'm so sorry. The teapot handle was unexpectedly hot."

"It must have been a heart attack," Mr. Smith suggested.

Mrs. Smith quavered, "But he was so young!"

The captain waited until comparative order was restored. Then he said heavily, "Mr. Forsyth Phair did not die of natural causes. He was murdered."

Mrs. Smith clutched her husband's hand. "No, no . . ."

Dr. Eisenstein said, "But who would—"

Dr. Wordsworth reached with trembling hands for her empty teacup, lifted it, set it back on the table. "It has to be someone on the ship. It may be someone in this room."

"Stop, stop!" Mrs. Smith wailed. "How can you suggest such a thing? Who could possibly have wanted to murder Mr. Phair?"

Mr. Smith put a restraining hand on his wife's knee. "Somebody did, Patty, and that's a fact."

Simon moved almost deliberately into the state of numbness which had protected him at the time of his parents' deaths, although now there was no grief and outrage, only shock. And he had had too much of death; he would be involved in no more. He did not hear what anybody was saying. He did not want to hear. But after a while he felt that somebody was trying to penetrate his shell of protection, and he turned and saw Mr. Theo looking at him, his eyes fierce under bushy brows. Before Simon could drop his gaze Mr. Theo nodded at him reassuringly. It was almost as though Aunt Leonis were with him and expecting him to behave like a man and not like a child.

He listened to the captain telling the passengers about the vanished portrait, about talking on the radio with the police, and when the shocked exclamations had died down, Poly raised her hand for permission to speak, as though she were in school.

Van Leyden said, "Yes, Miss Poly?"

"Aunt Leonis—Simon's Aunt Leonis. She's the only one who might possibly know."

"Know what, Miss Poly?"

"Why Jan's Quiztano name, Umar, is on the back of the portrait. It might give us a clue."

"What? What's that?" Dr. Wordsworth demanded.

Simon closed his eyes and mind during the explanations.

"A detective in our midst," Mr. Theo said in approval. "You could get in touch with Miss Leonis through the radio officer, could you not, Captain?"

"Yes. That is an intelligent suggestion. In any case, I would inform her of—what has happened." The captain nodded. "You would like to speak to her, Master Simon?"

Simon opened his eyes and the captain had to repeat the question.

"Oh, yes, please, sir! But the nearest phone is quite a way down the road at the filling station by the bus stop. There's usually someone there who's willing to drive over to Pharaoh and fetch her."

The captain's grim face relaxed slightly as he looked at the boy who reminded him so strongly of his own fair son at home in Amsterdam. "All right. We will start the wheels turning as soon as possible." He rose and spoke to the assembled group. "You are free to go where you please, though I expect you not to go below this deck." He looked at Poly and Charles. "It is a hot day, but I do not think that you would wish to go to the prow."

"No," Poly said. "No."

Simon's mind's eye flashed him a vision of the hearse, and the strange still body there, and he shuddered.

The captain dropped his hand lightly on the boy's shoulder. "Come, Simon, we will go to the radio room."

It was over an hour before Aunt Leonis reached the filling-station phone, during which time both Dr. O'Keefe and Mr. Theo made calls, Dr. O'Keefe to Benne Seed Island, Mr. Theo to Caracas, to say he would be delayed but hoped to arrive in good time for Emily's first concert, which was still a full week off. Then he put in a call to England, and for this he asked Simon to step outside. Why would Mr. Theo be calling England? At this moment it did not seem to Simon to be very important. The captain talked again with the police in Lake of Dragons and put in a call to Holland.

When Aunt Leonis was finally on the phone the captain spoke to her first. He told her, briefly, what had happened, then listened carefully. Then he said, "I am glad that you will come. I know that my government would wish to see this—more than unpleasantness—this dreadful event—resolved as soon as possible. We will make arrangements to have you flown here at your earliest convenience. . . . You will come at once? That is good." He handed the headset to Simon.

Aunt Leonis's voice crackled strangely but was quite comprehensible. "I will be with you by tomorrow evening, Simon. I have read Quentin Phair's letters. There was more than *Umar* on the back of the portrait, but we will not talk of it till I arrive." Then static took over and he could make nothing out of the last garbled words.

No matter, Aunt Leonis was coming. There was still horror, but if Aunt Leonis was going to be with them in Venezuela, then somehow she would manage to bring order out of chaos as she always had done.

The O'Keefes were with Mr. Theo in the salon. Simon was being taken care of by Mynheer Boon. Dr. O'Keefe said, "I think it will be better if Simon sleeps with Charles in my cabin, and I'll take his. We may well be detained for a few days in Port of Dragons. You kids will help make the transfer, won't you?"

"Of course, Daddy," Poly said. "Let's find him and get him settled, and then let's put on our bathing suits and splash around in the pool. I'm not being cold-blooded. I just think it would make us feel—feel cleaner."

Mr. Theo nodded. "How many of us will fit in, do you think?" Then he looked at Dr. O'Keefe. "I'm an old man, Doctor, and I've never been very patient. At the end of my life I find that I can't wait for the prudent moment for things. I have to snatch the time when I have it."

Dr. O'Keefe looked at him inquiringly.

Mr. Theo said, "When I suggested to you that we call Tom Tallis in London you felt that we should wait. I must confess, I have called him."

Dr. O'Keefe asked quietly, "And?"

"I was very cryptic. When he got on the phone I said, 'Tom, this is Theo. I will be delayed in getting to Caracas but hope, with help, to be in time for Emily's concert. You will want to come.' Then I hung up."

Poly clasped her hands. "Oh, Mr. Theo, do you think he'll come?"

Mr. Theo said, "Tom and I have known each other since we were both rather wild young men in Paris. It is not my wont to be cryptic. Tom will come." He turned to Dr. O'Keefe. "I hope you're not angry with me for going over your wishes?"

"I think I'm relieved," Dr. O'Keefe said.

The passengers of the *Orion*, with the notable exception of Mr. Phair, were gathered on the aft deck. Mr. Theo, in an old-fashioned one-piece black bathing suit, stood in one corner of the wooden pool and let the rolling of the ship splash salt water over him. Whenever there was a heavy swell the water sloshed over the sides of the pool onto the deck. Simon, Poly, and Charles joined him. The salt water felt cool and delicious.

Mr. and Mrs. Smith found the steep wooden sides of the pool difficult to climb over. They reclined in deck chairs. Mrs. Smith wore white terry-cloth shorts, a white sleeveless shirt, and white sneakers and socks.

Despite her softly wrinkled skin she looked as fresh and clean as a kitten.

"It's all right, Patty," Mr. Smith whispered. "He can't hurt us now."

She shuddered. "What a terrible thing to say! Who could have—oh, Odell, I'm frightened, I'm so frightened . . ."

The two professors had pulled their chairs to the opposite side of the deck from the Smiths. Dr. Wordsworth glistened from sun-tan lotion; she wore orange shorts and a flowered halter and her back glowed with copper and was smooth and supple, though the slack muscles of her upper arms betrayed her age. She brought out a white nose guard and put it over her nose to protect it from the sun, adjusted her straw hat to shade her eyes.

Dr. Eisenstein had pulled her chair into the shade of the canvas canopy.

Dr. Wordsworth's whisper was explosive. "Why don't you say it?"

Startled, Dr. Eisenstein looked up from her notebook. "Say what?"

"What I can see that you're thinking."

Dr. Eisenstein looked sad and tired. "No, I'm not, Inés. I'm numb with horror that such a thing could have happened, but I don't think that you had anything to do with it."

"You know that I hated him."

"I know that you're not a murderer."

Inés Wordsworth held out her hands and looked at them wonderingly. "I could have murdered him, I think, if I'd been angry enough. If he'd raked up the past publicly—but he couldn't do that without implicating himself, and to do him justice I don't think he would have. We did love each other once." She let her hands fall into her lap, the nails like blood. "Odd, to admit that I could kill if I were angry enough. But I didn't kill him."

"I know you didn't," Dr. Eisenstein said gently.

Dr. Wordsworth readjusted her nose guard. "Oh, Ruth, I admit I wished him dead that first day he got on the ship—but not this way. A nice lingering death from some excruciatingly painful disease would have been fine with me—so why am I so squeamish about murder?"

"Maybe because the murderer is still on board. It's unbelievable. It can't be one of the passengers—"

"Why not?"

Dr. Eisenstein shook her head. "I find it impossible to believe that *any*body on this ship, passenger or sailor, is a murderer. And yet somebody is."

"Let's hope it's a sailor."

"But a sailor—what could a sailor have against a passenger? someone he's never met before?"

"Quite a few of the sailors are from South America. And I've told you that Fernando Propice, or Forsyth Phair, was involved in all kinds of minor underworld stuff when I knew him, and a leopard doesn't lose his spots. It may be some kind of private smugglers' vendetta."

"That would be understandable, at least," Dr. Eisenstein said. "I suppose the *Orion* will be swarming with police tomorrow morning when we dock."

Inés Wordsworth was white under her tan. Her hands clenched. "Oh, God! the police always look into everybody's background in the case of murder. They'll find out about me."

"Not necessarily. You have an American passport."

"But don't you see how vulnerable I'll be if the police get hold of my record?"

"There's no reason they should."

Dr. Wordsworth relaxed slightly, letting her hands unclench. "Thank you, dear Ruth. Jail once was enough for me. And there are the officers to consider. Lyolf Boon, for instance, watching the bridge games but refusing ever to take a hand. It was F.P. he was watching, not you and the Smiths."

"And the captain," Dr. Eisenstein continued. "You mentioned only last night that the captain was formidably polite with Phair, the kind of rigid courtesy one reserves for someone one heartily dislikes."

Dr. Wordsworth smiled wryly. "In my youth I used to think I might like to be a spy or a secret-service agent. I don't think I'm cut out for it after all. You'd better use some of my sun-tan lotion, Ruth. Your nose is getting red. You get a lot of reflection from the sun even under the canopy. Oh, God! I wish we were with your Quiztanos and all this behind us!"

On the bridge the Master of the ship looked out to sea. Lyolf Boon was at the helm. Van Leyden said, "You were on the bridge this morning. Are you certain there was nothing on the radar?"

"There were the usual fishing ships, but only a few, and they did not approach us; they remained well on the outer range of the radar."

Van Leyden's jaw tightened. "My heart sank when I recognized the man, but in my most extreme pessimism I never thought of murder. It would seem that somebody attempted to steal the portrait, was caught by Phair, who was then murdered, and the portrait removed—do you have any ideas?"

"Jan is the only person we know to have an interest in the portrait. But I cannot bring myself to believe that Jan ten Zwick would murder. But I do not know what his Quiztano blood might make him do."

"Jan is only a quarter Quiztano," the captain said. "He is essentially Dutch."

"In looks. But there are many qualities in him which come from the Quiztanos."

The captain looked broodingly at the radar machine of which he was so proud. "That doesn't make him a murderer."

"Of course not. I didn't mean to imply—but I do not understand why he had the key to cabin 5. And why invent this wild tale of my having found the key on Phair's crossword puzzle? His lying disturbs me greatly. Never before have I known Jan not to tell the truth."

"Nor I," the captain said.

"Geraldo should keep his key cupboard locked."

"I daresay he will from now on. But there has never before been an occasion to be concerned when we have been at sea."

"Perhaps the possibility of further trouble has occurred to Dr. O'Keefe? You remember, he's changing cabins with Simon."

"A wise decision," Van Leyden said. "But I do not wish the boy to be alone at any time until we're certain no one wishes—wishes him harm. I'm not sure that such was in O'Keefe's mind, otherwise wouldn't he himself have shared his cabin with the boy? It seems likely he merely reasoned that it would hardly be pleasant for Simon to sleep alone in that cabin; that's how I'd feel if it were my son. I think, Boon, that we must be careful not to make any assumptions about anything, or anybody."

Boon agreed. "It is a matter for the police."

Van Leyden put his hand heavily on the radar machine. "Yes. It's all going to be very unpleasant. The police will be waiting when we land. And then Miss Phair's plane from La Guaira will arrive by late afternoon tomorrow. I suppose the police will have her met."

"Yes," Boon nodded thoughtfully. "It is all going to be very untidy. Was Phair a U.S. citizen?"

Van Leyden hit the palm of his hand against his forehead. "No, as a matter of fact, he was not." —How easily, he thought,—the *is* has become *was* on our tongues. "He carried a Venezuelan passport."

"How long do you think we'll be detained? This plays havoc with our schedule."

"I wish I could give you an answer. I have no precedent for this experience. I had no fondness for Mr. Phair, but this is hardly the revenge I would have contemplated."

"You would have contemplated revenge?"

Van Leyden looked surprised. "That was merely a figure of speech. My captain did not need a raw young sailor to avenge him. It was, in any case, not my prerogative. It's nearly time for lunch. I doubt if it will be a pleasant meal."

It was not. In the dining room the fans whirred heavily through the silence. The passengers picked at their food. The meal was over early, and nobody lingered in the salon for coffee.

After lunch the children did not know what to do. They could not go to the Dragon's Lair, past the hearse with its terrible passenger, even had the captain not put the lower deck out of bounds. The adults, instead of repairing to their cabins for a siesta, went out on the aft deck, seeking the breeze, too uneasy to rest. Dr. Wordsworth and Dr. Eisenstein went up to the boat deck and grimly began their pacing, up, down, around, up, down, around.

Poly went off to talk with Geraldo.

Charles followed his father around.

Boon took Simon into his office and showed him a tattered book of pictures of Venezuela. Simon leafed through it politely, pausing to study a large colored photograph, taken from a plane, of Dragonlake, with the Quiztano huts high on their stilts, far out into the lake.

There was a knock on the doorframe and Mr. Theo looked in.

"Come and amuse me, young Simon."

Boon nodded. "I have work to do. I must lock my office." He spoke heavily. "We are locking everything as though we were in port."

Mr. Theo took Simon out onto the deck. "It is hard-hearted of me," he said, "but my main concern is that I get to Caracas in time for Emily's concert."

"I guess I feel pretty hardhearted, too," Simon said. "I didn't want him to die or anything, but he did make me feel very uncomfortable, and I didn't want him taking the portrait away from Aunt Leonis and me, and I felt that he was glad to be getting me away from Poly and Charles, and that he didn't want me ever to see them again. And he frightened me."

Mr. Theo asked quickly, "How?"

Simon shook his head slowly. He could not say that it was because Dr. Wordsworth had made him realize that Cousin Forsyth was somebody very different from the elderly bachelor, overly tidy, impeccably courteous, that he had appeared to be during the month in South Carolina. So he said, "He was always quiet and polite, but there was something underneath."

"What?"

"Poly and Charles think he didn't like me, and I think they're right."

The wind blew through Mr. Theo's hair, ruffling it leoninely. "Let us be grateful for this breeze. We may not have it after we dock. Have you noticed how quiet the ship has become? No more music."

"I guess they don't feel like singing."

"The sound of guitar and flute was part of the breathing of the ship. I feel an emptiness."

"Me, too."

"Come on, then. Let us gird up our loins. The captain suggests that I bring you to the bridge. There'll be fishing boats for you to see on his radar machine."

It seemed to Simon that the captain was careful to see that he was always with an adult, never left alone. It was this which made him accept the unpleasant fact that somebody had already tried to take his life, that this somebody might be as interested in disposing of him as of Cousin Forsyth—but why? why? none of it made sense. He began counting the hours until Aunt Leonis would arrive. It was no more than twenty-four hours, now, or hardly more, only a day.

But would a frail old woman be able to protect him? Was she, too, coming into danger?

At bedtime Simon felt strange in the O'Keefe cabin, no matter how easy he was with Charles. But Charles was in one of his silences; he seemed to be completely withdrawn from Simon; his face was cold and forbidding.

It was not until the lights were turned off, earlier than usual, that Charles spoke. "Simon, I think I have to talk to you." He paused.

"I'm listening," Simon said after a while.

"What I have to tell you doesn't seem to have much to do with Cousin Forsyth and the portrait, but it does have to do with you." And in a cold, completely emotionless voice he told Simon all he had learned from Jan. "Of course it's all muddled," he concluded. "It's an old story and stories tend to get exaggerated and changed. But too much of it fits in with my dreams, and Jan said the Englishman is called the Fair—Jan said he's always thought of it as spelled F-a-i-r—but it's too close to Phair for comfort, isn't it?"

"Nothing's comfortable," Simon said, "and it does have to do with the portrait, since *Umar* is written on the back."

"Yes, I suppose it does. It's just Cousin Forsyth who doesn't seem to fit in. Simon, I'm sorry."

"It would be more of a shock," Simon said in a small, chill voice, "if Poly and Geraldo hadn't suggested it to me already. I tried to put it away as speculation and dream and not reality. But so much has happened, I don't seem to know which is which anymore."

Charles said softly into the darkness, "It doesn't mean Quentin wasn't—wasn't—I know how much he means to you—how you admire—"

The cabin fan whirred softly and steadily.

"It means he wasn't the kind of person I thought he was. And that changes me, too." The breeze lifted and blew gently through the open windows. Then Simon asked, "Do you think somebody killed Cousin Forsyth in order to get the portrait?"

"Maybe. But who? And where did the portrait vanish to?"

"The only person who . . ." Simon paused, said, "Jan . . ."

"If Jan were going to steal the portrait and kill Cousin Forsyth he'd hardly have told me all he did . . . but either he or Mr. Boon is lying about the key."

"All this wanting to be revenged on—on the Phair—I don't really understand."

"I do," Charles said quietly. "You may remember that Poly told you that two years ago a friend of ours was murdered in Lisbon. And Poly and I wanted him avenged, all right. There were several people we hated ferociously. And then we ended up with Daddy having to help the person who was most responsible for his death. So I understand. I just don't understand its going on and on this way."

"No."

"Uncle Father. It's important for him to know all this."

"I suppose so."

"Maybe Quentin had a reason for not coming back, Simon."

"Niniane," Simon said bitterly.

"But you love Niniane. And Aunt Leonis talks to her."

"I'm very confused," Simon said. "Quentin broke his word."

"Words sometimes do get broken, Simon."

"Not Quentin Phair's! I know a lot of politicians nowadays, and even presidents, don't take promises seriously, and even lie under oath, but I was brought up to speak the truth. My father's newspaper was sometimes in trouble because he uncovered truths, and cared about honor. And Quentin Phair was always our ideal of a man of perfect honor, who cared for the truth above all things, and who spent his youth helping to free an oppressed continent."

"Well, he did do that," Charles pointed out. "He spent his youth with Bolivar."

Simon was silent.

After a while Charles suggested, "Why don't you cry?"

"I'm too old."

"Mother says it's silly for men to feel they shouldn't cry at appropriate times."

"Have you ever seen your father cry?"

"At appropriate times."

"Do you consider this an appropriate time?"

"It's a death."

"I don't feel like crying about Cousin Forsyth."

"Quentin. The man you wanted to be like is dead. He never was. As Poly said, he was too good to be true. So maybe if you cry about him, then you'll be ready to find the real Quentin Phair."

"I'm not sure I want to."

Charles pointed out, "He's brought us all into quite an adventure, you'll have to say that much for him."

IX

PORT OF CALL

Simon woke up suddenly, not knowing where he was. The early-morning light shimmered on the white ceiling of the cabin—not the cabin he had shared with Cousin Forsyth, where drawn curtains kept the light to a minimum, where Cousin Forsyth's snores were now only an echo. No. He was in Dr. O'Keefe's cabin. He was in Dr. O'Keefe's bunk.

He raised himself on his elbow and looked across to the other bunk. Charles was lying there, eyes open, staring at the ceiling. When Simon moved he sat up and smiled.

Simon smiled back. But he still felt empty; something was missing; the loss of Quentin Phair was far larger than the loss of Cousin Forsyth. He did not want to talk about it, so he said, "It's now nearly time for breakfast." He stretched. His pajamas were slightly damp with perspiration. The cabin fan was whirring and they had slept without even a sheet.

"The Herald Angel is probably in the galley making early coffee for the Smiths." Charles assumed his Buddha position and lapsed into silence.

Simon broke the silence by asking, "Is he one?"

"The Herald? I think so. You know the clouds we've been watching after lunch? Very light and transparent, and they seem to be throwing themselves into the wind, and we've all said they look as though they're having such fun . . . ?"

"I remember. I've never seen clouds like them before."

"Well, I dreamed last night that Geraldo and Jan both had wings of clouds and that they were flying above the ship—but flying is too heavy a word. It was a lovely dream to have had last night. Geraldo and Jan—they're on the side of the angels, as the saying goes. Don't worry about Geraldo. He won't do anything to hurt Poly."

Simon thought about this for a moment. Then he said, "Thank you, Charles. I've been being jealous. I know Poly's still my friend even if she's friends with Geraldo in a different way. That was a lovely dream."

A shadow moved across Charles's eyes. "They're not always lovely. But Canon Tallis tells me that I may not reject the gift, because God does not give us more than we can bear."

"If there is a God."

"Poly was very upset when Daddy wouldn't cable him."

"God?" Simon asked in surprise.

"Uncle Father—Canon Tallis. But I think Daddy was really very relieved that Mr. Theo just went ahead and phoned. You'll like Uncle Father, Simon."

"I suppose if you and Poly like him, then I will."

"He's not going to be like anybody you've ever met before. One of our friends described him as looking like a highly intelligent teddy bear, but that's not a very good description, because teddy bears are hairy, and he's completely bald—I mean completely, even to having ridges of bone showing above his eyes where most people have eyebrows."

"How come he's completely bald?"

Charles was standing by the washbowl, starting to

brush his teeth. He took his toothbrush out of his mouth and spat. "He was tortured, way back in some war—one of those awful ones in the Far East. They used electric shock on him and it was so strong that it killed all his hair follicles, and it almost killed him, but he didn't betray his men."

"He was a soldier?"

"A chaplain. But he went with the men wherever they went. That's the kind of person he is. And that's why Poly wanted Daddy to send for him, and it's also why Daddy didn't want to. Shall we get dressed and go out on deck?"

"Is it all right?" Simon asked. "Your father told us to keep the door locked . . ."

"I think it's all right as long as we stay together. Let's see if the pool is filled. Salt water's much nicer than a shower."

They made their way along the quiet passage. The passengers were still in their cabins behind the chintz curtains. The rest of the ship was silent. No early-morning sounds of laughter, of music. The silence was as oppressive as the heat, and Simon tried to break it by whistling a few bars of "I met her in Venezuela," and broke off in mid-melody, thinking that Quentin might almost have been the man in the song. The song was even more painful now than it had been after his mother's death. The words would not leave him alone.

> *When the moon was out to sea,*
> *The moon was out to sea,*
> *And she was taking leave of me,*

I said, Cheer up, there'll always be
Sailors ashore in Venezuela,
Ashore in Venezuela.

Was that all it had meant to Quentin? It could not have been all. Simon pushed open the screen door to the promenade deck with a furious gesture.

Much of the water in the pool had splashed over the wooden sides during the night. Nevertheless, Simon and Charles chose the foot of cool ocean water rather than the cabin shower. When they had rolled about till they were thoroughly wet, one of the sailors climbed up to the deck and indicated to them that he was going to drain and refill the pool. Simon and Charles got out and stood at the deck rail, looking across the water to a long dim shadow on the horizon.

"South America," Charles said. "It's really very exciting."

But Simon felt nothing but an aching sadness.

He continued to be passed from person to person, never left on his own. He was silently grateful. He did not want to be left alone with his thoughts. His flesh prickled with apprehension. He was sure that Mr. Theo was not a secret murderer. His pheromones told him that Dr. Wordsworth had a violent temper and cause to dislike Cousin Forsyth but that, except in a moment of passion, she would not murder. The carefully stacked wood from the portrait's crate spoke of premeditation, or at least a kind of cool surrounding the murder which he did not think was part of Dr. Wordsworth's personality. But that left everybody else on the ship to be afraid of. Nobody and nothing was to be trusted, not even his memories.

Shortly after ten o'clock in the morning Lyolf Boon took Simon up to the bridge. "You are privileged," Boon said. "The one time the passengers are never allowed near the bridge is when we are taking on the pilot and bringing the ship in to dock. You must stand out of the way and not ask questions."

The captain gave Simon the briefest of preoccupied nods. Simon stood just outside the bridge cabin and watched a small bug of a boat approach them from the direction of land. The bug sidled up beside the *Orion,* and a man sprang out, clambered up a rope ladder, and landed lightly on the lower deck.

"The pilot. Keep out of the way," Lyolf Boon warned Simon. "He'll be up on the bridge in a minute. Stand here. Don't ask questions. The captain has a very short temper when we're docking. Watch, and anything you want to know I'll tell you later."

"Yes, sir." Simon pressed against the rail, where he could see everything and not be underfoot. Ahead of him was the busy harbor of Port of Dragons; above it rose what appeared to be hundreds of tiny shacks crowding up the steep hillside above the harbor. The wind was sultry and saturated with moisture. He pulled Geraldo's cap farther forward to keep his hair from blowing in his eyes, and to shade them from the brilliance of sun on water. Under the cap he could feel perspiration. His shirt began to cling moistly. The weight of the unknown future lay on him as heavily as the heat.

* * *

The other passengers stood in little groups on the promenade deck.

"I don't know what's the matter with the pilot," Dr. Wordsworth remarked to the Smiths. "We've been backing and filling in a most inept manner. I gather the captain has a low tolerance for fools. This certainly must have broken his tolerance level."

"It seems to be a problem in parallel parking," Mr. Smith said. "I find parallel parking difficult with an automobile, and it must be far more of a problem for a ship. There's only one berth left free, with a freighter on either side. Port of Dragons surely is a busy harbor."

Mr. Theo and Dr. O'Keefe stood side by side. "The fork lifts are just sitting there," Mr. Theo remarked. "I suppose we won't be allowed to unload anything until the police have been all over the ship. I expect Tom by mid-afternoon."

His words were drowned out by shouting on the dock. Sailors from the *Orion* threw heavy ropes across the dark water between ship and shore; the ropes were caught by longshoremen and hitched around iron stanchions. Slowly the ship inched landward to bump gently against the old tires which were fastened to the wooden pilings of the dock—primitive but excellent bumpers.

On the quay stood a bevy of uniformed officials, talking loudly and with much gesturing and flinging of arms, shouting to the longshoremen, who in turn shouted to the sailors on the *Orion*, until the gangplank was dropped with a clatter and ship and shore were connected. The officials bustled into the ship and disappeared.

Charles said to his sister, "Jan and Geraldo have drinks and cigars set out in the salon."

"For the customs men," Poly said. "Geraldo says they always do, not just when there's a murder. Ouch. That sounds awful, doesn't it? 'Just when there's a murder.' Oh dear, are we getting hardened?"

"Inured, maybe."

"Isn't that the same thing?"

"Not quite. You can get used to something without being hardened. The cigars and stuff aren't just for the customs officers this time," Charles said. "I wonder what they'll do?"

"The customs officers?"

"The police."

Poly said in an overly matter-of-fact voice, "They'd better get Cousin Forsyth out of that hearse and onto some ice pretty quickly. In this weather by this time he stinketh."

Charles said, "Will they want an autopsy?"

"I suppose so. It's what's done. But there wouldn't seem to be much doubt about the cause of death. Not much point in sticking a dagger into the heart of someone who's already dead, for instance. And the dagger doesn't afford a clue. It's Venezuelan, the kind that can be picked up in any port, and most of the sailors have them, because they're decorative, and they take them home for presents. Oh, Charles, I've been trying to look at it all objectively, like Uncle Father, but the thing that throws me is that I thought Cousin Forsyth was after Simon, and now—"

Charles spoke quietly. "I still think he was. I have the strongest feeling that if Cousin Forsyth hadn't been got out of the way he might have succeeded in killing Simon."

"You mean maybe someone killed him to save Simon?" Poly asked hopefully.

"I don't know. There are a whole lot of threads and they're all tangled up. But I still think Cousin Forsyth boded no good for Simon." He help up a hand and pointed.

All the passengers hurried to the rail and watched as a short, excited official ran down the gangplank to the dock and began shouting and gesticulating. A large elevator lift maneuvered alongside the *Orion*. The passengers could not see what was happening on the foredeck, but it was obvious from the increased shouting and excitement that it was something important.

A great yellow metal arm reached out across the dock and over the *Orion*. Then it moved slowly back and the hearse, in a cradle of ropes, wavered in the air over the oily water between the *Orion* and the pier. The passengers watched in fascination as the hearse swung back and forth, tilted, righted, and finally, with a bump, was set down on the dock. A second official ran down the gangplank, shouted in unintelligible Spanish to the men on the dock, ran to the first official, shouted some more, and then the two chief officials got into the hearse and it drove off.

"Could you understand what they were saying?" Charles asked.

"Only a few words. It was some kind of dialect. I think they're driving right to the morgue."

Charles poked her, and she looked up to see Boon coming out to the promenade deck with Simon, and then going back into the ship.

Simon hurried toward them. His voice was studiedly casual. "I wish yawl could have been up on the bridge with me. I had to stay way out of the way, and even so, the captain got in a towering rage and yelled all kinds of things in both Dutch and Spanish at Mynheer Boon and the pilot—I couldn't understand a word, but he obviously was giving them Hades. Mynheer Boon says he doesn't really mean it, and this was a difficult docking and everybody is all uptight—I mean, even more than usual." Then he said in a voice so low that they could hardly hear him. "He's gone. Cousin Forsyth."

"Yes, Simon," Poly said. "We saw."

His eyes looked dark in his pale face. "It seemed so strange to think of him being in the hearse when it was swinging there, over the water and the edge of the dock and it tilted and—"

Poly said in a matter-of-fact way, "A freighter doesn't have a hospital, and it was the most prompt and effective way to get him directly to the morgue."

Charles said, "Simon, just remember that Aunt Leonis is coming, that she'll be here before dinner. Do you think you'll be allowed to go to the airport to meet her?"

"The captain says it depends on the local police, but he'll try to arrange it."

"Think about that, then."

The heat bore down.

After lunch the captain came out to the promenade deck and called Simon. "El señor jefe de policía Gutiérrez, chief of police in Port of Dragons, will take you out to the airport to meet Miss Phair." He smiled at the boy. "Come."

Simon followed Van Leyden, through the ship,

down the gangplank, to an official-looking black car with a seal on the door. A small, potbellied man with shiny dark hair and a perspiring face was introduced as el señor jefe de policía Gutiérrez. His black waxed moustache was far more impressive than Cousin Forsyth's had been, its points curling up to the middle of his cheeks, but it was the only impressive thing about him. His white summer uniform was wrinkled and dark with sweat, and he was dancing about impatiently.

Simon shook hands. "How do you do, sir?" he queried in careful Spanish.

Simon's Spanish words evidently relieved el señor Gutiérrez, who began to gabble away until Simon stopped him and asked him please to slow down. This appeared to be a difficult request. Sr. Gutiérrez blew a small silver whistle and was almost immediately surrounded by excited subordinates. He exhaled a stream of incomprehensible Spanish, his voice rising to a high pitch. Minions ran in every direction, and then Gutiérrez bowed politely to Simon and said, "We will drive to the airport now, and you will answer me some questions, yes? It will not be difficult for you. Then we will arrange a happy meeting with the elderly lady, yes?"

"Yes, please, sir."

Gutiérrez opened the right-hand door to the front seat for Simon. Then he got in behind the wheel. "I myself will drive so that we will be private." He took out a large silk handkerchief, flicked some imaginary dust off the steering wheel, and mopped his brow.

Simon reached out to make sure that his window was open. The car was a hot box.

Gutiérrez took a cigar from several in his breast

pocket—Dutch cigars—and lit up. The smoke made Simon feel queasy, but he tried to think only that he was on his way to meet Aunt Leonis.

Gutiérrez drove rapidly away from the port, waving in a lordly fashion at the soldiers with machine guns who stood formidably at the exit. They drove along a narrow road above the sea.

Gutiérrez snapped, "Where is this portrait of Bolivar?"

"It has been stolen, sir."

"Aha!" said el señor jefe de policía Gutiérrez. "This is what the Captain van Leyden and the señor Boon have told me. The wooden crate was found open, and the portrait had vanished, and all this at sea!"

"Yes, sir."

Gutiérrez drove with his foot down on the accelerator until they were traveling on a lonely road with jungle above them to the left, sea below to the right. "How did this portrait of our general come into your possession?" It was an accusation. Gutiérrez obviously did not think that Simon had any right to a portrait of Bolivar.

But the boy answered courteously. "Not my possession, sir. It belonged to my Aunt Leonis and she sold it to Cousin Forsyth."

"Sold it. Aha! Ahem! Why would she sell such a valuable thing?"

"Well, because it *was* valuable, sir, the only valuable thing she had left, and she had no money."

"Impossible. All Americans are rich." The cigar smoke blew heavily through the car. "If she had no money, how could she have bought such a valuable portrait in the first place?"

"She didn't buy it, sir. It was hers. It has always been in our family."

"Always? Incredible. How would an aged American have had a portrait of Bolivar in her family? This is a most unlikely story." Gutiérrez spoke around the cigar. Simon's nausea began to be acute. "Why do you speak Spanish?"

Simon countered, "Would you prefer me to speak English? It would be much easier for me."

"That is not what I am asking. Where did you learn Spanish?"

"From my Aunt Leonis—sir."

Simon had decided definitely that he did not like el señor jefe de policía Gutiérrez, who gave him no more confidence in the police than had Dr. Curds in the ministry.

"Your cigar is making me sick, sir," Simon said, "and I don't think I can speak any more Spanish for a while."

Gutiérrez frowned his disapproval, but put out his cigar. "You are withholding information."

They drove in silence for perhaps five minutes. Simon felt sweat trickling down his back between his shoulder blades. Gutiérrez's face glistened like melting lard. The landscape widened out and flattened, with a broad savannah between the road and the forest. Gutiérrez made a long U-turn, and there was the ocean on their left, pounding into shore. "We are here," Gutiérrez said.

The airport for Port of Dragons was little more than a short runway along a strip of dirty beach. The surf was pounding in heavily, and the spume was a mustardy yellow instead of white. Everything brassily reflected the heat of the sun. There was a bird's nest in the wind sock. A small plane was parked like a clumsy bird on the airstrip: Aunt Leonis's plane? If so, where was she? Across the airstrip from the ocean was a small wooden shack outside which a soldier lounged, a rifle swung from his shoulder. By the shack a hearse stood, black and shining and hot.

The hearse.

The sun smacked against the bullet hole in the windshield, and light burst back.

"The hearse—" Simon's throat was dry. "Why is the hearse—"

Gutiérrez did not reply. He drew the car close up to the rear of the hearse.

"Is—is Cousin Forsyth—"

"No, no," Gutiérrez answered soothingly. "He is in the morgue. It is all right. Come, I will show you."

"Aunt Leonis—"

"Her plane is not yet in. There are head winds. We have time. Come." He opened his door and pushed himself out from under the wheel.

Simon did not move.

Gutiérrez walked around the car and opened the door on Simon's side. "Come."

Simon pressed back, his bare legs below his shorts sticking to the seat. His dislike of Gutiérrez had turned to anger, and the anger to terror.

Gutiérrez reached in and took his arm in a firm grip. The rotund little man was far stronger than he looked. Simon was hauled forcibly out of the car, yanked from the stuffy, smoky, sweaty heat of the interior into the blazing broil of the sun. Was Aunt Leonis waiting in the shade inside the shack? Was Gutiérrez lying to him?—Please, please, be there.

He struggled to get loose and run to the shack, but

Gutiérrez's flabby-looking arms were like iron and he dragged the boy toward the hearse.

The Venezuelan's voice was gentle in contrast to his fingers, which were bruising Simon's arms. "Don't be afraid. Don't fight me and you won't get hurt. I just want to show you something."

The rifle-slung soldier moved swiftly from the shack over the short distance to the hearse and flung open the double doors. Then he and Gutiérrez together picked Simon up bodily and threw him into the hearse and slammed the doors shut behind him.

Simon landed on something. Something pliable.

A body.

X

THE BODY IN
THE HEARSE

His terror was so great that he could not even cry out.

The body gave a very living grunt as Simon almost knocked the wind out of—who was it? Not Cousin Forsyth . . .

The grunt was followed by muffled sounds, but no words.

Simon was almost thrown to the floor as the hearse began to move, accelerating rapidly. The shirred lavender funereal curtains covered the windows, and Simon precipitated himself across the hearse and struggled to open them, but they were tacked down. While he was trying to pull them loose his eyes adjusted to the dim light and he turned to the still-grunting body on the stretcher.

There lay a man, trussed up like a fowl; a blindfold covered his eyes, and a gag was rammed into his mouth. With trembling fingers Simon untied both, to reveal a rather pale face and a completely bald head.

"Uncle Father!" Simon cried.

Dark eyes widened in surprise. "Who are you? How do you know me?"

"You're Poly's godfather," Simon said, starting to work on the knots; he was slowed down by the rocking of the hearse, which appeared to be traveling much too rapidly for the state of the road.

"Make haste slowly," Canon Tallis advised as the hearse jounced over a rut and Simon was thrown against him. "And while you're working tell me who you are. And keep your voice down."

"I'm Simon Renier, Simon Bolivar Quentin Phair Renier, and I've been on the *Orion* with Poly and Charles and Dr. O'Keefe, and Mr. Theo, too, of course." The terrifying yet tedious job of loosening the canon's bonds was finally done, and Simon helped him to sit up.

Canon Tallis pursed his mouth as though to whistle, but his lips were so sore and bruised from the gag that only a small puff came out. He asked, "Where's the rest of the family?"

"Home, on Benne Seed Island. Dr. O'Keefe brought Poly and Charles with him when he was asked to spend a month in Venezuela—you really are Canon Tallis?"

The bald man nodded thoughtfully. "Curiouser and curiouser."

"I guess Mr. Theo didn't tell you much when he called you."

"So right."

"But you came anyhow. He said you would."

"When I got an unexpected and extremely cryptic phone call from him, I thought I'd better come see what was up. I shall want you to tell me what *is* up, Simon, but first we'd better try to look out and see where we're going." Between them they managed to loosen a corner of the lavender curtain, which had been tacked down very thoroughly indeed. They peered out. The hearse was bouncing along what was no more than a double rut cut through the jungle. Trailing vines brushed against the windows. A ferocious-looking wild hog tore through the underbrush and vanished into green.

"We're not moving as quickly as it seems," Canon Tallis said. "I wonder if we could get out?" He tried to open the rear doors. "We're locked in. Do you have a knife on you?"

"No, sir," Simon said. "I'm sorry."

"No matter. I doubt if it would help. This is a solid lock, not the thing one would normally expect on a hearse. It may be padlocked from the outside." The hearse jolted and veered violently to one side. "They're not going to be able to drive much farther. Not unless this path turns into a road, and somehow I doubt if it will. Can you tell me quickly what's been happening?"

As quickly as possible, prompted by astute questions, Simon told Canon Tallis what had happened since the fork-lift incident on the dock at Savannah.

The hearse continued to crash roughly through the jungle. Simon thought it was never going to stop. "Are we being kidnapped?"

"It would appear so. Though I'm hardly a kid."

"But why?"

"Somebody is still trying to dispose of you, it would seem."

"And somebody doesn't want you around to clear things up. But that policeman, Gutiérrez, he wasn't in Savannah or on the ship. He couldn't be the murderer. But he did throw me into the hearse."

"Knocking the wind out of me. It does appear to be a rather complex maze, though I begin to glimpse a pattern."

"What, sir?"

"Your not-overly-lamented late Cousin Forsyth seems to have been involved in one way or another with a good many people."

"Is—is Gutiérrez going to kill us?"

"Since he has not already done so, I somehow doubt it. And when I do not arrive and it's noticed that you've vanished there's going to be considerable excitement on the *Orion.*"

"But does anybody know you're coming—I mean, for sure?"

"I was puzzled enough by Theo's call to decide to leave London and come, and I was concerned enough to phone a friend of mine, Alejandro Hurtado, chief of police in Caracas, and ask him to make sure that the captain of the *Orion,* as well as Theo, be advised of the time of my arrival. Hurtado told me that he would arrange to have me met, so I somehow doubt if our present plight will go unnoticed by him." He put his hand out suddenly and touched Simon's shoulder. "We're slowing down."

The hearse jounced along for a moment, then came to a lurching halt.

After a moment the doors were flung open. The hearse had stopped in a small clearing where a helicopter was waiting. Gutiérrez peered in at them. "I am so sorry to inconvenience you," he said in his most unctuous manner. "The lips of someone must be closed, so I have taken you hostage." He grabbed Simon, and pulled the struggling boy out of the hearse and into the helicopter. The soldier with the rifle knocked Canon Tallis on the head, stunning him, and then slung the heavy body over his shoulder as though it were a sack of grain, and dumped it into the copter.

Gutiérrez was at the controls. In a moment the incredible noise of the blades deafened Simon, and then they were airborne.

* * *

Poly and Geraldo sat in the small shade up on the boat deck. The heat of port was so heavy after the breeze of open sea that even Dr. Wordsworth had given up her daily constitutional. Despite the shade, the whitepainted wood of the bench was hot against Poly's bare legs.

"Oh, Herald," she said, "things are so strange and my emotions are so mixed. If nothing had happened Daddy and Charles and I would have left the *Orion* forever, and you'd be getting ready to go on to Aruba and Curaçao and wherever you go before La Guaira, and the portrait would still be in the cabin, and Cousin Forsyth and Simon would still be on board, and Simon wouldn't be off with that oily policeman to meet Aunt Leonis. And yet I can't bring myself to wish that you and I weren't sitting here, being comfortable together."

Geraldo leaned toward her and kissed her.

When they moved apart she said, "I am gorgeously happy. How can I be happy when someone has been murdered?"

"I should not have kissed you," Geraldo said. "Forgive me."

"Why shouldn't you?"

"Because you're still a child."

"I am not!"

"And I am in no position to—oh, you understand, Poly-heem-nia. Sooner or later you will leave the ship and we will never see each other again."

Poly gave him her most brilliant smile. "I know. I can be quite realistic, Geraldo. But this was my first kiss and I will never forget it, ever, not when I am as old as Aunt Leonis."

"I will try to be realistic, too," Geraldo said, but he would have kissed her again had not Dr. O'Keefe called up to them.

Poly jumped guiltily. "I think Daddy feels he has to keep track of us all."

Geraldo touched her cheek lightly with one finger. "I want him to keep track of you."

"Geraldo, have you any ideas?"

He leaned toward her. "Many."

"No, no, silly, about Cousin Forsyth and the portrait."

"There are murmurs about Jan, but I know that it is not Jan."

"Of course not! Jan wouldn't murder."

"But we know of his interest in the portrait, and there is his lie about the key. The crew—everybody— we are all very disturbed. Most of us have worked on the *Orion* for years, and no one is on the ship for the first time this voyage. We find it impossible to believe that there is a murderer among us. But I heard Mynheer Boon defending Jan to Mynheer Ruimtje."

"What about the passengers?"

"It is not you or Charles or your father or Simon," Geraldo said firmly.

"Mr. Theo, Dr. Eisenstein, Dr. Wordsworth, the Smiths. Not one of them is strong enough to have got Cousin Forsyth into the hearse."

"Possibly two could."

"Mr. and Mrs. Smith certainly couldn't."

"The lady doctors?"

Poly pondered this. Dr. Wordsworth looked strong enough. "Wouldn't they have looked suspicious?"

"Anybody would have looked suspicious, if seen."

"It would be rather difficult to lug Mr. Phair from cabin 5, through the ship, out on deck, and into the hearse without being seen."

"He may not have been killed in the cabin."

Poly fondled Geraldo's hand. "If I were the murderer I think I'd have tried to lure Cousin Forsyth out on deck, get him behind the hearse or one of the big packing cases right by it, and done him in there so that I could have got him into the hearse inconspicuously."

Geraldo raised her hand to his lips and kissed her fingers. "You look so funny and adorable playing the detective."

"I'm not playing!"

"Sorry, Polyquita, sorry." He kissed her lightly and rose. "I have work to do, and you must go to your father."

She stood, too. "Simon and Aunt Leonis ought to be here soon. And my godfather. I know it's childish of me, but I keep feeling that when he gets here everything's going to be all right."

"May it be so," Geraldo said.

Simon and Canon Tallis watched the helicopter disappear, up through a tangle of leaf and vine, trailing long shards of greenery on its runners; the rotors chopped through the entangling jungle until the machine was free and high in the sky.

They had been dumped unceremoniously in a small clearing which would be visible from the air only to someone who already knew about it, and who was a superb pilot.

"In a cinema," Tallis said, "we'd have overpowered them and taken control of the copter."

"What would we have done then?" Simon asked. "Could you fly it?"

"I'm woefully out of practice, but I do have a pilot's license, and desperation can be a good co-pilot. That man knows his jungle and he knows his machine. Unfortunately they took my gun at the airport before they tied me up."

"You had a gun?"

"Something told me to be prepared. However, it seems that I was not prepared enough, or we wouldn't be here."

"Sir, are you all right?" Simon asked.

Canon Tallis rubbed his skull. "I have a nasty egg here, which will probably be a brilliant hue of purple by morning, but otherwise I'm fine."

"I thought he'd killed you."

"For some reason he only wanted to knock me out, and that he succeeded in doing. But no other harm done, thank God."

Green of leaf and vine hid the helicopter, though they could still hear the roar of its blades. Then sound, too, was lost in the enveloping murmur of the jungle. A bird startled Simon with a scream; deep within the tangle of green and brown and olive came a chattering which sounded like monkeys, and probably was.

Simon asked, "Why did they just dump us out here in the middle of the jungle?"

"I think your fat little man—"

"El señor jefe de policía Gutiérrez."

"El señor Gutiérrez for some reason did not want to kill us outright. Odd how squeamish some types can be. The thug with him would much have preferred to shoot me than knock me out, put a bullet through you, and then leave us here for the vultures."

"What are we going to do?" Simon asked.

"Try to survive until Hurtado finds us."

"Will he find us?"

"Hurtado is one of the best policemen in the world. If anybody can find us, he will."

Miss Leonis leaned toward the window in the little one-prop plane and watched the landing at Port of Dragons. Despite her exhaustion from the trip—the bus ride to Charleston, the long flight to La Guaira with a change of plane en route, and the bumpy trip in this old crate—she was excited. She peered out at the stretch of beach beside the runway, full of flotsam and jetsam, driftwood—and, as they came closer and she could see better, old sandals, tin cans, empty bottles. The water looked yellow and rough. Then the ground came up to meet them and they bounced several times and lurched to a stop. Her ancient heart was beating too rapidly; she could feel a flutter in her throat as though a small and frightened bird was caught there. Her hands, despite the heat, were cold.

Several solicitous officials helped her from the plane and set her down on the airstrip. She looked around. She was glad that she had not seen the bird's nest in the wind sock while they were landing; it hardly gave one a sense of confidence. Close to the plane was a low shack, and through the open door she could see a large set of scales, a soldier with a submachine gun, and two other semi-uniformed men with rifles. The three of them were playing some kind of card game, slapping cards and silver down on the table, which was spotlighted by the sun and looked even hotter than outdoors.

She felt a presence at her side, turned, and one of the officials who had helped her from the plane was bowing obsequiously. He was rotund and shiny with heat. "Miss Phair?"

She bowed in acknowledgment.

"Señor jefe de policía Gutiérrez of the Port of Dragons police, at your service."

She extended a white-gloved hand and he kissed it.

"I am here to escort you to the *Orion,* where you will be joyfully reunited with your nephew." He led her to an official-looking car with a gold seal on the door. "If you will be so kind as to sit in front with me, perhaps I can get some preliminary questions out of the way on the drive to the ship."

She did not like him. Her heart continued to thud. The car was stiflingly hot and smelled of stale cigar smoke. As he closed the door for her she decided that she was much too tired to speak Spanish, and so she sat and smiled courteously and vaguely at el señor jefe de policía Gutiérrez as he started the car and drove off, immediately firing a barrage of questions at her.

It took him some time to realize that she was not going to respond. Then he hit his forehead with the heel of his palm and moaned, as though to one of his minions, "But she is supposed to speak Spanish!"

The corners of Miss Leonis's mouth quirked slightly. She leaned back in the car and closed her eyes, making a concentrated effort to relax her travel-taut muscles, to slow the rapid beating of her heart. If she was to be of any use to Simon she must rest. Slowly and rhythmically, without moving her lips, she began to recite poetry to herself, Shakespeare's sonnets, her favorite psalms, the prelude to Chaucer's *Canterbury Tales*.

Her head drooped forward and she slid out of poetry and into a light slumber. She paid no mind to el señor jefe de policía Gutiérrez.

Defeated by passive resistance, he drove on.

The captain and Boon were waiting for them on the dock.

"But where is Simon?" Van Leyden demanded.

"Simón? But he has returned to the ship." Gutiérrez smiled at Miss Leonis, at Van Leyden and Boon.

"What are you talking about?" Boon asked.

"The English priest was at the airport when Simón and I arrived. He was waiting in an official car sent from the police department of Caracas. When he said that he wished to question the boy immediately I hesitated, of course, but he persuaded me. He is a man of much authority."

"Where are they, then?" Van Leyden tried to keep his voice calm.

"The Englishman said that they would talk on the way back to the ship. His driver was one of Hurtado's top men. How could I refuse? I was outranked. Surely they are here by now? They left half an hour before Miss Phair's plane arrived."

Miss Leonis asked sharply, "Where is my nephew? What is going on?" She felt old and bewildered and her lace parasol did little to keep the heat of the sun from beating down on her.

"It is of no moment, gracious señora," Gutiérrez burbled. "They will of course be here momentarily."

A large black limousine drew up, and a uniformed chauffeur sprang out. "Where is the Englishman? he demanded excitedly.

What had been confusion now turned to chaos. The limousine ordered by Hurtado had been delayed by a flat tire. When the chauffeur finally reached the airport he was told that his charge had already departed, that he had been met by an agent of Comandante Alejandro Hurtado—but that, declared the chauffeur, was impossible; he was the agent; the comandante had phoned him; he was always Hurtado's official chauffeur in Port of Dragons . . .

Van Leyden looked at his watch. His anger toward the dead man was even deeper than his anxiety; was history going to repeat itself? Was Phair, even dead, going to cause his resignation? He said, calmly enough, "We will wait half an hour. By then the Netherlands consul, Mynheer Henryk Vermeer, may be here. He was vacationing in the hills but he is already en route to Port of Dragons and should be here shortly. In the meantime, Miss Phair, while we are waiting for your nephew and the Englishman we will try to make you comfortable in the ship's salon, which is considerably cooler than the deck. Please be so kind as to follow me." He took her parasol and held it over her until they reached the cover of the ship.

Miss Leonis was not sure that she was not going to faint before she got to the salon. Van Leyden, seeing her tremble, put his arm about her and helped her upstairs and into a comfortable chair where she would get what little breeze there was.

"I do not understand what is happening," she said.

Van Leyden rang the bell for Geraldo. "Miss Phair,

when there has been a murder, things are apt to be incomprehensible temporarily."

"Who is this English priest with whom Simon is supposed to be?"

"Is with, I am sure, is with. He is a friend of one of the passengers, who sent for him."

"Isn't it a bit late for a priest?"

"It appears that he has worked for Interpol and has a reputation as someone who can solve difficult problems."

"Let us hope that he can. Would it be possible for me to have some tea?"

"I have already rung for it."

"Thank you. You are very kind."

"Please try to rest, Miss Phair. You have had a difficult journey."

"Yes. Thank you."

"Simon will be most happy to see you. He is a good lad. Ah, here is Geraldo. Tea for Miss Phair, please, Geraldo, and something light to eat. Please excuse me, Miss Phair. I will send Simon to you the moment he arrives." The anxiety with which he looked at his watch as he crossed the threshold belied the confidence in his voice.

Poly hurried out onto the promenade deck and went to Charles, who was reading in the shade of the canvas canopy. "Aunt Leonis is in the salon."

He dropped his book. "What!"

"Aunt Leonis is in the salon."

"Who told you?"

"I saw her."

"Are you sure?"

"We did see her in Savannah, Charles. Who else could it be?"

"Where's Simon, then?"

"If he's not with Aunt Leonis he should be here with us. Have you been in the cabin lately?"

"It's too hot."

"Let's look for him."

Charles closed his book and put it down on his chair. With a worried look he followed his sister.

Simon was not to be found.

Poly said, "It's like when we were looking for Cousin Forsyth and couldn't find him. Do you suppose—"

"No, I don't. Let's go to the captain."

The captain was on the bridge, with Dr. O'Keefe and Mr. Theo. Quietly he told the children that Simon was supposed to have left the airport in a government car with Canon Tallis. He did not say that the Englishman and Simon were already gone when the official chauffeur reached the airport. Instead, he made his voice reassuring. "No, we must not become alarmed too soon. I've had word from el comandante Alejandro Hurtado, chief of police in Caracas, who is coming today. Evidently Comandante Hurtado is an old friend of the Englishman's."

Dr. O'Keefe nodded. "Yes, Tom has friends all over the world. If he has been met by a government official we needn't worry."

But Mr. Theo shook his head so that his white hair flew about wildly. "They should be here if all is well. They should have been here an hour ago."

The captain did not deny this. "Let us not alarm the

old lady. It is possible that the government driver is not familiar with the route. They may have lost their way."

"Tom Tallis does not lose his way," Mr. Theo said.

It had to be conceded that something had gone wrong. Canon Tallis and Simon ought to be on the *Orion* and they were not and there had been no word from or about them.

Walking up and down the promenade deck Gutiérrez wrung his hands. His face streamed with sweat like tears. "But it is impossible, impossible," he kept repeating.

Van Leyden told the assembled passengers and Aunt Leonis, "Vermeer will be here any moment. Hurtado is flying in from Caracas and will arrive after dinner. They will order everything." His face was pale and all the lines seemed to have deepened.

Dr. Wordsworth whispered to Dr. Eisenstein, "This must be hell for Van Leyden." She drained her glass and shook the remaining ice.

Dr. Eisenstein whispered back, "And for the old lady. She must be wild with anxiety over the boy."

Van Leyden said, "I think that we should all go to the dining room now. The cook has prepared an excellent meal for us. We must eat, you know."

Mr. Smith took his wife's hand. "This is more than Phair's murder, Patty."

"That nice young boy." She squeezed his hand. "I hope he hasn't come to any harm."

Poly said, "I'm not hungry."

Charles answered, "Neither am I. But the captain's right. We have to try to eat."

* * *

Passengers and officers ate in strained near-silence. All fragments of conversation sounded unusually loud, though voices were kept low. When Dr. Wordsworth asked, "Pass the salt, please," in a quiet voice, everybody jumped.

Miss Leonis sat in Simon's place. Cousin Forsyth's chair had been taken away. She ate a little because she knew that she had to, but she did not talk. She was silent not only because she was exhausted, and worried beyond belief about Simon, but because she bore the burden of Quentin Phair's journal, and she did not want to talk until she knew who it was she should talk to. The O'Keefes, she knew, were as anxious about Simon as she was. She had spent an afternoon with Mrs. O'Keefe and the younger children. She trusted the O'Keefes. It might be that she should talk to Dr. O'Keefe. She would wait and see. The two professors and the Smiths she sensed to be preoccupied with problems of their own which might include the disappearance of Simon and the English canon, but went beyond them. The old Greek organist she felt to be a friend; he obviously cared about Simon, and it was he who had sent for the Englishman. He was attentive to her in a quiet, unobtrusive way, not talking, but seeing that her teacup was filled, that she had salt and pepper, butter.

At the other table Charles whispered, "Where is Aunt Leonis going to sleep?"

Poly answered, "Geraldo says they've booked rooms for her and for Uncle Father at the Hotel del Lago in Port of Dragons. Charles, where are they? Simon and Uncle Father?"

"I wish I knew."

Jan came into the dining room and whispered to the captain, whose somber face relaxed slightly. He spoke to the assembled company. "Vermeer and Hurtado are both here. May I ask you, please, to stay in the dining room after dinner, just for a short while, until I know their wishes?" He bowed and left, speaking in a low voice to Jan, who closed the glass doors between dining room and salon, thereby cutting off the breeze. The passengers waited in tense silence, which Mr. Theo broke.

"If this Comandante Hurtado is a friend of Tom Tallis's he'll find Tom and Simon in short order."

Miss Leonis looked at him gratefully.

Geraldo hovered, refilling their water glasses. "Perhaps I should bring coffee?" he suggested.

"It's too hot," Dr. Wordsworth said.

Then Jan reappeared. His expression seemed to have set into a heavy mask of apprehension. Now that he was not smiling, Charles remembered that Jan's usual expression was a pleasant smile.

"Captain van Leyden would like to see you all on the promenade deck. It is cooler than the salon. We will serve coffee there, Geraldo."

"Yes, sir."

The colored lights around the awning on the promenade deck were lit, giving it a carnival appearance in macabre contrast to the mood of the assembly. On shore, small lights blinked on in the huts, moving in the wind and trembling like Christmas-tree lights up the mountainside. A single, very bright star pulsed in the blue-green sky. The dock was brightly lit with bulbs on cords stretched from warehouse to warehouse, and from telephone and light poles. Under one of the light poles was an ancient Hispano-Suiza, highly polished, parked beside a large black limousine.

The captain and two men rose to greet the passengers. They had been sitting at one of the small tables on which stood a bottle of Dutch gin and three small glasses.

Van Leyden made the introductions. The consul, Henryk Vermeer, was a heavy, straw-haired, bulldog of a man in crisp white shorts, crested blazer, and solar topee. Charles heard his father whisper to Mr. Theo, "He looks more like an Englishman in India than a Dutchman in Venezuela."

Mr. Theo whispered back, "Did you see the Hispano-Suiza? Bet it's his."

The comandante from Caracas, Alejandro Hurtado, was tall for a Latin, a dark man in dark clothes, with a dark, sharp jaw which would be purply-black almost immediately after he had shaved.

Vermeer shook hands all round, beaming affably, as though this were a purely social occasion. Hurtado revealed no expression whatsoever, but he looked at each passenger intently when he was introduced, as though memorizing name and face.

—I'm glad I have no secrets to hide from him, Poly thought as Hurtado bowed over her hand. —And I'm glad he looks a hard person to fool.

Gutiérrez was not there.

"Where is Simon?" Aunt Leonis demanded of Hurtado.

Simultaneously Mr. Theo asked, "Where is Tom Tallis?"

* * *

In the dimness of the jungle evening Canon Tallis rubbed his hand wearily over the painful lump on his bare pate. "Now, Simon, we had better prepare for the night. Are you a hand at camping?"

"No, sir. Camping wasn't exactly Aunt Leonis's thing."

"Not exactly mine, either, but necessity is an excellent teacher." The priest had taken off the dark jacket of his clerical suit and had rolled up his shirt sleeves. "The first thing to do is to collect enough dry wood for a fire, heat or no heat. It's a good thing we're shaded here; my unprotected head sunburns overeasily. First thing tomorrow I'm going to have to make some kind of head covering—my panama is somewhere in that hearse."

"I can make a sort of hat for you, sir," Simon said, "that's something I know how to do, by weaving palm fronds together."

"Good lad. I shall be much obliged. You do that, and I'll try to get a fire going."

"But why do we need a fire, sir, when it's so horribly hot?"

The canon smiled. "Not for warmth, certainly, though we may be grateful for it during the night. If we can keep smoke going up through the trees it will be an indication of our whereabouts which could be spotted by a helicopter—Gutiérrez is not the only one with a whirlybird. I'm certain that Hurtado will have the jungle searched."

By the time the canon had a small fire burning in the center of their clearing, Simon had woven him a passable head covering which he tried on at once.

"Yes, this will do admirably tomorrow."

He should have looked ludicrous—his bald head covered by the green palm hat, his clerical collar formally about his throat, his arms scratched and bleeding in several places from his endeavors. But all Simon thought was, —I know why Poly loves him. He does make me feel that everything's going to be all right.

In their little clearing it was already night. The canon squatted by the fire, carefully feeding it, "as I wish I could feed the two of us. Tomorrow we'll have to look for nuts and berries, and maybe we can crack a coconut between a couple of stones. But we'll have to be careful. I'm no expert on the edible roots of the Venezuelan jungle."

"Maybe I can help there," Simon said. "We have a lot of the same plants at home, sir, and Aunt Leonis and I eat a lot of wild stuff."

"Good, then. The two of us make an intrepid pair. All shall be well. Now, what I would like us to do this evening, to quell the pangs of hunger, is to go over in detail everything you have already told me, and more. Don't be afraid to repeat yourself. Remember that nothing you can tell me is trivial, no matter how unimportant it may seem. If I can get a clear picture of what went on at sea, possibly I'll have an idea about my unexpected reception at the alleged airport, and why you and I have been dumped here like two babes in the wood. Whose mouth has to be kept closed by Gutiérrez, and why? Start with—no, let's go even further back. Start with the arrival of Cousin Forsyth at Pharaoh."

* * *

On the promenade deck of the *Orion* the passengers sat in a stiff circle. Geraldo had brought out the coffee tray and had been asked by the Dutch consul to serve cognac and liqueurs, and to make lemonade for Poly and Charles.

Miss Leonis, too, chose lemonade. "Where is that little policeman who met me?" She disposed of Gutiérrez by her tone of voice.

"Gutiérrez. I have taken over the case," Hurtado said calmly.

"I'm so glad!" Mrs. Smith clasped her small hands together. "He was trying to question us in such a bullying way."

Dr. Wordsworth said, "He appeared to be the kind of small-town policeman who immediately gets puffed up with the enormity of his own insignificance."

"Murders and missing persons are hardly in his line." Vermeer beamed. "A little smuggling here and there is more the kind of problem he comes up against. More cognac, my dear madame?" He gazed admiringly at Dr. Wordsworth's dark good looks.

"Thank you, no." She gave him a bright smile.

Deftly, Hurtado led the conversation in what seemed a casual way, ably seconded by Vermeer. In a short time they had found out a good deal about the passengers. Hurtado began questioning Dr. Eisenstein about the Quiztano Indians. "It is interesting, is it not, that you should be planning to visit these people who seem, in some way, to be connected with the stolen portrait?"

"And therefore, possibly," Vermeer said jovially, "with the murder."

"I cannot understand it!" Dr. Eisenstein exclaimed. "Why would a Quiztano name be written on the back of Mr. Phair's portrait?" She turned to Miss Leonis. "He bought the portrait from you, I believe?"

"Yes," Miss Leonis said, "but I am afraid I can tell you nothing."

"My dear madame," Vermeer pursued, "nothing?"

"Nothing. I have undertaken this journey because I, too, need information."

Hurtado noted the determined set of the old woman's jaw, the bone showing clearly beneath the soft, finely wrinkled skin.

Dr. Eisenstein continued, "And why didn't Jan tell me that he's part Quiztano, when he knows that the entire purpose of this trip for me is to visit the settlement on Dragonlake?"

"You did not ask him?" suggested Vermeer.

"But who could guess? He looks completely Dutch."

"True, true," Vermeer agreed amiably. "On a happier occasion you and I must chat, my dear doctor. I, too, am interested in the local Indians, and I have found Jan most helpful. Perhaps, later on, I can be of service to you."

"Oh, thank you!" Dr. Eisenstein said. "There are so many things I would have liked to ask Jan."

"It would have been so interesting for all of us," Mrs. Smith said. "When we lived in—" She stopped herself in horror, putting her pudgy hand up to her mouth.

Vermeer asked with sociable interest, "When you lived where, Mrs. Smith?"

"Ver—Vermont. Burlington, Vermont."

Hurtado said, "Your Spanish is excellent, Mrs.

Smith, both yours and your husband's. I congratulate you."

"Thank you . . . " Mrs. Smith began to knit rapidly.

"Did you learn your Spanish in Vermont?"

Mr. Smith took off his spectacles and began to polish them. "We frequently visit our granddaughter and her family in Costa Rica."

"You've never been to Venezuela before?" Hurtado asked.

"Certainly we have been to Venezuela." Mr. Smith put on his spectacles. "When we come to South America we always spend a little time visiting and sightseeing in places other than Costa Rica—which is where we learned to speak Spanish. Although our grandson-in-law speaks excellent English."

"Your grandson-in-law is Costa Rican?"

"Yes."

"And yet your accent is that of Caracas," Hurtado said.

Mrs. Smith burst into tears.

Vermeer sprang to his feet and held a large white linen handkerchief out to her. "My dear madame, please do not upset yourself so! What has happened?" He patted her clumsily on the shoulder.

"I can't bear it!" Mrs. Smith sobbed. "I can't bear being terrified of being found out like this!"

"Patty!" Mr. Smith tried to stop her.

"My dear madame," Vermeer said, "found out about what? You have nothing to fear as long as you speak the truth."

Hurtado held up a hand to stop Vermeer. He spoke in his quiet, unemphatic way to the weeping woman. "Would you like to speak to me alone?"

She shook her head. Her soft old face was streaming with tears. "I'd like everybody to hear. It's better that way."

"Patty, please—"

But she could not stop.

—Why doesn't Hurtado take her away? Poly wondered, and then answered her own question. —She might not talk unless she does it right now, right here. But it's horrible.

Charles reached out and took his sister's hand and held it tightly.

Miss Leonis had thought that she was beyond embarrassment. But she was not. She looked at Mr. Theo, who was scowling ferociously at Hurtado.

"He's an honorable man, my Odell." The words flowed from Mrs. Smith like her tears. "A fine man. No one finer. But when we were young he had a problem, a gambling problem."

Mr. Smith stood up, knocking over his chair, and moved away from them. Vermeer moved swiftly toward him, but Mr. Smith only went to the rail and looked out to sea. Vermeer said, "My good man, if this has nothing to do with the murder it will quickly be forgotten by us all."

Mrs. Smith dabbed at her eyes. "He worked in a bank in Caracas. He had a fine position for a young man. We were doing well, I was teaching English, and we had a lovely little house in Macuto—that's a suburb, a nice one. Then—he lost a lot of money and he—he borrowed from the bank."

"Borrowed?" Hurtado asked.

"He told me—he told me what he had done. I made him go immediately to the president of the bank, and he paid it back, Odell did, with interest. He worked hard and he paid back every penny. He wasn't asked to leave his job; the president of the bank was like a father to us, and everything was all right, and ever since that one time there's been nothing, nothing, he's never gambled again, ever, and he was vice-president of the bank in Burlington; they gave him an engraved silver tray when he retired, it was all behind us . . ."

Dr. Eisenstein, who was sitting nearest Mrs. Smith, tried to stop her. "Dear Mrs. Smith, why are you telling us all this? There's no need."

"There is, there is. We had forgotten it. It was past. But then there was that night at bridge—you can't have forgotten that night."

"No."

"Maybe he suspected—"

"Who suspected?" Hurtado asked.

"Mr. Phair. Maybe he suspected about Odell, and was testing. I don't know how he found out—how would he find out?"

"People like Mr. Forsyth Phair have a way of finding out things," Dr. Wordsworth said, and was given a sharp nudge by Dr. Eisenstein.

"However he found out, he found out, and he went to Odell."

"Mr. Phair went to your husband?" Hurtado prompted.

"Yes. He went to Odell."

Mr. Smith turned from the rail and moved back into the light. "He threatened me. He said that if I did not pay him he would tell everybody what had happened, and he would spread the story in Costa Rica, and it would hurt our granddaughter—" He stopped. Then he said, very quietly, "I told him that as far as I was concerned he could jump overboard. I do not want the past reopened. I do not want our granddaughter to think less of me. I do not want anybody hurt. But I will not live under the constant threat of blackmail. I knew that if I were to give him money the demands would never stop. So I had a motive for murdering him. But I did not."

"Of course you didn't!" his wife cried. "You couldn't have."

"Of course, of course," Vermeer said, full of cordiality. "Do have a drink, Mr. Smith. We all wish you well."

Hurtado looked at his watch. "This will be all for tonight. I am grateful to you, madame." He bowed. "If you will all be equally forthright we will sift this matter through in no time. Miss Phair, it would be my pleasure to escort you to your hotel."

She nodded acquiescence.

"I will see the rest of you after breakfast. Out here, or in the salon, whichever is cooler."

"Señor comandante," Dr. Wordsworth said, "may I suggest that the murder and the theft may not have been committed by one of the passengers?"

"My dear lady, I am quite aware of that. I shall be questioning the officers and crew after you have retired." He spoke affably enough, but there was admonition behind his words. "Vermeer, come with me, please. I will return you to your small appliance which will surely not seat three of us."

Miss Leonis moved numbly between the two men, who helped her down the gangplank. Hurtado seated her carefully in the limousine, saying, "The hotel, alas, is not air-conditioned, but I think you will find it reasonably cool."

"Thank you. Heat does not bother me. My only concern is Simon."

"He is my concern, too, madame. I will pick you up after breakfast, say ten o'clock. That will give you an opportunity for a good rest."

"I am much obliged. I realize that what happened on deck tonight was probably a good thing—but—do you have any idea as to the whereabouts of my nephew and the English canon?"

"Believe me, Miss Phair, I'm as anxious to find them as you are. Tom Tallis is an old friend. And a highly competent man. If Simon is with him, he is in good hands."

"Do you think they are together?"

"At this moment I see no reason to doubt it."

Vermeer said, "We will try to find the supposed chauffeur who met Tallis. It should not be too difficult."

Miss Leonis asked, "You think that someone impersonated the official chauffeur and then kidnapped Simon and Canon Tallis?"

Hurtado said, "It is as plausible a theory as we have right now. My chauffeur thinks that his flat tire was not accidental."

"And the wool was pulled over Gutiérrez's eyes?"

"So it appears."

"Forgive me, señor comandante, I do not believe in teaching professionals their own business, and if you're not telling me all that you are thinking I quite understand. But I don't think that Gutiérrez is a fool, although I agree with Dr. Wordsworth that he has a somewhat enlarged estimation of his own importance."

"Quite," Hurtado said.

"And I do not trust him."

"Why not, Miss Phair?"

"Sense of smell. A long life has sharpened mine."

"I will bear that in mind. But please try to let us do the worrying, Miss Phair. I shall not be going to bed tonight. But you must rest."

"Yes," she said. "I know that. Señor comandante, I wish to go to Dragonlake tomorrow."

He looked at her, his eyes for a fraction of a second betraying astonishment. "Madame, it is a difficult trip."

"Will you make arrangements for me, please?"

Vermeer began to protest, but Miss Leonis cut him off. "Since I am not under suspicion for murder, theft, or kidnapping, there is no reason you should not allow me to go. If you would care to accompany me, Mr. Vermeer, that would be my pleasure."

Hurtado looked at Vermeer with a slight nod. "It shall be arranged, madame. But you will be kind enough to tell us why you wish to make this excursion?"

"There is, after all, a Quiztano name on the back of a portrait which once belonged to me. And I have a feeling that it may help us to find Simon and your friend."

The limousine drew up before the broad patio of the hotel. Hurtado and Vermeer escorted her into the lobby. The chauffeur carried Miss Leonis's suitcase to the desk.

"My dear madame." Vermeer beamed. "The comandante and I have not eaten. Would you care to join us for a small collation?"

"Thank you, no. The ship's dinner was more than adequate. I should like to be shown directly to my room."

Hurtado said, "Of course. But there is one question I would beg you to answer first. What is written on the back of your portrait of Bolívar?"

She answered, "It once had painted on it, *For my son, born of Umara*. Time, or effort, or both, have blurred and faded the writing, so that now the only letters that show clearly are U-M-A-R."

"What does this mean—Umar, or Umara?"

"Umara is always the name, the inherited name, of the princess of the Quiztanos."

"How do you know this?"

"It is written in Quentin Phair's journal, and referred to in his letters to his mother, and to his wife, Niniane."

"You have these letters?" Hurtado asked.

"I do."

"With you?"

"Yes. In his will Quentin Phair requested that they not be read for six generations. It had always been my intention to leave them for Simon, but during the days since Simon and Forsyth boarded the *Orion* I have dishonored Quentin's request and read the letters and journals. It is because of this, as you can see, that I wish to go visit the Quiztanos tomorrow."

Hurtado said, "I assume that you felt you could give Dr. Eisenstein no information because you did not wish to confide in the assembled company."

"I would have had no right to make such a confidence."

Hurtado's voice was quiet and courteous. "But you will tell us what is in the letters and journals?"

"I will tell you, perhaps, after tomorrow."

"We may have to ask you for the letters and journals."

"I understand. But I am not yet ready to give them to you. They are extremely personal."

"Madame, a policeman is completely impersonal."

"I am not a policeman. But I will not withhold from you anything which might help you in your inquiries." She poked in her reticule and drew out a small bundle of documents. "These are the papers which Forsyth Phair gave me to establish himself as a member of the branch of the family which moved north, and then west, after the War between the States. I would appreciate it if you would check on them for me."

Hurtado held out his hand. "Certainly."

Vermeer asked, "Do you have any reason to doubt the authenticity of these documents?"

"Yes."

Hurtado raised his brows.

"The check Mr. Forsyth Phair gave me for the Bolivar portrait—money which was to see me through the rest of my days—was a piece of paper, no more. Since it was for a large sum of money it was investigated by the bank. The check is worthless. If the man were not dead I would suspect him of absconding with my nephew, and I would place a rather large bet that he is somehow behind Simon's disappearance. There's no doubt that Forsyth Phair, whoever he was, was murdered, is there?"

"No doubt at all."

"Now I wish to retire," Miss Leonis said. "You will,

of course, phone me at any time during the night if there is news of Simon?"

"Of course, Miss Phair. Mynheer Vermeer will call for you after breakfast. You are fortunate in your choice of escort. Vermeer is somewhat of an anthropologist and knows Dragonlake and its Indians as deeply as anyone who is not a native of this area. The Quiztanos do not welcome strangers to their village, but Vermeer is known to them as a friend."

"Thank you." She bowed gravely. "That is the first piece of good news I have had in a long time."

"I trust you will rest well." Hurtado called the night clerk and asked him to see Miss Phair to her room.

"*À demain madame.*" Vermeer bent over her hand.

"Good night, gentlemen."

They watched after her. Her walk was stiff with fatigue, but her body was erect.

In his pajamas, Charles went to Jan's cabin.

The steward looked troubled. "It is not good for you to be too much with me."

"Am I bothering you? I'm sorry."

"No, no, it is not that. I know that I am under suspicion."

"That's nonsense."

Jan ran strong, blunt fingers through his fair hair. "I did not murder him. But it is true that I am the only one to have a special interest in the portrait. Mynheer Boon says he never saw the keys, and this I do not understand because he gave them to me to return to Mr. Phair."

"I don't understand either," Charles said.

"I know only that I am suspected."

"Who suspects you?"

"Hurtado. He is the one who is important. I am not worried about Gutiérrez. I know his type. While he was questioning us in the salon he pocketed half the cigars—he's worse than the customs men—and blew and blustered at us, but he did not know what he was doing. But Hurtado is different."

"I hate it, I hate it!" Charles cried with vehemence, more like his sister than himself. "I know you didn't kill Cousin Forsyth, but I can't bear to think that *anybody* on the *Orion* could have done it."

"Nor I," Jan said. "It is a bad business. I do not know how it will end."

As Charles crossed the foyer to go to his cabin, el señor comandante Hurtado came briskly up the stairs. "Young man, I must talk with you."

Charles waited.

"Shall we go to your cabin?"

In the cabin Charles looked at the bunk in which Simon had spent only one night. He asked, "Where are Simon and Canon Tallis?"

Hurtado lowered himself onto the chair and regarded Charles with his steel gaze. "I wish that I could tell you, Charles. But they are not off my mind for one moment. Tom Tallis is my friend." He touched his breast pocket and indicated a small two-way radio. "If there is any news we will know at once. Now, Charles, I want you to tell me about your dreams."

"How do you know about my dreams?"

"You seem to have discussed them with a good many people."

Slowly Charles crossed his legs. "Dreams are—dreams. They aren't evidence. They don't hold up in court."

"We're not in court. Anything may be important. A reaction to a dream may give me the clue that I need. It may help me to find Simon and Tallis as well as the murderer."

Charles closed his eyes. "All right, I'll tell you. If Canon Tallis phoned you from London to make sure that you would know he was coming, that tells me two things."

"And they are?"

"That you are his friend. And therefore to be trusted. And also that he must have suspected something might happen. He takes my dreams seriously, by the way."

"I take most things seriously," Hurtado said.

When Charles had finished talking, his voice as unemphatic as Hurtado's, the comandante said, "I would like you to tell this to Miss Phair."

Charles nodded.

"If she were not old, and exhausted from travel and worry, I would take you to the hotel tonight. But that will not do. I will pick you up first thing tomorrow morning."

"You're going to take me to her, rather than bringing her to the *Orion*?"

"You are an intelligent boy. Yes. I have reasons. Get to bed now. Perhaps you will dream."

"Perhaps I will," Charles said. He did not sound happy.

* * *

Simon and Canon Tallis lay on the rough ground of their clearing. They had tried to soften it with leaves and grasses, but it was still hard and uncomfortable. Their fire burned brightly. But they were grateful not so much for the warmth as for the light. Around them the jungle was alive with noise. Some of the noises Simon recognized from South Carolina, but there were new and strange noises which he had never heard before, breathings and cluckings and hoots. Once he sat upright in terror as the firelight was reflected in two large amber eyes.

Canon Tallis put another piece of wood on the fire. "We have just about enough till morning; then we'll have to collect more."

"What was that?" Simon asked.

"Some jungle creature. I don't think that we'll be disturbed as long as we stay right here and keep the fire going. We'll take turns sleeping. You try to sleep now, and when I get too sleepy to be alert I'll waken you."

"I don't think I'm sleepy," Simon said.

"No. But close your eyes and perhaps sleep will come."

"Do you have any ideas who took the portrait, and who killed Cousin Forsyth, and why Gutiérrez kidnapped us?"

"It appears to me that they are all connected," the canon said.

"Do you think that my ancestor—Quentin Phair—do you think he really did go to Dragonlake and fall in love with the Umara, and then leave her?"

"It seems likely."

"I wish it didn't."

"All human beings break promises, Simon."

"Not Quentin Phair."

"The Quentin Phair of your dreams wasn't a real person."

"No, but—I was brought up to believe that a gentleman does not break promises."

"That's not a bad way to be brought up. It's good to take promises seriously. Then we're not apt to make or break them lightly. I would guess that your ancestor did not make his promise lightly, but that when he got away from Venezuela and Dragonlake it was almost as though he were waking from a dream. Dragonlake may well have seemed more like a figment of his imagination than anything else, once he reached cold and reasonable England. And then when he came to the North American New World and met Niniane the dream must have seemed even further away. I do not say that this excuses him, but perhaps it does explain him?"

"I guess so. You mean, he didn't break the promise in cold blood. It was what Aunt Leonis would call a sin of omission rather than commission?"

"Quite."

From somewhere in the jungle came the scream of a small animal, a series of hooting calls, a cry that sounded like shrill laughter. "Not much like Piccadilly," the canon murmured. "Do try to close your eyes and rest for a while. No use both of us staying awake all night. We'll do better at solving the murder and getting ourselves out of this predicament if we get some rest."

Simon closed his eyes. He had expected that the canon would lead them in prayer, rolling out pompous words as Dr. Curds had been wont to do. But if the canon did any praying it was in silence. Simon suspected that he had prayed before the boy lay down, but he could not be sure. But Canon Tallis, he understood, prayed the way Aunt Leonis prayed, and this kind of praying was something he respected, even if he did not understand it.

He tried to listen to the fire rather than the noises outside their small clearing. After a while he slid into a doze.

While the boy slept Canon Tallis took a sharp stone and slowly and carefully sharpened the end of a strong branch into a rudimentary spear.

XI

THE LAKE
OF DRAGONS

Charles and Aunt Leonis sat at a small round table on
the terrace of the Hotel del Lago, eating breakfast.
Hurtado had urged them to speak as openly and fully
as possible; one never knew what small clue might
lead to the murderer, or the whereabouts of Simon
and Tallis. Then he left them alone and stood at the
far end of the terrace. He had his back turned to
them, and had taken himself out of earshot of their
conversation, but they both knew that any untoward
movement or word would not escape him.

After a while they forgot him.

"You dreamed true," Miss Leonis said when Charles
had finished. "It is all in the letters and the journals."

"You've read them?"

"After the accident with the fork lift, which you
took as seriously as I did, I kept having the feeling
that something was wrong, that I should not have allowed Simon to go with Forsyth—so, yes, I read them.
And I learned more than I wanted to know about
Quentin Phair. He was not the white knight *sans peur
et sans reproche* I was brought up to believe him to
be—though neither was he a scoundrel. For all his
folly and over-idealism he was a man of uncommon
valor, vision, and a great deal of charm." She poured
herself another cup of lukewarm tea. "I do not understand why Hurtado has no news of Simon."

Charles said, "If he's with Canon Tallis he's all right."

Miss Leonis beckoned to Hurtado, who joined them. "Have you found anything out about the papers I gave you last night?"

"Madame, I am not a magician."

"I am over-impatient. Forgive me."

"I understand your concern. I should have information on the papers for you by this evening."

"Good. It occurs to me that it might also be wise for you to call the museum in Caracas and see if Forsyth did make arrangements there about the portrait."

Hurtado looked at her with admiration. "One of my men has already been instructed to do so."

"Sir," Charles said, "wouldn't it be a good idea for Aunt Leonis to go to Dragonlake?"

Miss Leonis smiled at the boy. "I am going. This morning. Mynheer Vermeer is to accompany me. He'll be here shortly?"

"He's waiting in the lobby," Hurtado said. Then he looked directly at Charles. "What did you dream last night?"

Charles's face closed in. Miss Leonis and Hurtado waited. Finally the boy said, "There may be something in one of the Quiztano dwellings which Aunt Leonis ought to see."

"And what is that?" Hurtado asked.

"I didn't dream clearly enough. If Aunt Leonis is going there, she can look."

"Will I be able to?" the old woman asked.

"If what I think is there is there, and if you are meant to see it, you will be able to," Charles said.

Hurtado spoke in a deceptively gentle voice.

"Young man, you do understand that if I wish to, I can make you tell me whatever it is that you dreamed?"

Charles gave an unexpected smile. "You're Canon Tallis's friend. So I know there are certain things you won't do."

Hurtado's jaw did not relax. "I wouldn't be too certain of that."

Charles said, "You know that I can't tell you something deadly serious when I'm not sure. When Aunt Leonis gets back from Dragonlake, then I'll tell you."

Hurtado said, "The two of you are a pair. I'm surprised that you are not the nephew; you will tell me what you feel like telling me when you feel like telling me." He snorted. "Please understand that a man has been murdered, the murderer is at large, and we do not know where Simon and Tom Tallis are."

"I do realize that," Charles said somberly. "That's why I can't tell you anything which might be misleading."

"Let me be the judge of that," Hurtado said.

Charles only shook his head. "Tonight."

Hurtado tucked Aunt Leonis into the Hispano-Suiza beside the benevolent Vermeer, who wore, instead of his solar topee, an English straw boater. Miss Leonis had on the thin blue and white dress described by Charles, an ancient leghorn sun hat, and carried her lace parasol.

Vermeer started the engine, revving it fiercely, then nosed uphill, through a narrow street, the houses brightly painted with warm, sunny colors, reds, oranges, yellows, and cooler summer colors, varied shades of greens and blues. Despite her anxiety, Miss Leonis looked about with pleasure.

Vermeer pointed. "If you look through the open doors you can see courtyards and gardens. I live in such a house. It's very pleasant, though hotter in summer than a Dutchman is accustomed to." He drove around the corner into a large square, with a rococo bandstand, flowering cactus, tall, lush trees, towering palms. "Plaza Bolivar." After the cool beauty of the plaza they drove through what appeared to be the main street. Vermeer pointed out bank and post office.

"All the soldiers and policemen with guns," Miss Leonis said, "in front of the bank and the post office, and there—that policeman controlling traffic with his rifle slung and ready—is this the custom in Port of Dragons?"

"Port of Dragons is close to the border, and bandits come across too often for comfort. There's also a sizable band of Cubans in the hills, and the city officials are afraid of revolution."

"With reason?" she asked.

Without answering, Vermeer turned the car and drove rapidly down a long street of brightly colored row houses; suddenly the houses began to be separated and set in flower-filled gardens, and then they drove past prosperous and beautiful villas cheek by jowl with shacks made out of rusty corrugated metal and a few planks. The well-kept and imposing houses became fewer and farther apart, and without warning they were driving through a camp of rickety shacks. A sour and acrid stench assailed their nostrils.

"It looks like a refugee village." Miss Leonis held her handkerchief to her nose.

"It's not. It's the barrio—*ciudad de pobres*—the poor of Port of Dragons."

"Is this—exceptional?"

"Oh, no, you will find this everywhere."

"I understand why you did not answer my question about revolution," she said. "At home we see a few shacks, but never a whole city of them like this. They certainly can't be waterproof."

"They're not."

"What happens in a heavy rain?"

Vermeer's perpetual grin seemed to widen. "A lot of them wash into the sea."

The grin did not deceive her. "How do you stand it?"

He shrugged. "I do what I can. It is not enough."

She looked at the shacks. They seemed to steam in the heat. The laundry hung limp and dirty-looking on the lines.

"There's no easy answer," Vermeer said. "At La Guaira the government built several beautiful high-rise buildings on the waterfront. The people moved out of their shacks and into the apartments, and shortly thereafter most of them moved back to the shacks, where they can have their goat and their garden patch and where the home, bad as it is, is theirs."

A group of naked children with bloated bellies waved at the car. Miss Leonis and Vermeer waved back.

Then the barrio was behind them, and Vermeer drove along a super-highway through a scrubland not unlike some of South Carolina. Vermeer said it was called *monte*. On either side of the highway were booths where Indians were selling touristy gifts—though Miss Leonis wondered how many tourists would come here; it was hardly a resort area. There were also a number of booths with roofs of palm and banana leaves where native men were stopping to drink.

Miss Leonis disciplined herself to observe what was going on around her and not to think about Simon, or what was going to happen when they reached the Quiztano village. She asked, "What are they drinking?"

"Coconut milk." Vermeer slowed down as they passed the next stand, so she could see that the milk was not sold out of the coconut but was poured in and out of two pitchers. "They add sugar water and ice, so that the coconut milk gets dirty and diluted."

She watched as the server hacked several coconuts open with a machete, unplugged them, poured the milk into one of the pitchers, and threw out the coconut with all its meat.

"It looks highly unsanitary," Miss Leonis said as Vermeer accelerated. "But the countryside reminds me of home. No wonder Quentin Phair was happy to stay in North America. We don't have these tall cactus trees, but we do have the palms, and the oleander and bougainvillaea."

The highway narrowed and they drove through a village which Vermeer told her was typical of the area. It was gaudy and crowded, houses, shacks, villas, all crammed in together with no plan or pattern. In the center of the town was a square with a big, beautiful church. In front of the carved wooden doors was a little huddle of old men and women in black.

Miss Leonis regarded it carefully. "In North Florida where some of Quentin Phair's property was, there is Spanish architecture, too."

Vermeer pointed. "Pigs."

She looked, and several large pigs were wandering around the central fountain of the square. Shops crowded out onto the street, with Christmas-tree lights still strung up—possibly, she thought, —they never take them down.

"The houses are interesting," Vermeer said. "Look at that one, so shabby and poor—and yet you can see through the open door that the furniture is new and chrome. And it has always seemed strange to me that the largest and most prosperous villas front directly onto the street, just like the shacks, instead of facing the river, which flows behind them."

"What kind of people live here?" Miss Leonis asked. "And what do they do for a living?"

They left the village and drove across a long suspension bridge. "Most of them are involved in the oil industry in one way or another," Vermeer said, and ahead of them they could see what appeared to be hundreds of round oil tanks.

Suddenly the lake was on their right and Miss Leonis drew in her breath in surprise. Far into the lake sprouted the tall metal towers of oil wells. Vermeer drew up to the shore and stopped his Hispano-Suiza with a flourish, sprang out, and opened the door for Miss Leonis.

She stood beside him under the completely inadequate shade of her parasol. She felt that she was in some kind of hell. Not only was the heat fierce, but excess gas from one of the wells burst in flame from a pipe just a few feet away. Around the spouting flame, heat quivered visibly in the air. Nearby were several official-looking buildings outside which armed soldiers lounged.

Miss Leonis said, "I can see why there have to be men with rifles. All these oil wells must represent millions and millions of dollars. If there should be a revolution it would be quite a coup, and the United States would be just as upset as Venezuela. We depend on all that oil. No wonder even the traffic cops seem ready to shoot on the slightest provocation."

Vermeer nodded. "There is great wealth here. Next to Maracaibo it is the greatest wealth in Venezuela. Nor should one forget that the oil wells provide a reasonable standard of living for a great many people who would starve otherwise."

Miss Leonis looked down at her feet where black sludge oozed heavily out of the lake. "It looks to me as though the oil industry is raping the lake."

"That is for people like Dr. O'Keefe to decide. One thing I have learned in three years at Port of Dragons is that there are no easy solutions."

"It's like something out of Dante's *Inferno*," she said. "Some of those towers look as though they might be able to stride across the water like robots."

"I have had nightmares of them legging across the land and through the town," the Dutchman said. "But it makes me think of the English H. G. Wells rather than Dante. Shall we continue our journey now? I thought it a pity not to show you the oil wells since our route goes right by them."

They got back in the car. Miss Leonis settled herself. "I am glad to have seen the oil wells, although I do not find them reassuring. And I feel in need of reassurance."

The road narrowed, so that two cars would have had difficulty in passing. The *monte* pressed in on it.

Through trees on their left, Miss Leonis could see glimpses of the lake. They were beyond the oil wells now, and the water shimmered in the sunlight.

She pulled her leghorn hat forward to shade her eyes from the glare. Her heart ached. There should have been word of Simon by now. Perhaps she and Charles were both wrong to hold back information; they could have no idea what might mean something to Hurtado; and Vermeer had a keen intelligence behind his idiotic grin.

Vermeer turned toward her. "Only a few miles now, and then we will make the rest of the journey in a canoe."

"Splendid."

"You do not object to the canoe?"

"My dear young man, I was canoeing in the cypress-black waters around Pharaoh long before you were born. I can tell an alligator from a log. In an emergency I am still a good swimmer."

"Perhaps, during the next few minutes, you will tell me why this trip to Dragonlake is so important to you?"

"I will tell you," she said.

For the first time Vermeer looked at her without a smile.

On the *Orion* Hurtado moved from passenger to passenger, officer to officer, sailor to sailor. His jaw appeared to grow darker with each interview, but his eyes retained their sharpness, and his expression remained impassive. He spent more time with Jan than with anybody else.

* * *

In the jungle Simon and Canon Tallis struggled to keep their fire going.

"Will we have to spend another night here?" Simon asked.

"It's possible. Not to worry about it now. We managed last night."

"Some of those animals came pretty close to us."

"We'll have to keep the fire going."

"Do you think anyone's seen our smoke?"

"The jungle is extraordinarily thick and our smoke is fairly thin."

"What kind of animals do you think they were last night?"

"Could be many different kinds, from wood mice to wild boar."

"Snakes?"

"We have to watch for snakes as we collect wood, Simon. I don't think they'll bother us at night. How about looking for some more berries? Our frugal breakfast seems a long time ago."

"All right, sir."

Canon Tallis handed him one of the two spears he had fashioned during the night. "You're not apt to need this as long as you're careful, but you might as well take it with you. And do not go out of sight of the fire. Better to be hungry than separated."

"Is it going to be all right, sir?"

Canon Tallis adjusted his palm sun hat. "In terms of eternity, of course it is going to be all right."

"But in terms of right now?"

"No use borrowing trouble, Simon."

"You think Hurtado will find us?"

"Yes. I do think that he will find us. But I can't promise that he will."

Simon turned away. "Aunt Leonis doesn't make promises unless she's positive, either. But if you think he's going to find us that's good enough for me. I'll try to find us more berries. If I climb up and get a coconut do you think we can get into it?"

"I think so," the canon said. "I've found two good flat rocks we could use for crushing purposes."

"We're really managing very well, aren't we?"

"We're an extraordinary pair."

"Aunt Leonis is going to be very worried about us, and so are Poly and Charles and Mr. Theo. I'm very glad your señor comandante Hurtado knows about us."

Miss Leonis sat in the center of a large dugout canoe. Vermeer was in front, and occasionally turned around to nod reassuringly. A young man from the Quiztano village sat in the stern and paddled deftly and swiftly. He was long-limbed and fine-boned, and the golden-bronze of his skin seemed to be lit from within. He wore a short orange tunic, belted in leather, with a knife case. The acathine folds of his eyes slanted up toward the temples on either side, reminding her of the eyes of young warriors in early Greek sculpture.

He told them that his name was Ouldi, and that he had been sent by Umar Xanai to guide them, and that he spoke English and Spanish. But that was all the information he gave them. His face was as impassive as Hurtado's, and he paddled swiftly and in silence, his oar knifing the water without a splash.

The trip on the lake was cooled by a light wind which ruffled the water. If Miss Leonis had not been beset by anxiety and misgivings she would have enjoyed it. Now that they were nearly there she felt herself trembling in anticipation. She could not escape the thought that Simon might be the next young Phair to be cut down. She tried to eradicate this horror by thinking of Charles: What did he expect her to see at Dragonlake? Could it possibly be Simon?

"Look." Vermeer pointed.

Ahead of them in the lake, small round buildings on high stilts stretched out in the water, somewhat like the oil wells. But where the oil wells had seemed alien and sinister, the Quiztano village appeared to her to be natural and delightful. —It is probably very much the same way it looked when Quentin first came here, she thought.

It was certainly exactly as he had described it. Her old eyes rested on the pleasant scene almost with a sense of déjà vu. Half of each circular building was enclosed by a panel of loosely woven straw screening. As they approached the house farthest out in the water Miss Leonis saw a young woman slide the matting around so that the interior of her dwelling would be protected from the sun. All around the circumference of the small and airy building, flowers were blooming. The whole village, she realized, was bright with flowers. The roofs of the small dwellings, like those of the coconut sellers, were covered with palm or banana leaves. Small boats were tied to the slender pilings of many of the dwellings.

Ouldi paddled swiftly toward the shore, past the stork-like dwellings, under several of them. On shore many canoes were pulled up onto the beach out of the water, and she could see a sizable group of people assembled to watch their arrival. No sign of Simon.

Four young men detached themselves from the group and ran splashing through the water to pull the canoe high up onto the sand. Vermeer jumped out, holding out his hands in greeting.

Ouldi, still expressionless, picked Miss Leonis up and set her down gently on the beach. She stood there and looked about her. Had she really expected to see Simon? Not really; it was a forlorn hope. If it had been Simon, Charles would have been more definite. Then what did he expect her to see?

There were not as many houses on land as in the water; a few of the round, stilted dwellings, and, most impressive of all the buildings, two long rectangles with flower-filled verandas. Between the two large buildings, in the center of the greensward, was a large statue. From a distance she could not tell whether it was carved from wood or stone; it was the figure of a woman, inordinately tall, flowing in graceful lines from earth to sky, so that it seemed to belong to both. Quentin had mentioned the statue of a goddess, and that her religion was important to his Umara, and it seemed to him no worse than any other form of worship. Religion, to Quentin, was woman's work.

Behind the greensward the jungle reached upward to become a mountain, looming high into the sky. There was a fresh, flower-scented breeze blowing through the village, and a sense of calm and cleanliness. Though the stilted dwellings had a light and windswept look, they were far more substantial than the hovels in the barrio. The mountain itself protected the village, rather than overwhelming it.

The villagers reflected the exuberant colors of their flowers; the young men wore short, colored tunics; on the older men the tunics were longer. The women wore flowing, brightly patterned gowns; everywhere was poinciana scarlet, jacaranda azure, laburnum flame.

—No wonder Quentin could plan to make his life here.

Vermeer was shaking hands with the assembled group, and seemed to know some of them intimately. He bowed low to an old man in a long white robe who came from one of the round dwellings on the greensward. The old man embraced Vermeer, kissing him first on one cheek, then on the other, and thirdly, ceremoniously, on the forehead.

The Dutchman returned the three kisses with joyful formality. "I greet you, Umar Xanai. And I bring to you one who has news of the long-gone One. Her name is Miss Leonis Phair, for she herself is of the line of the Phair."

The old man bowed courteously. "You bring us news, Señora Phair?"

She shook her head. "Sir, I come hoping for news. Do you know where my nephew is?"

Umar Xanai replied, "We know nothing of a nephew. We await the Phair."

Miss Leonis's disappointment was acute, but she said only, "Yes, I know. That is why I am here. I have come to find the past. And now I look for Simon, Simon Bolivar Quentin Phair Renier, a descendant of your Phair."

The old chieftain gestured and two young men ran lightly up the steps to the larger of the round houses and returned with a chair made of young trees laced together with vines. When Miss Leonis was seated one of the young men took her parasol and shaded her with it, while a boy barely past childhood, no older than Simon, fanned her with a palm leaf. Again Umar Xanai bowed over her hand with Western courtesy.

She stiffened as she saw a litter being carried out of the dwelling from which her chair had come. On the litter was a small figure in a silvery-blue robe.

Ouldi said in his rather flat voice, "It is the Umara. She is so old now that she can no longer walk. She eats and drinks little. She spends her time in fasting and prayer."

The Umara was attended by two women in long gowns of silvery-blue, like moonlight. The litter was carried close to Miss Leonis's chair and she could see that the woman sitting on it was indeed very old, much older than she herself. The skin did not have the interior glow of the other Quiztanos, but was the grey-brown of a coconut. She wore a turban and Miss Leonis suspected that she had little or no hair. Her skull showed clearly through the almost transparent skin. Her eyes were sunk deep in their sockets, but they seemed to pierce.

Umar Xanai beckoned to Ouldi. The young man hurried to him, and the old chief dropped one arm lightly on the shoulders of Ouldi's orange tunic. "Your escort, Señora Phair, is one of my great-grandsons."

"Several greats, I should say," Vermeer remarked. "Ouldi is barely out of boyhood."

"You should not worry so much about the bindings of time," the old man said, then turned to Miss Leonis.

"Ouldi has just returned to us. He has been away at the big university. Our friend Vermeer arranged for it. So, Ouldi, now you will serve as interpreter. I am too old for long conversing in strange tongues. And the Umara tires even more easily."

The ancient Umara spoke a few words, and began to laugh.

Ouldi said, "She says that she was told that an Old One was coming, and she laughs because the Miss Phair is so young." He stopped, cocking his head to listen as the Umara spoke again, this time with no laughter. "She wants to know if you have the memory that goes beyond death."

"Perhaps."

Ouldi listened again, his head on the slender stalk of neck cocked like a bird's. "She wants to know where the Phair is."

Miss Leonis was surprised to have Vermeer speak to her without even a trace of a smile. "Please be careful how you answer," he said.

She turned to Ouldi, thought for a moment, then said, "I do not know where he is, and this causes me much anxiety."

The Umara nodded in satisfaction at her response. "Again we have sent hunters out to look for him. As they found him before, so they will find him now."

"The jungle is very large," Miss Leonis said. "How will they know where to look?"

"They will go to where they found the Phair the first time."

"And if he is not there?"

"He will be there. Already we have had messages that smoke has been seen. He will be there."

Despite her misgivings, Miss Leonis caught hope from the strength of the Umara's conviction.

The ancient woman continued, "And now we two must speak alone together. You will come to my dwelling, with Ouldi to speak for us." She waved her stick-thin arm imperiously and the litter was raised. The two moonlight-clad women came immediately to her side; now Miss Leonis noted that, though both seemed to her to be young, there must be over a generation separating them. She guessed that they were being trained in the duties of the Umara, from whose point of view anybody under a hundred must be young.

Ouldi helped Miss Leonis rise from the low and supple chair which had been gentle to her tired bones. He spoke in the strange liquid syllables of Quiztano, which reminded Miss Leonis of flowing water and which was completely different from the flat intonation with which he spoke English. The two youths who held parasol and fan moved along with them over the greensward, which was soft and springy under their feet. She moved as though in a dream. Perhaps fatigue and the automatic anesthesia of over-anxiety accounted for her lack of emotion at this extraordinary situation.

She asked, "What are the two long rectangular buildings on either side of the statue?"

"They are the Caring Places, the Caring Places of the Phair."

"What does that mean?"

Ouldi repeated, "They are the Caring Places. For those who are dying. For those who are ill and may, with care, recover."

She stopped. The two youths with parasol and fan

quickly stepped back to shade her. "What did my ancestor—the Phair—have to do with all this?"

"It was his thought that the Quiztanos should have special places in which to provide care. We have always had the Gift, but the idea of the Caring Places came from the Englishman, and it was with him that we made the first one."

Miss Leonis looked at the great statue. She could see now that it had originally been carved of wood, but it was so old that the wood had acquired the patina of stone. The face was serene; the lips were quirked in a slight smile which gave a feeling of delight. The carved eyes, however, were as dark and enigmatic as Ouldi's. "What—who—is—?"

Ouldi looked up at the statue and returned its smile. "Until I went away for my studies I understood better than I understand now. She is the one through whom we see the stars and hear the wind."

"Your goddess?"

"Perhaps I would call her that now, though I think I would be wrong. For she is not what she is; and she is more than she is. We do not worship her or pray to her as some of the people in the cities pray to their plaster saints in the gaudy churches. The Umara prays through her, and so does Umar Xanai."

"And the rest of you?"

"Prayer, too, is a gift. We do not all have it. But we benefit from those who do."

Still Miss Leonis did not move toward the dwelling of the Umara. She looked at the two long airy Caring Places. "These—we would call them hospitals today, would we not?"

Ouldi laughed, but there was no pleasure in his laughter. "I think not. When I was at the big university I got a terrible pain in my side and I was taken to the hospital and my appendix was removed. I would not want anybody I love to be ill in a big city hospital. No. These are Caring Places."

"Two Caring Places for a small village—are the Quiztanos often ill, then?"

"Seldom, seldom. We are strong and live long, not as long as the Umara, for we do not have her need and promise to keep, but long, long."

"But who are the Caring Places for, then?"

"For any who may need them. When the Phair and his Umara started them it was for those injured in the wars—liberator or royalist, it did not matter. Many men who were left to die lived because they were brought to us for caring. And those who died did not die alone. We helped them make the journey from here to there."

"Us—we—you talk as though you had been there."

"It is part of the Memory," Ouldi said. "I share in it."

Miss Leonis looked again at the statue. "There isn't war here now. Who is in the Caring Places?" She looked toward the long buildings. The porches were bright with flowers, and the screens were adjusted to provide shade.

Ouldi followed her gaze. "Those who are ill, hungry, filled with the diseases of poverty and starvation. There are some ill from the fish in the far section of the lake. You must have driven by the barrio?"

"Yes," Miss Leonis said. "What happens when the Caring Places are full?"

Ouldi shook his head. "They often are, but they hold as many as we can care for at one time. The people from the barrio come to us; they bring their babies to us. They know that we will care for them and help them make the journey through the valley of death if that is the destination."

"Who does the caring?"

"Those men and women of the Quiztanos who have the Gift, those who have been called to give their lives to the Caring Places. One must be very strong to go through the other side of night with the dying and then return."

"And Quentin Phair—he started all this?"

"I don't know about Quentin, but the Phair started many things," Ouldi said, "both good and bad. He made promises and broke them and there are those who are still angry."

"Here, among the villagers?"

"No. The Umara and Umar Xanai will not permit anger and hate to remain in our midst. Each generation there are those who leave here and make their way in the cities. Some of them have been filled with a sick desire for vengeance, and although they are no longer Quiztanos, they drink and talk about the Quiztano revenge and their lost heritage. Hatred is not the way to bring the Phair back."

She said, "You have left the village and gone to the city and you did not stay there—you returned."

"I am betrothed to an Umara."

"Would you have returned otherwise?"

"I think that I would. At the university I learned much, including that I do not like much of what is supposed to be civilization. Now, Señora Phair, I have talked with you for too long. We must not keep the Umara waiting." He took her arm and urged her forward. When they reached the Umara's dwelling place he gestured to the youths with parasol and fan to wait outside, and helped Miss Leonis up the steep steps. The Umara's two waiting women were adjusting the screens to provide the maximum shade and breeze, and as they slid the screens around, a shaft of sunlight pierced the interior and spotlighted a man's face.

Miss Leonis felt her heart thud crazily within her chest.

The man was not alive. It was a portrait. The portrait of Simon Bolivar.

Hurtado and Vermeer sat on the boat deck.

"You saw the portrait yourself?" Hurtado asked the Dutchman.

"Yes. It is a fine portrait, and an excellent likeness of Bolivar in his prime."

"And on the back?"

"*For my son, born of Umara.* Actually, one had to know that that was what was there. It looked to me as though someone had tried to sand and chip the words away. The wood on which the portrait is painted is thin in places and some of the letters were cut so deep that it would have been impossible to eradicate them without cutting into the portrait. Only the letters U-M-A-R are still clear."

"How did the old lady explain them?"

"She said that until she had read the journals and letters there was no reason to be curious. Unless one has heard of the Quiztanos at Dragonlake, U-M-A-R is only a meaningless jumble of letters. She said that she had thought it might be the mark of the artist."

Hurtado's jaw seemed to darken. "I need to talk to her."

Vermeer nodded sympathetically. "She could not have made the trip back."

"Are you positive?"

"I myself felt her pulse. It was weak, and far too rapid, and very uneven. Her zeal to learn the truth was greater than her strength. And she is half ill with anxiety over the boy."

"With cause. I have learned that Forsyth Phair died two years ago in Salt Lake City, Utah. The passport and all else that the impostor gave the old woman are excellent forgeries. So it is conceivable that the murderer murdered the wrong man."

Vermeer rubbed his nose. "The plot thickens."

"The murderer may not have known that Phair was an assumed name, and it may have been a Phair he was after."

"The ancient Quiztano vendetta against all Phairs?"

"I am a Latin, Vermeer, and I take such things more seriously than you do. Hate does not die easily around here. Nor the passion to bring past crimes to judgment. Don't forget that there are at this moment Israelis in Argentina tracking down Nazis."

"Yes. That, too, is a long time to hold hate."

"Hate dies less easily than love. How did the Quiztanos explain the portrait in their village?"

Vermeer said, "I would like a beer. How about you?"

Hurtado rose and went to the call bell.

When he sat down again, Vermeer said, "Umar Xanai said that they do not know how the portrait came to them."

"Oh?"

"It was brought to the village, it seems, by a fisherman who has Quiztano blood. He could not or would not tell them how he got it."

"Could not?"

"According to Umar Xanai, he was in a state of terror. All he wanted was to unload the portrait."

Both men were silent as they heard steps. Jan climbed up from the promenade deck. "You rang, sir?"

"Yes, Jan, two beers, please." Vermeer's smile sprang back to his face. He looked after Jan, running down the steps, and asked, "What are you going to do about him?"

"Jan? Tonight, nothing."

Vermeer said, "It was Jan who took me for my first visit to the Quiztanos, otherwise I shouldn't have been welcomed. I feel that I am betraying my friend."

"If he is innocent he has nothing to fear. If he is involved in smuggling—"

Vermeer cut him off. "No. I can't think of Jan as belonging to the world of smugglers, even the more innocent kind."

"Is there an innocent kind?"

"The early smuggling—tea, sugar, spices—I cannot think of such goods in the same category as drugs and chemicals."

"What about the art racket?"

"Art what?"

"Racket. An American idiom."

"It's bad. But it's still not quiet as contemptible as drugs, as antibiotics and steroids cut with poisons, as chemicals misused to destroy life for the sake of greed. Smuggling is far worse today than it used to be."

"It is a sin to steal a pin."

"What?"

"An English idiom. Smuggling is smuggling. One step leads to another."

"Jan has not stolen a pin."

"How well do you know him?" Hurtado asked calmly.

"I thought I knew him extremely well, but of course I see him only when the *Orion* puts in at Port of Dragons, and when he takes me out to Dragonlake—but I have always sensed in him a deep innocence."

"Perhaps that very innocence makes it possible for someone less innocent to use him for less than innocent purposes."

"Gutiérrez?" Vermeer suggested hopefully.

"Have you got anything on him?"

"Not yet. Remember, I'm only a consul, and I don't have an army of policemen and detectives and secret-service people at my beck and call."

"You might be interested to know that he has flown the coop."

"Has what?"

"An English idiom. I sent for him this morning and was told that he has gone to visit his mother, who is very ill. Marvelously convenient how mothers can get ill when the heat is on—another English idiom."

"Where is this alleged mother?"

"In one of the small villages deep in the jungle. He preempted a helicopter. No telephone, of course. He cannot be reached."

Vermeer pulled up one of his knee socks and straightened the garter. "He has a reputation for knowing the jungle well, including places that can be reached only by canoe or copter. I prefer to think of oily little Gutiérrez involved in dark doings rather than one of my compatriots. Jan does have a Dutch passport. No, no, he wouldn't do anything to hurt Van Leyden."

"It will look bad for Van Leyden if someone on his ship is dealing in narcotics on the side."

"Narcotics is only a small part of it. Chemicals, including mercury."

"Mercury. Yes," Hurtado said. "You know, Vermeer, if Dr. O'Keefe had been murdered I could have understood it better than Phair."

"Because it is an ill-kept secret that he has been brought to Venezuela to investigate Dragonlake?"

"There have been several cases of mercury poisoning among the people who live near one of the chemical plants. The oil wells are the obvious pollutant, but not necessarily the most dangerous one."

"Industrial effluents containing mercury absorbed by fish which are then eaten by the people of the barrio? Yes, I've heard. Ouldi said something."

"It's one of the nastier forms of poisoning, with neurological damage and intense pain." Hurtado looked grim. "I'd better have O'Keefe watched, then. Does he have any idea he may be in danger?"

"He's no fool." Vermeer suddenly looked as grim as the policeman.

Jan appeared with a tray, two bottles of beer, and two glasses. He set it down on the bench between the two men. Instead of leaving immediately he asked anxiously, "Is there any news of Simon?"

"Not yet," Hurtado said.

* * *

Miss Leonis sat on the veranda of the Umara's house. The Umara had been placed on a low couch, and Umar Xanai sat on the floor, as did Ouldi. A large round tray was set on a low table between them. It contained a graceful bowl of fruit, and a corresponding pitcher of a cool and delicious drink which seemed to have been made from a combination of fruits and herbs.

Umar Xanai passed a glass of the pale-green beverage to Miss Leonis. "This is a restorative. It will give you strength and calm your heart."

She sipped it appreciatively. "Thank you. I had not realized quite how tired I am from my journeyings."

The Umara spoke in her strange, ancient voice, and Ouldi translated. "Your journey through time as well as space?"

Miss Leonis sipped again. "Yes. I am learning that I share in your Memory. It is our loss in my world that we no longer value the memory of our people."

Umar Xanai replied, "Those who do not share in the Memory are only a part of themselves. It is good that you have come to fulfill what has been lost."

Miss Leonis sighed. Her heart pained within her. As she sipped the cool liquid the grey look receded from her face, but her eyes were dark with pain.

Ouldi said, "The Phair is safe. The Umara promises."

Miss Leonis bowed. "I am grateful. And grateful, too, for your kindness and hospitality. I understand from Mynheer Vermeer that you do not encourage strangers."

Umar Xanai replied, "We have a work to do. It is easily misunderstood. If the wrong people come with modern investigations we might be forbidden to do our work—or they might want us to make it bigger, and that would destroy it. And then"—he pointed toward the great carving—"she would no longer smile."

Miss Leonis set down her empty glass. Her breathing was no longer agony, but it still rasped. "It is very kind of you to keep me here tonight. The trip back to Port of Dragons would have been too much for me. And I am not sure when—or if—I will be able to leave."

Umar Xanai smiled. "It is our honor to have you with us, for as long as need be. We knew that you were coming to Venezuela even before the Dutchman made the arrangements for you today, so we have been expecting you."

"How did you know?"

"Jan, the steward on the *Orion*. I have in my Memory a picture of his Quiztano grandmother when she was young and beautiful and in love with the big blond youth from Holland. Jan has become dear to my heart with his love of the Quiztano part of his heritage. He knows our way of sending messages—a whistle here, the beat of a drum there, another whistle, and it is quicker than your modern machines."

"How did Mynheer Vermeer make the arrangements for today?"

"Thus. Through Jan. Jan feared the trip would overtax you, so even before you arrived we had made preparations for you to stay." A twinkle came into the old man's eye, and he spoke swiftly to Ouldi, the liquid syllables bubbling like a brook in early spring.

Ouldi said, "Grandfather says that you will be more comfortable here than at the new so-modern hotel. Always at night a breeze comes over the lake and the forest lends us the coolness of its shadows and the mountain gives us the strength of its peace. And"—he gestured toward the statue—"she gives us her blessing."

"Your Lady of the Lake," Miss Leonis said.

Ouldi translated, "Not of the lake only. She speaks to us not merely of the waters, but of the wind and the rain and the mountain and the stars and the power behind them all."

Miss Leonis looked out over the peaceful scene. "I, too, trust the same power."

The Umara, who seemed to have fallen asleep, spoke.

Ouldi listened carefully. "She says that this Power is the Power which has all Memory. Even her Memory is as nothing compared to the Memory of the Power behind the stars."

Miss Leonis said, "To be part of the memory of this power is for life to have meaning, no matter what happens." She had based her life on this faith. She could not begin to doubt it now.

Simon and Canon Tallis sat by their fire.

"But you don't think we're going to have to stay here more than one more night, do you?"

"No, Simon. If nobody has found us by tomorrow morning I think we will have to start heading toward the sea. We've run out of edible berries within moderate radius of our campsite. But you did nobly indeed to get us those coconuts. I was beginning to feel dehydrated."

"So was I," Simon said. "I don't think anything has ever tasted so good." He looked at his scratched hands. His thighs were scraped from the descent from the high tree. Why did the coconuts have to be at the very top? But they still had two coconuts for morning.

Tallis said, "I've been given too many warnings about the water in South America streams and rivers to risk drinking, no matter how clean that nearby stream may look. There are tiny organisms which bite and then lay eggs in one's bloodstream, for instance, which cause a slow death. It's not worth the risk."

The dark seemed to increase around them. Simon broke the silence to ask, "When Quentin Phair came to see about his mother's inheritance in North Florida and Georgia and South Carolina, was it like this?"

"It was probably more like this than like the country you grew up in. Our ancestors braved considerable danger without making any fuss about it."

"We're not making much fuss, are we?"

"You're not," Canon Tallis said. "I'm doing a good deal of grunting and groaning over my physical exertions. I'm woefully out of condition. Now, Simon, you take the first watch tonight, and I'll sleep for an hour or so. Don't hesitate to wake me if you see or hear anything."

"Are you ever frightened?" Simon asked as the canon arranged himself on his bed of moss and fern. He was a large man, a little too heavy. His bald head caught and reflected the light from the fire.

"Frequently."

"Are you frightened now?"

"No. There doesn't seem to be any particular reason to be frightened. But I am tired from our labors. Good night, Simon."

"Good night, Uncle Father." Simon noticed that the priest kept his wooden spear under his hand.

The night seemed even more alive with sound than

had the night before, or perhaps his ears were more attuned to it. He thought he could even hear insects moving along the rough bark of the tree trunks. The birds settled down for the night, but more noisily than the canon. They seemed to be passing along messages to each other. He was sure he recognized the chittering of monkeys, although they had seen none. The day had been brightened by the wings of birds, but the only animals they had seen were a kind of squirrel, and many lizards of varying sizes.

Simon stiffened and put his hand on his own spear as he saw two eyes reflecting their firelight. He threw another piece of wood on the fire, but he couldn't use too much wood or it wouldn't last until morning. The eyes retreated.

Simon looked over at the canon, whose body was relaxed. The palm-leaf hat was over his eyes. He was breathing quietly, not snoring, but the relaxed breathing of sleep.

The boy turned and the eyes were there again, this time closer. He took a stick and stirred the fire, but the eyes did not go away. He took a small stone and threw it as hard as he could. Whatever beast it was, it moved heavily, with a crackling of twigs, but retreated only a few inches. The eyes looked small and ugly in the firelight, but Simon did not think the animal was as small as the eyes would indicate. He tried staring it down. The eyes blinked, but opened again. There was a small snap of twigs as the beast moved forward until Simon could see what it was: a wild boar.

With trembling hands he grabbed the spear, shouting, "Go away!"

Canon Tallis was awake and on his feet in seconds, holding his spear lightly in his right hand.

There was a horrendous noise of grunting, screeching beast, and the canon shouting, "Out of the way!"

Simon stepped back, spear in hand, ready to move in, but keeping out of the way of the canon's feet. The snarling of the animal was the most repellent sound he had ever heard, but then the snarling changed to a scream which was worse. The canon, too, was breathing heavily with effort. His spear was deep in the boar, but the animal thrashed wildly and with enormous strength, and Simon could see that the canon was beginning to tire.

Suddenly the boar turned so that Simon, putting all his weight into his action, could thrust his own spear into the leathery hide.

But the raging beast was stronger than both of them, although it no longer wanted to attack. With two spears buried deep in its flesh it burst away from them and crashed into the forest.

"Will it come back?" Simon panted.

Canon Tallis was taking great gulps of the dark, humid air. "I doubt it. I think we wounded it pretty badly. That was good work, Simon. I'm not sure I could have kept up much longer. Are you all right?"

"Yes, sir."

"You're a brave boy." Canon Tallis stretched one leg toward the fire. The dark cloth of the trousers was ripped from thigh to ankle, and blood dripped on the ground.

"Oh, sir, he hurt you!"

The canon examined an ugly gash along his calf. "It's only a flesh wound. But I ought to wash it."

"Not the stream," Simon said. "It would be as dangerous as drinking it."

"Bright lad. You're quite right. I'll let it bleed a bit, and the blood itself will clean it. See if you can gather me some clean ferns and I'll stanch the blood with them."

When the wound was covered with fresh green, and the bleeding stopped, the canon said, "I doubt if either of us will do much sleeping for the rest of the night. Let's go over, once more, everything we know about the theft of the portrait and the murder of the Phair. Each time you tell me, you remember something new."

Dr. Wordsworth and Dr. Eisenstein were playing cards in the salon. All the portholes were open and the fans going but it was still hot and stuffy. Dr. Wordsworth slammed down her cards.

"I'm going to Hurtado."

"Inés, no!"

"I should have gone immediately and I was too involved in myself, as usual, to realize."

"But why? What good will it do?"

"Don't you see that if Hurtado knows Phair was involved in smuggling, it may be of immense importance?"

"Yes, I suppose it may be, but then you will have to tell him . . ."

"Everything. It's all right. As far as society is concerned, my time in jail has paid my debt, and my life has been impeccable since. I left for the United States as soon as I got out of jail and not a thing that I've done in my new country cannot be looked at in the light of the sun. And my American passport will help." She stood up. She looked tall and elegant in a long white skirt slit up the sides to show her shapely legs. She smiled at her friend. "Hurtado is a man. When I dressed for dinner I think I already knew what I had to do."

"Would you like me to come with you?"

"No. Thank you. Though he will probably want to talk with you afterward. You've known me longer than most people. So perhaps you'd better stay here and be available."

"Of course. You're very brave, Inés."

"Hurtado may think it a trifle late." Dr. Wordsworth left the salon.

Miss Leonis lay in the fragrant dark of Dragonlake. The high dwelling was, as Umar Xanai had promised, far cooler than the hotel had been. Air flowed beneath, above, through. She could hear the water lapping gently against the pilings of the dwelling huts in the lake. Somewhere nearby a night bird was singing sweetly. Whatever she had been given to drink had indeed helped her. For a while she had thought that her over-taxed heart was giving out, that she was going to die then and there among a strange people in a strange land with Simon who knows where.

Now she thought that she would be able to hold on until Simon was found at any rate and some of the confusions were straightened out—not only about Forsyth Phair, but about Simon and the Quiztanos.

But why was her portrait of Bolivar in the Umara's

dwelling place? It still stood there, although she could not see it in the dark.

—They will not be satisfied with the portrait, she thought. —They want Simon. What are we to do?

XII

THE RETURN
OF THE PHAIR

In the morning el señor comandante Hurtado assembled the passengers and told them that he had arrested Jan for the theft of the portrait and the murder of Forsyth Phair.

Simon slept fitfully toward morning. When he woke up, the canon was putting the last few twigs on the fire. His face looked flushed and feverish.

"Sir, are you all right?"

Tallis indicated his leg. "It seems to be a bit infected."

"Can you walk on it?"

"I don't think so, Simon."

"Well, then," Simon said after a moment, "I'd better try to find us some berries and stuff for breakfast. We've got another coconut, so we won't be dehydrated. I'll have to go a little farther afield for the berries, sir."

"Not until daylight."

"No, sir."

"And then stay within voice hail, Simon. It would be very easy to get lost. Call out every few seconds, and I'll call back."

"Yes, sir. I will. I'm sorry about your leg. Does it hurt much?"

"A bit."

"You were like St. George killing the dragon last night."

"A far cry, I'm afraid."

"You were close enough to St. George for me. Wild boars are probably more dangerous than dragons. Hurtado or someone should be along to find us any moment now."

"Yes, Simon. They ought. It should be daylight soon."

Miss Leonis rose early at Dragonlake, as she did at Pharoah. She awoke feeling refreshed, although her heart still seemed to rattle like a dry leaf.

With considerable effort she dressed in her blue and white dimity, and folded the soft gown she had been given to sleep in. Then she climbed carefully down the steps of the Umara's dwelling place and walked across the greensward to the lake's edge. Her breath came in small, shallow gasps.

Umar Xanai was there before her, alone, sitting in Charles's favorite position.

The old woman sat down silently, slightly to one side and behind him. Around her she could sense the sleeping village. Someone was moving on the porch of one of the Caring Places. Soon Dragonlake would be awake. All around her she heard bird song. A fish flashed out of the lake and disappeared beneath the dark waters. Above her the stars dimmed and the sky lightened.

When the sun sent its first rays above the mountain, Umar Xanai rose and stretched his arms upward. He began to chant. Miss Leonis could not understand the velvet Quiztano words, but it seemed clear to her that the old chieftain was encouraging the sun in its rising, urging it, enticing it, giving the sun every psychic aid in his power to lift itself up out of the darkness and into the light. When the great golden disc raised itself clear of the mountain the chanting became a triumphal, joyful song.

At the close of the paean of praise the old man turned to the old woman and bent down to greet her with the three formal kisses.

She asked, "You are here every morning?"

He nodded, smiling. "It is part of my duties as chief of the Quiztanos."

"To help the sun rise?"

"That is my work."

"It will not rise without you?"

"Oh, yes, it would rise. But as we are dependent on the sun for our crops, for our lives, it is our courtesy to give the sun all the help in our power—and our power is considerable."

"I do not doubt that."

"We believe," the old man said quietly, "that everything is dependent on everything else, that the Power behind the stars has not made anything to be separate from anything else. The sun does not rise in the sky in loneliness; we are with him. The moon would be lost in isolation if we did not greet her with song. The stars dance together, and we dance with them."

Miss Leonis smiled with joy. "I, too, believe that. I am grateful that you help the sun each morning. And when the moon wanes and the sky is dark—you are with the dying moon, are you not?"

"When the tide ebbs and the moon is dark, we are there."

"My tide is ebbing."

"We know, Señora Phair."

"It will be an inconvenience to you. I am sorry."

"Señora Phair, it is part of our Gift. We will be with you."

"I am not afraid."

"But you are afraid for the Phair."

"I am afraid for Simon."

"Do not fear, Señora 'Phair. You have come to redeem the past."

"That is not in my power," she said sadly.

He looked at her calmly. "You will be given the power."

"I can make no decisions for Simon."

"But you will allow him to make decisions for himself?"

"I have always tried to do so. I will not try to influence him by telling him that I will not be returning to South Carolina. I wish I shared your certainty that he is all right."

Umar Xanai nodded calmly. "He will be here before long. The Englishman with him has been hurt, and has to be carried. A litter will be made for him in the same way that a litter was once made for the Phair."

"How do you know all this?"

He smiled, all the wrinkles in his tan face fanning upward. "We have our own ways of seeing. They will be found today, your boy and his friend. I am not sure when. But today."

"I am grateful."

"Come." With amazing agility he sprang to his feet. "It is time that we broke our fast. You have need."

Miss Leonis accepted his strong hand; she could not have risen without him. "Thank you. I am grateful to have a few more days. It would ease me if I could be certain about Simon. Can you keep me going that long?"

He looked at her steadily. "You will have that much time. It is our Gift. Sometimes when we have sent out young men to the cities, to the hospitals and medical schools, the Gift is laughed at. Sometimes our young men laugh, too, and do not return."

"I know." She sighed. "The Great God Science. It has failed us, because it was never meant to be a god, but only a few true scientists understand that."

Again he smiled. "There are things that you must teach us, Señora Phair. The young Umaras seek time with you."

"They will teach me, too."

He held out his arm to support her, and together they walked slowly back to the village.

To the passengers on the *Orion* it seemed even hotter and more humid the second day in port than it had the first.

But now that Hurtado had made an arrest, the unloading of the ship began. No one was allowed on the foredeck, though the passengers could watch through the windows in the salon. One of the sailors sat in his high cab and manipulated the levers which controlled the great yellow cranes. From the promenade deck the passengers could see the station wagon hover over the dock, as the hearse had hovered, then drop down gently, all four wheels touching earth simultaneously.

Dr. Wordsworth and Dr. Eisenstein left the salon for the deck, seeking what little breeze there was. They leaned on the rail and watched a large crate swing onto the waiting mandibles of a fork lift. "They know what they're doing," Dr. Wordsworth said with considerable admiration.

Dr. Eisenstein turned from the dock and toward her companion. "Inés, do you really think it was Jan?"

"Hurtado's no fool," Dr. Wordsworth said, "but I confess I was surprised. However, since I've been unable to come up with a prime suspect myself, I have to assume that he knows what he's doing."

"But after what you told him about Mr. Phair being Fernando—"

Despite the heat Dr. Wordsworth shivered. "Interesting," she remarked casually, "how heat can affect one like cold. Hurtado was extraordinarily courteous with me. I have great respect for him. But has it occurred to you that what I told him may have been what he needed to put his finger on Jan?"

"But Jan is so open and friendly, and almost as vulnerable and innocent-seeming as Geraldo."

"Don't you realize, Ruth, that the innocent and the vulnerable are the very ones preyed upon by types like F.P.?"

"But Jan—!"

"I don't like it, either. But I'm grateful it's over."

Dr. Eisenstein glanced at the chair where she had put her straw bag of notebooks and academic periodicals. "Mr. Hurtado says we will be allowed ashore, soon. I'm glad he wasn't too hard on you last night."

Dr. Wordsworth laughed, a more spontaneous laugh than her companion had heard in some time. "Hurtado is an intelligent and successful and highly desirable man. I think he found me attractive—though if he had suspected me of murder that would have made no difference. But, do you know, Ruth, it's funny, theatrical

Vermeer I'm drawn to. Human beings are the most peculiar of all creatures."

Dr. Eisenstein smiled. "The feeling between you and Mr. Vermeer appears to be mutual."

"Here you go, matchmaking again. No, Ruth. Vermeer beams on the entire world and only he knows what goes on behind that smile. And I certainly have no desire to lose my heart to a Dutch consul in an obscure backwash of a country which is no longer mine."

"He knows a lot about anthropology—"

"Which makes up for all deficiencies in your eyes. Oh, I know he's not the idiot he appears. But all I meant was that Hurtado has the machismo and it doesn't even touch me. I'm sorry about Jan. I liked him. But Fernando Propice was a master at corrupting innocence."

Dr. Eisenstein put a restraining hand on Dr. Wordsworth's arm. "Look—"

Jan, his face pale, was walking down the gangplank, somewhat awkwardly, because he was handcuffed. A policeman walked in front of him, another behind him. The two women watched as he was pushed into a police car and driven off.

There had been scant pickings for breakfast, or for lunch, as Simon and Canon Tallis carefully called the bare handful of berries that made up their meals. They drank the milk from the last coconut, and chewed on a few greens which Simon recognized as being like the edible greens around Pharaoh, picked by Aunt Leonis and cooked with a little white bacon. But cooked greens and greens raw are quite different;

these tasted bitter, though at least they contained a little water and were worth chewing for that alone, for the coconut milk did little to assuage their thirst. Simon knew that if it had not been for Canon Tallis, he would long ago have cupped up water from the brook.

"If Gutiérrez is the type I think he is," the canon said, "he would choose a place with no safe water supply. Murder by indirection is what he's after."

"We've got to have something more to eat," Simon said. "I'll have to go a little farther."

"No, Simon. You went beyond voice range last time, and almost got lost."

"But I didn't get lost. I got back."

"You might not, the next time. It's not worth the risk of being separated. I know neither of us cares if we never see another coconut, but we can survive on them for a while longer, if you'll climb another tree. And by tomorrow I'll be able to walk."

Simon knew that Canon Tallis did not think much of the boy's chances of surviving alone in the jungle. —And I've never been a Boy Scout or anything, he acknowledged. —Aunt Leonis and I have led very sedentary lives.

He could recognize a water moccasin or a rattler or a coral snake. He did not think much of his ability to fight off a wild boar singlehanded.

By mid-afternoon it was apparent to both of them that the priest's wound was worsening. Despite frequent fresh dressings of cool leaves the wound became steadily more inflamed and suppurating. The flush of fever rose boldly in the canon's cheeks.

He reached up to the woven sun hat covering his bald pate. "I think I must have a touch of sun."

"You have fever, sir."

"Yes. Perhaps I have."

"You're not going to be able to walk by morning, sir."

The priest did not answer. Around them the jungle noises seemed to increase, to draw closer. They heard hoots, clucks, cackles; hisses, screeches, growlings.

"They smell my wound," Canon Tallis said. "If Hurtado has not found us by tomorrow you had better leave me here and head for the sea. Do you know how to guide yourself by sun and wind?"

"I've never had to, but—as you said—necessity makes a good teacher. I'll do my best to—" He broke off as there was a crescendo of noise and activity, and a sudden screeching of birds flying high up into the air above the jungle. Near their clearing twigs crackled, leaves rustled, a branch creaked.

Then, above them, Simon saw eyes, great obsidian eyes in a cat-shaped face. The body was spotted and rippled with muscles tensed to spring.

"Run!" Canon Tallis ordered. "Simon, run!"

Blind with terror, Simon ran.

Geraldo would not leave his hot box of a galley. He stood at the sink and washed cups and saucers which did not need washing. His face was stained with tears.

Poly hovered. "I know he didn't do it, Herald."

Tears gathered again in Geraldo's dark eyes. He blew his nose.

"But"—Poly asked hesitantly—"why did he lie about the key to cabin 5?"

"Jan does not lie."

"You still think he's covering up for somebody?"

Geraldo shrugged.

"You think he'll go on covering even if he's hanged for it—or whatever they do in Venezuela?"

Geraldo hunched his shoulders upward again.

"And the portrait—" Poly said. "How did the portrait get off the *Orion* and into the Umara's house at Dragonlake?"

"It could be done," Geraldo said slowly. "A fishing boat could come close enough so that a strong swimmer could get to the *Orion* unseen."

"Unseen by radar?"

"Yes. It is possible."

"And then what?"

"From the lower deck, where the pilot comes on, from there the portrait could easily be lowered into the water. And you said that it is painted on wood."

"That's what Simon said."

"So it would float."

"But wouldn't the salt water hurt it?"

"Perhaps not if it were only for a short time and if it were to be cleaned off immediately."

Poly looked at him admiringly. "You've really thought it all out, haven't you?"

"It seemed necessary."

"Have you told Comandante Hurtado?"

Again Geraldo shrugged. "I did not think that it would help Jan."

"You mean, it's something Jan could have done?"

"Jan—or the man who tried to push Simon overboard. And I have no doubt that the señor comandante could figure this much out for himself. He does not need me to tell him."

"But we don't know what he said to Jan, or what Jan said to him."

"We know enough. Jan was not quiet. He was heard. He swore he had nothing to do with it, any of it."

"And Simon and Uncle Father?"

The tears began to flow down Geraldo's cheeks. He spoke over a sob. "I do not understand the comandante Hurtado. I thought he was a man of wisdom. Why has he not found them and brought them to the *Orion?* We do not even know if they are alive."

Poly put her hand over Geraldo's mouth. "Stop! Stop!" She wondered at her own dry eyes.

Charles sought out Hurtado and was finally summoned up onto the bridge, where the policeman had been talking with the captain.

"You want to see me?" Hurtado asked.

"Yes, please. I had a dream last night."

Hurtado wiped his hand over his somber jaw. "It is late for dreams."

"Please—I saw a man being handcuffed, and it was not Jan, because Jan was crying, crying for the man."

"Who was it, then?"

"It was a man in a winter uniform, with his cap pulled down. I do not know who it was. But it was not Jan."

"Your dreams do not tell you enough."

"But my dreams have never lied. And it was not Jan who was being handcuffed, because Jan was there, weeping for whoever it was."

Hurtado spoke heavily. "Charles, I have to trust the evidence."

"But it was not Jan, I know it was not Jan."

Hurtado reminded him, "You yourself said that dreams do not hold up in court. I'll speak to you later, Charles. I have work to do."

"Simon and Uncle Father?" Charles asked. "Have you found them?"

Hurtado looked over the boy's head, not meeting the blue eyes. "A party of Quiztanos is searching for them, and they can move in the jungle where no white man can manage."

"But you think they're all right?"

Now their eyes met. "I will not think otherwise."

Simon did not know how long or how far he ran in his panic, crashing through underbrush, not thinking of scorpion or snake, not feeling the lash of vines cutting across his face. At last the density of the jungle itself stopped him. He had run into a wall of trees and bushes laced together by vines.

He stood still, panting, his heart thudding wildly. Sweat suddenly poured out of him, while his mouth and throat were parched.

He had run away.

He had run away from Canon Tallis with his wounded leg. He had run away from whatever kind of wildcat it was which had been about to leap on them.

He had abandoned Canon Tallis, incapable of protecting himself, left him to be killed. He had thought only of saving his own life.

Suddenly he was furious, furious with Quentin Phair.

—If you hadn't run away from Dragonlake I'd never have run away from Uncle Father. If you'd been where you ought to be, then I'd never have deserted my friend. It's your blood in my veins that's responsible—

No. He could hear Aunt Leonis as clearly as though she were there in the jungle beside him. 'Ultimately your decisions are yours, Simon. You have a goodly heritage, but it is up to you to live up to it. Quentin Phair cannot make you brave in an emergency. You have to condition your own reflexes of braveness.'

If Quentin Phair could not make him brave, neither could he make him a betrayer.

—But I'm blood of your blood, Quentin, he thought bitterly.

His anger ebbed, leaving him spent and heavy of heart. He began to walk. He had no idea in what direction he had run, or if he was heading toward or away from the clearing. He was afraid of returning to the clearing, afraid of what he might find there. But he had run away, there was no evading that, and the only thing left to do was to return. He knew that it would be too late, but it was still what he had to do.

Shortly after lunch Gutiérrez appeared. His mother had recovered from her illness; the sight of her son had given her renewed strength.

Vermeer, staying on the *Orion* in Hurtado's absence, greeted him effusively, rejoicing over the miraculous recovery of el señor jefe de policía Gutiérrez's beloved mother. "And I am happy to tell you, my dear Gutiérrez, that Hurtado has made a definitive arrest. All our troubles are over."

Gutiérrez's surprise was as enlarged as Vermeer's sympathy. "But who can it be? Never have I known so complex a problem!" When Vermeer told him, he said,

"Of course, I should have guessed. I have been suspecting that young man of indulging in smuggling for some time, but could not pin anything definite on him."

"Smuggling as well as murder and theft and kidnapping!" Vermeer exclaimed.

Gutiérrez rubbed his pudgy hands together. "It explains much."

"Does it? Why does smuggling explain the murder?"

"The Bolivar portrait," Gutiérrez said. "That is an extremely valuable portrait. If Jan were caught stealing the portrait by Mr. Phair, then he would be forced to dispose of him. There is much profit to be made from stolen art treasures."

"You think Jan was part of a ring of art thieves?"

"It is likely, is it not?"

"And what about the boy and the Englishman?"

Gutiérrez moved his face into distressed lines. "They have of course been found?"

"Not yet. We know more or less where they are; the Quiztanos saw smoke in the interior of the jungle, and a party is out looking for them. We expect them to be found shortly."

"A happy issue to all our problems," Gutiérrez said, but he did not sound happy. "Pray do excuse me, señor consul, but I must get back to my job. I wanted to come directly to the *Orion,* but now there is work to be done, all the daily routines to be picked up."

When Gutiérrez had bustled off, greeted at the gangplank by what seemed to be hundreds of waiting minions, Vermeer went out onto the dock and spoke to a man who was lounging in the shade of his truck.

* * *

During the afternoon the pain in Canon Tallis's leg had become so acute that he knew he was not going to be able to keep it from the boy much longer. As his fever mounted, his mind began to remind him of a movie camera; sometimes everything was close up, clear, each detail visible; then the camera would move back so that all was far away. When he became aware of the beast in the tree above them, crouched to spring, he viewed it as from an incredible distance, as through the wrong end of a telescope. He knew that he could not run. He heard himself calling to Simon to run, and then he crossed himself and prepared to die.

His life did not flash before him—after all, he was not drowning—but he had a quiet feeling of pleasure that his life had been rich in experience and friendship and the love of God.

He closed his eyes.

Then he heard a thwack, and a scream, and a thud, and the wildcat dropped from the tree, dead, an arrow piercing its heart.

The Smiths sat in the shadow of the canvas canopy on the promenade deck. "That nice Jan," Mrs. Smith said. "It is hard to believe."

"Not many people who knew us in Burlington would ever have suspected that I was once so involved in gambling that I nearly ruined our lives."

"But—murder! I cannot see Jan as a murderer."

Mr. Smith patted her hand gently. "The human heart is too often an ugly thing, Patty. There are not many gentle souls like you. If it hadn't been for you I *would* have ruined us."

"I knew what you were really like," Mrs. Smith said. "You're a good man, Odell, and I love you."

"You've made me what I am, Patty. You gave me the courage to stand up to Phair and refuse to be blackmailed. I love you, too, and just as much as I did fifty years ago."

They sat holding hands, and smiling at each other, and did not even notice Dr. Eisenstein looking at them with a rather wistful expression.

It was blunder and stubbornness and sense of smell and possibly pheromones which guided Simon until finally he broke out of the undergrowth and into the clearing. The jungle closed quickly over his tracks.

The fire was there, no more than smoldering ashes. That was all.

No Canon Tallis. No beast crouched to spring, ruby eyes gleaming.

Simon's heart began to pound again. Could this be someone else's clearing?

No. This was the branch from which the puma—or whatever it was—had prepared to attack. This was the small pile of green wood and leaf mold he had collected for the fire. There were the coconut husks. These were the beds of grass and fern which they had made, Canon Tallis's still bearing the imprint of his body. And there was the palm-leaf hat Simon had woven for the priest.

For a moment Simon had a horrible vision of wildcat, lion, leopard, snake, scorpion, vulture, all feasting on the ample body of the priest.

But something would have been left: white clerical collar, silver cuff-links, belt. Or buttons; there would at least have been a button. He scrabbled about on the ground.

Nothing.

Absolutely nothing.

He sat back on his heels in perplexity.

What to do?

Then he stiffened. In the distance he heard a motor, completely incongruous amid the jungle sounds. But it was approaching, and it came from above. Leaf and vine had quickly closed over the tearing by Gutiérrez's helicopter. The smoke signal which might once have penetrated the green was dead ash. If this was a helicopter sent out by Hurtado there would be nothing to see.

The sound came closer, high above his head, then lower, lower.

He began to tremble. Only Gutiérrez or one of his men would know how to get here without a signal from the ground, and a landing strip.

The noise of the rotors was deafening.

Monkeys screeched, birds flew up in the air. Then there was a sound of ripping and the helicopter dropped through the vines. The blades quivered to a stop.

Simon pressed back into the surrounding tangle of jungle, but there was no point in running away. This time there was to be no escape. He had abandoned Canon Tallis and anything that happened to him now was his own fault. He waited.

Gutiérrez climbed out of the machine.

He was followed by the soldier with the rifle who

had thrown Simon into the hearse and the priest into the copter.

Simon did not move. He would have welcomed boar or wildcat.

"Where is he," Gutiérrez demanded, "the Englishman?"

"I don't know."

"What you mean, you don't know?"

"I don't know," Simon repeated.

Gutiérrez grabbed him by the arm. Simon tried to jerk away, but he could not.

The soldier kicked him in the belly. "Where is he?"

The wind was knocked out of Simon. He gasped like a fish out of water. He saw the boot raised to kick again.

He closed his eyes.

When Hurtado reached the dock at Port of Dragons, a message was waiting for him. A man who seemingly had been asleep all day in his hammock had received a message from the Quiztano village. The English priest had been found, and the boy was not with him.

Vermeer and Hurtado were closeted in the captain's quarters. "This is serious," Hurtado said. "You actually told Gutiérrez that smoke was seen in the jungle?"

"I did."

"Vermeer, I do not understand you."

Vermeer's smile had a slightly fixed look. "I did not forget what you said. It was the only way I could think of to force Gutiérrez's hand."

Hurtado wiped the back of his fist across his sharp

blue jaw. "Gutiérrez left the *Orion,* went to the police barracks, got in a small police car, and took off. One of his subordinates reports that Gutiérrez was called to meet someone at the airport."

"You have called the airport?"

"Gutiérrez did, in fact, go there. He stopped only long enough to collect one of the soldiers who hangs about the place, and preempt a helicopter."

"Are you having him followed?"

"Vermeer, I am only a policeman. He has a good start on us. I have three helicopters out, but I cannot cover the entire jungle. If Gutiérrez has gone back to his mother's village there'll be no tracing him."

Vermeer asked, "Alejandro, what else is on your mind?"

"Tom Tallis has been found. He has a badly injured leg, where he was gored by a wild boar."

"And the boy?"

"We don't know where the boy is."

"But why?"

Hurtado told him.

"Tallis is with the Quiztanos?"

"Yes. His leg is evidently in bad shape."

"But what about Simon?"

"The Quiztano party has gone back into the jungle to look for him. He evidently ran in terror. He will have left traces. But they must find him quickly. There are dangers in the jungle."

Vermeer said, "Alejandro, you have to get hold of Gutiérrez."

"Why is Gutiérrez so important at this moment?"

"I have a hunch that he has something to do with the kidnapping, and that he and the murderer are—what do you say—"

"In cahoots," Hurtado said. "An American idiom. It is possible. But why do you say 'the murderer' that way?"

"I am not at all convinced that you have arrested the right man."

Hurtado's dark eyes sparked. "As you tried to trap Gutiérrez, so have I tried to trap the murderer. Jan has everything against him. But I am convinced of his innocence."

At Dragonlake, Miss Leonis and Canon Tallis tried to hide their anxiety about Simon. Tallis lay on a chaise longue made of young trees and vines in the same way as Miss Leonis's chair. It had been placed on the porch of Umar Xanai's dwelling. The crude couch was amazingly gentle to his tired and aching body. His leg wound had been cleaned and dressed and he had quickly withdrawn his first request to be taken immediately to a hospital. The agonizing pain was gone and if he did not attempt to move he was quite comfortable. The hectic flush had left his face.

Miss Leonis's chair had been placed so that they could talk easily. The life of the village flowed about them like a cool stream. Birds sang. On the porch of one of the Caring Places they could see a young Quiztano male in a bright, belted tunic, helping a little boy to walk. At the far end of the porch a young Quiztano woman, in softly patterned, flowing robe, tended an old man.

"I have muscles I never even knew existed," Tallis said. "Why didn't they put me in one of their hospitals?"

"Caring Places," she corrected. "You have a wound,

but it's not that serious, now that it's been cleaned and the infection controlled. Umar Xanai says that you were absolutely right not to touch the water in the stream. It's full of lethal amoebae."

"What have the Quiztanos used on me? I cannot tell you how much better I feel."

She smiled. "They have ministered to me, too. They have ointments and powders which have been used by them as far back as the Memory goes. I would guess that what they put on your wound must be some equivalent of an antibiotic. After all, penicillin comes from bread mold."

"It was like a dream," he said, smiling. "There I was, my leg being cleaned and dressed by a gorgeous young creature who told me that she has her M.D. from the university in Caracas. Quentin Phair would be pleased."

"Yes. I think he would. I hope that Niniane would be pleased, too."

He changed the subject. "I noticed that the young men who rescued me carried bows and arrows, or spears, not firearms."

"The Umara and Umar Xanai do not permit firearms, and those who wish to use them leave the tribe."

"The Umara and the old chieftain—they rule together?"

"I believe the Umara carries the ultimate authority. They are a strange and fascinating people, and I hope that I am not putting too much trust in them when I expect them to find Simon."

"They found me."

"But this is not the first time on this journey that Simon has come close to death."

"It would seem to me," Canon Tallis said, "that Simon has been saved for a purpose. And if he has been saved for a purpose, he will be all right now." ⸱

"He should not have run away from you."

"I ordered him to."

"But you were wounded and helpless."

"He couldn't have helped. What use two of us dying? And your lad is no coward. He was extraordinarily brave and resourceful about the boar."

She shook her head slowly. "He shouldn't have run."

Canon Tallis said gently, "Miss Leonis, all we must concentrate on now is having Simon found and brought here to us."

"He will try to get back to the clearing. Once he comes to himself he will know he shouldn't have run, and he will try to get back."

"The Quiztanos have returned to the clearing, and they will ray out from there. They will be able to follow his tracks no matter how quickly the jungle covers them for untrained eyes."

"It will be night in a few hours."

Tallis corrected her. "It will not be night for a few hours. We will pray that during that time Simon will be found."

She sighed. "Sometimes I think I am prayed out."

"I doubt that."

She looked at him, at his bald head, his warm, dark eyes, at the lines of pain on his face, pain which did not come only from his injury. "I have learned that no is an answer to prayer, and I have come to accept a great many noes. I cannot accept a no about Simon."

"You will accept what you have to," the priest said quietly. "Meanwhile, you must hope. Simon is to be saved for a purpose. That is the best help you can give those who are looking for Simon. Prayers of hope."

"Yes." She shut her eyes. For a long time the two of them, the middle-aged priest and the old woman, remained in silence. The sounds of the village mingled gently with their quiet. From the lake came splashing and the laughter of children. From somewhere behind them came a woman's voice raised in song almost as clear and high as a bird's, and her song was joined by bird song. The breeze lifted and moved through the trees with a sound like rain.

After what seemed an eternity, Miss Leonis opened her eyes.

Canon Tallis was looking at her, his dark eyes compassionate.

She asked him, "Do you know who murdered the man who called himself Forsyth Phair?"

"Yes. I think I do."

"It was not Jan?"

"No. Not Jan."

The afternoon sun beat down on the *Orion*. Dr. Eisenstein nodded in her deck chair.

Dr. Wordsworth poked her. "Ruth. Come look at this." She pointed down at the dock.

Dr. Eisenstein pulled herself out of her chair and went to the rail; she laughed with pleasure as she saw a man asleep in a rope hammock which was slung under the side of a large truck, so that the man slept in the shadow of the truck as comfortably as between two trees.

"We should take a nap, too," Dr. Wordsworth said.

"But Englishmen detest a siesta."

Dr. Wordsworth stretched slowly, languorously. "My English blood grows thinner by the hour. I have discovered that I love my country. Why doesn't Hurtado let us leave the ship? Vermeer said that permission should come through any moment."

Dr. Eisenstein moved to the shade of the canvas canopy. "It does seem odd. I understand that Dr. O'Keefe has been allowed off."

"Official business," Dr. Wordsworth said. "He's here at the invitation of the Venezuelan government, and now that Jan has been apprehended I guess it was easy enough to relax regulations for him. He went off with several pompous-looking officials."

"Where did you learn all this?"

"Vermeer. Oh, Ruth, I wish there was something we could do."

"Do you want to play cards?"

"I mean about finding Simon. Let's go take a siesta."

Dr. Eisenstein leaned back in her chair. "I was having one when you woke me up."

"Sorry. Go back to sleep."

Dr. O'Keefe returned to the *Orion* hot and depressed. Charles and Poly were not in their cabins. Poly, he assumed, would be with Geraldo. He undressed and took a cold shower. His preliminary investigations of the lake had not been encouraging, and the head of department who accompanied him had not been optimistic. Most worrying was a chemical plant from which O'Keefe guessed that a dangerous amount of mercury was escaping into the lake, although "Any amount is dangerous," he said to his guide, a distinguished-looking man from Caracas with the incredible name of Geiger, pronounced Hay-hair.

Geiger told him that to keep the poison from infecting the lake would be enormously expensive. He himself was highly alarmed because the chief of public health had reported cases of mercury poisoning.

"And I very deliberately drove you through the barrio," Geiger told O'Keefe. "You have seen for yourself what conditions are like there, and you will guess that there may well have been other cases which have not been reported. Life is less important to the business barons than their profit sheets."

It was going to be difficult to shake up this greed so that a beautiful lake would not be destroyed, taking along with it a great many human lives.

"What about the water by the Quiztano settlement?"

"It is unpolluted thus far, but unless the industrial effluents are expelled elsewhere it is inevitable that the whole lake will suffer. We are further handicapped by the fact that there are many people in high official positions who consider that the people of the barrio are themselves pollutants, and that if a great many of them should happen to die off, it will be helping to curb the population explosion."

"I gather that you do not sympathize with this view?" O'Keefe asked.

Geiger shook his head. "No, but it makes it more difficult for us to impress the business barons with the seriousness of the situation. Add to this that many foreign powers have interest in our oil wells and chemical plants, and you will see that our efforts could be turned to provoke an international incident."

"But you will make the efforts anyhow?"

Geiger nodded. "This is why we asked you to come.

Words from a man of your reputation will hold more weight than anything one of our own scientists could say."

—Greed, Dr. O'Keefe thought angrily, as he stood under the cold shower. —Is the same kind of greed behind the murder of Phair and the kidnapping of Simon and Tom?

When he was dressed in clean shorts and shirt he went to check on his children. Geraldo told him that Poly had gone back to her cabin, and he found her there, scowling at her little icon.

She looked up. "St. George isn't killing dragons anymore, is he, Daddy? He's not going to be able to save Simon and Uncle Father. He's only a piece of paper pasted on wood. I hate him."

Dr. O'Keefe said, "You never thought your icon was a miracle-worker, did you?"

"No. But it used to make me feel that dragons could be killed if there was a St. George around."

"Don't you still feel that way?"

"Most of the St. Georges I know have been killed by the dragons. Like Joshua. And Quentin Phair was never a St. George at all. Daddy, if Simon and Uncle Father are all right we should have heard by now."

"This isn't like you, Poly," her father said. "The worst thing you can do for them is to give up hope."

"Okay. I'll try to hold on. You'd better go look in on Charles. I think he's upset about something."

"Where is he?"

"In the cabin."

Dr. O'Keefe left his daughter and walked up the starboard passage to the cabin. He looked in and saw Charles lying face down on his bunk.

Dr. O'Keefe touched him lightly on the shoulder. "Charles."

Charles turned over and startled his father with his pallor. His eyes were red from weeping.

"Charles, what is it?"

"It has been an appropriate time for a man to cry," Charles said.

He turned over, and once more buried his face in his pillow. Dr. O'Keefe watched him for a few moments, then left. When his children were very small there was usually something which he could do to ease whatever was troubling them. Both Poly and Charles had moved beyond that stage, and he felt helpless and heavy of heart.

He went to the salon, looking for Mr. Theo.

Simon crouched, eyes closed, waiting for the boot to kick him again. It was not going to be an easy way to die, and he was certain that the soldier was going to kill him.

Then he heard a *twing* and a shout.

He opened his eyes and the soldier was dancing about in pain, an arrow through the hide of his boot and into his foot.

From every direction, it seemed, came bronze young men in bright tunics, carrying spears, and bows and arrows.

If Gutiérrez knew the jungle, so did the Quiztanos. In single file they walked through what appeared to be impenetrable undergrowth. Gutiérrez was marched between two of the Indians, as was the soldier whose boot had so nearly killed Simon. The arrow had been removed.

Gutiérrez screamed and howled and cursed. He was the chief of police of Port of Dragons. The Indians would pay for this. Here he was, rescuing Simon; didn't the fools realize that he, with his helicopter, had found the boy first and was there to save his life? and for this he was treated like a criminal. They would all shortly be behind bars.

At last he ran out of wind.

The soldier moved along without emotion. His rifle had been taken from him and left in the copter. If the arrow had hurt his foot he gave no sign.

Simon walked with a young Indian, who identified himself as Ouldi and told him that Canon Tallis and Aunt Leonis were waiting for him. After that there was little conversation. The trip through the jungle used all their lung power and concentration. Simon followed in Ouldi's footsteps, and it took every ounce of his failing strength for him to keep up. The heat of the jungle which hardly affected the Indians had Simon streaming with sweat. His mouth was so dry that the dryness was pain. Occasionally Ouldi reached a hand out to help him through a difficult place.

Simon tried to conceal the fact that he was so exhausted he was not certain one foot would continue to follow the next. His breath came in short gasps. He had a stitch in his side which threatened to double him up. Just as he was about to pant out to Ouldi a plea for a moment's rest, the undergrowth cleared, the trees and shrubs were behind them, and they faced the deep blue of Dragonlake.

Two large open wooden boats were waiting on the

beach. Ouldi told Simon to get into the first. Gutiérrez and the soldier were hustled into the second, and Gutiérrez again began to scream threats and abuse. Instinctively Simon put his hands over his ears.

"It is all right," Ouldi assured him. "He cannot hurt you now. He will be taken directly to Port of Dragons where Mynheer Vermeer and the police from Caracas will be waiting."

"Señor Hurtado?"

"His men. Señor Hurtado is at Dragonlake. And we have the information he and Mynheer Vermeer were seeking. Gutiérrez"—Ouldi spat the syllables—"he was not born with that fine name. One look at him and I could tell that he is an Indian from across the border—"

"Not Quiztano—"

"No, no, a tribe of short, stupid people who have almost completely vanished because they have betrayed their own ways. They have no Memory. As for that Gutiérrez, he is a smuggler."

"But he's a policeman."

"So? Not all policemen are Hurtados, any more than all consuls are Vermeers. Being a policeman simplified his dirty work—very dirty."

Simon looked at Ouldi with respect. "Canon Tallis suspected he might be into something like that." He gazed somberly as the boat with Gutiérrez and the soldier was rowed away.

Four Indians were in the boat with Simon and Ouldi. They rowed swiftly, in the opposite direction from the other boat. Ouldi sat in the prow, his back turned to the water so that he was facing Simon. "We are glad you have come, little brother."

"I'm glad, too. You saved my life. Gutiérrez wasn't rescuing me. That soldier was going to kill me and

Gutiérrez wasn't about to stop him. You came just in time." His throat was so parched he could scarcely speak.

Ouldi took a small skin bag from his belt and handed it to Simon. "There are only a few swallows, but that is all you should have right now."

The swallows were sheer bliss, and Simon handed the empty skin to Ouldi with gratitude.

The Indians rowed strongly and swiftly but it seemed a long time before Simon saw ahead of them the round dwellings on high stilts stretching out into the lake. It was exactly as Charles had described it, exactly like the picture he had seen in Jan's book.

"Uncle Father—Canon Tallis—is really there? And Aunt Leonis?"

Ouldi smiled slightly. "How many times do I have to tell you? Yes, they are there." The boat swept past the dwelling farthest out in the lake. Ouldi pointed toward it proudly. "That is my dwelling. That is where I will bring my betrothed on the night when we two are made a new one."

When the boat neared the beach he held up his hand for silence.

A large group was assembled. Simon looked about eagerly, but at first he could not see Aunt Leonis or Canon Tallis. Hurtado was clearly visible standing a little apart from the Indians, with his dark hatchet face and city suit.

Ouldi jumped from the boat and helped pull it ashore, then held out his hand to Simon, who jumped out onto the soft sand.

From the clearing a young girl came running out of the large central building, her patterned dress flowing

like butterfly wings. She carried a goblet which she
offered to Simon. It was half filled with a pale liquid.

"We know that you are still thirsty," Ouldi said, "but
you have been very long without enough water, and
so you must drink only a little at a time. This will
help."

He drank thirstily, and the golden liquid cooled and
healed his throat far more than water would.

"Thank you," Simon said. "It has helped." He gave
the goblet back to the girl.

"Now," Ouldi said. "It is the moment."

The group on shore had turned away from Simon
and the boats and were looking back to the greensward. Simon followed their gaze, past an enormous
stone-grey statue of a beatifically smiling woman, to a
litter being carried by two young Indians. A small figure was crouched on the litter; at first he thought it
was a child. Beside the litter walked two women, one
middle-aged, one young. When the litter came closer
he realized that the small figure was not a child but a
very old woman, much older than Aunt Leonis.

A man in a long white tunic, with white hair down
to his shoulders, detached himself from the group and
went up to the litter and spoke briefly to the occu-
pant, who raised her hand imperiously, and spoke in a
cracked, almost whispering voice.

The man returned a few words, and Ouldi whispered to Simon, "Umar Xanai and the Umara."

The litter bearers carried the old woman up to Simon.

He felt a strange constriction in his chest. He held
his breath until he thought his lungs would burst, but
his grey eyes met the probe of her dark ones. He felt

that he was moving out of time and into eternity, that this meeting of eyes would never end, that time had stopped and would never begin to flow again.

Then the ancient Umara spoke three words in a language completely foreign to Simon, a language fluid as water.

Umar Xanai came to her and asked her something in the same deep, dark tones.

Again she spoke three words.

The words were whispered from person to person, and then the whole village burst into cries, cries which had a harmonious, musical quality, cries which were certainly sounds of joy.

And then Simon saw Aunt Leonis, standing in the background, next to Canon Tallis, who had been carried out on his light and flexible couch. Simon ran to them, and then he and Aunt Leonis were holding each other, and he was crying, and so was she, and they held each other and rocked back and forth as they had not since the night Simon's mother had died, but this time the tears were tears of joy.

So it was some time before he realized that Ouldi was speaking to him, trying to get his attention, speaking formally for the whole village. "She says that you are the One. The Umara says that you are he for whom we wait."

Simon pushed the words away. "No, no. I'm only Simon Renier, from South Carolina, tell them, Ouldi, please, I can't possibly be the one . . ."

Ouldi repeated calmly, "The Umara says that you are the One."

"Aunt Leonis—Uncle Father—"

Ouldi kissed Simon ceremoniously on each cheek and then on the forehead. "We welcome you, Phair."

"I'm Simon. Simon Bolivar Renier."

Umar Xanai stepped forward, giving Simon the three ritual kisses. "You are the Phair."

"Oh, Aunt Leonis, Uncle Father, please tell them!" Simon cried. "I'm not—you mustn't let them think—"

Umar Xanai said, "The Phair promised that he would return. Now the Phair has kept his word and the long waiting is over."

"But he was a grown man," Simon protested, "and I'm only a boy." There was a darkness before his eyes which was only partly the darkness of approaching night.

"You are blood of his blood," Umar Xanai said.

Simon paused, then said slowly, "Yes. I am. I, too, have run away when it was my obligation to stay."

"And now you have returned," Umar Xanai said.

The Umara had been sitting impassively on her litter. Now she gestured again and the bearers brought her back close to Simon. She put her small and ancient hands up to his face and gave him the three kisses of benediction. Then she gestured regally toward her dwelling place and the bearers carried her away.

"Aunt Leonis—"

"Yes, Simon."

"Well, tell them, ma'am, please tell them."

"What do you want me to tell them, Simon?"

"That I am not Quentin Phair."

The old woman looked at the chieftain. "I think they understand that."

"And Aunt Leonis, I couldn't possibly just stay here and leave you to go back to Pharaoh all alone."

"I'm not at all sure that I could make the trip back to Pharaoh, Simon. I'm too old for jet travel. I don't think that my heart could stand the journey back."

"But Boz—what about Boz? We can't just desert Boz!"

"Boz is dead, Simon."

The boy put his hands over his eyes. No. It was too much. Bitter tears forced their way through his fingers.

He felt a gentle but firm pressure on his shoulder, and Umar Xanai said, "It is late, and the Phair is tired from his ordeal. He needs refreshment and rest. He will be ministered to by one of the Umaras, and then he will spend the night with Ouldi in his dwelling. Tomorrow, when he is rested, he will see more clearly."

"What am I to do!" Simon cried. He turned desperately to Umar Xanai. "Sir, Quentin Phair is my ancestor. He is long dead. I am his descendant. I have all—all his faults."

Umar Xanai smiled placidly. "And you have returned to us, as you promised you would. The Umara recognized you as the One. We welcome you."

Hurtado and Tallis remained on the beach after the village had settled down. The dark night of the jungle was heavy around them.

"But there are hardly any insects," Hurtado exclaimed. "What do they do?"

"Whatever it is, if they could bottle it they could make a fortune," Tallis replied.

"You really are all right?" Hurtado asked. "Don't you think you should see a doctor?"

"I have. And these people with their Gift have something that hasn't been around in modern medicine for a long time. Whatever they used on my wound has completely taken away the infection. I'm convinced that I could walk on my leg now, but they will not permit it, and I trust their judgment. Hurtado, if you wish to remain my friend you will say nothing about their Caring Places."

"There is really no reason why I should say anything," Hurtado said. "Vermeer, too, would take it ill, and I wish to remain friends with both of you. So Vermeer was right about Gutiérrez. There are two young men, of Quiztano blood, who are willing to testify against him."

"An unpleasant character," Tallis understated "He certainly never expected that Simon and I would survive the jungle. And we nearly didn't."

"But it doesn't get us any closer to finding the murderer."

"Doesn't it? I rather think it does. From all the bits and pieces I've gathered, I've been able to get a pretty clear picture."

Hurtado looked at him and waited. Tallis's face gleamed whitely in the starlight.

"We know that Forsyth Phair was not, in fact, Forsyth Phair, but Fernando Propice, a Venezuelan of mixed blood, largely Levantine, long involved in smuggling, extortion, and any nasty business that came to hand. Right?"

"Correct," Hurtado agreed.

"And that no bank in Caracas has either a Forsyth Phair or a Fernando Propice on the records."

"Correct."

"The murderer, I would guess, dabbled in smuggling and got involved with Propice, who tried to drag him in further than he wanted to go. The murderer wanted out, and the only way out was to dispose of Propice."

"And who is this person? Do you know, or is it all guesswork?"

"It's largely guesswork."

"Are you going to let me in on it, or do I have to find out in my flatfooted way?"

Tallis's smile gleamed. "Phair/Propice was the boss in this smuggling operation; he was almost making it. Gutiérrez was his sidekick. The murderer got tangled with them, but he didn't want to kill anyone, or to get involved in drugs or chemicals. When he told Gutiérrez that he no longer wanted to play his game, Gutiérrez took off with Simon and me and told the man that he would kill us if he didn't keep his mouth shut. The murderer, being more squeamish than Gutiérrez, was forced to keep quiet to avoid further bloodshed."

"Go on."

"Back to Propice. It seems more than likely that what little Quiztano blood remains in his veins went back a long time—to Quentin Phair, in fact."

"I know that's what the old lady thinks."

"Umar Xanai and the Umara corroborate this. They knew him to be an evil and vindictive man, like Edmund in *Lear,* dwelling on rights he felt he ought to have, and willing to do anything to get what he thought he deserved. At one time he took himself to Dragonlake to claim the jewels Quentin Phair had left the Umara, and which Propice thought were his due."

"What did happen to the jewels?"

"They were sold and the money used for education—universities, medical schools. So Propice felt abused there, too. As Quentin's heir, he was due everything that befits the heir—the long-spent fortune, the portrait, of course the portrait, and the ancient grudge."

Hurtado looked across the lake at the peaceful stork-like dwellings. Violence and vengeance seemed out of place. He sighed. "I think you're probably right, Tom. There are natures warped enough actually to be more proud of the ancient grudge than any other part of the inheritance. And it fits in with what Dr. Wordsworth told me. But you still haven't pointed to the murderer. Half of Venezuela would have a motive."

"Simon gave me the first clue with the story of the key to cabin 5."

"The cabin with the portrait, yes. And Jan's foolish lie. Geraldo is convinced that Jan is lying to protect someone."

"I think that Jan did not lie."

"Then—?"

"Boon did."

"Where's your evidence?"

"I don't have enough. But Boon's winter uniform vanished. A winter uniform is less visible in the tropical dark than summer whites. It would have been easy for Boon to weigh it down and dump it on the bottom of the ocean. The key story was an attempt—a successful one, as it turned out—to implicate Jan, and so was the planting of the portrait here."

"How did he manage that?"

"Easily enough. If he was on the bridge in the small hours of the night he could have lowered it into the water without being seen."

"So could anybody else."

"It was Boon who was alone on the bridge, the only one watching the radar scan. A fishing boat could eas-

ily come right up to the *Orion;* the portrait could be
lowered, and no one the wiser."

"This is guesswork."

"Back to Propice for a moment, then. It's all part of
the pattern. He paid or blackmailed someone to run
Simon down with the fork lift, and that little scheme
was foiled by Poly. So then Propice ordered Boon to
push Simon overboard. Boon probably refused to kill,
and then Propice threatened him until he thought he
had no choice."

"Geraldo's talk of reluctance," Hurtado said. "Yes, it
fits."

"I see Boon moving slowly to the boy with a heavy
heart—for he appears to be a foolish rather than an
evil man, Alejandro. And when Geraldo stopped him
and he did not have to complete an action which was
totally repugnant to him, he decided the only way out
was to kill Phair."

"What about the portrait?"

"It's probably Propice's hold over him. If Boon
didn't play along, Propice would pin him for smuggling, easy enough to do if he was already in Propice's
and Gutiérrez's net. My theory is that Boon intended
his smuggling to be a strictly on-shore business. It
seems that his tastes are fairly expensive and he
wanted to pick up a little extra cash. Also, he knows
something about art."

"Plausible," Hurtado said. "We're fairly certain the
art ring is centered in Port of Dragons."

"It probably seemed innocent enough at first. But the
innocent don't stay innocent when they think they can
stay on the edge of crime. Drug dealers aren't worried
about anybody's conscience, nor would it concern a

Gutiérrez that Boon would try not to do anything which would reflect on the Master of the ship."

"You have a vivid imagination, Tom," Hurtado said. "Imagination does not hold up in court."

"No, but you agree with me," Tallis said. "You arrested Jan on the gamble that the murderer would then betray himself. Or that he would not let someone else hang. I think your gamble will pay off."

"There's not much time."

"I don't think Boon will let Jan take the rap. He got into deeper waters than he intended, and he ran scared. I think he will stop running."

"He'd better stop soon, then. I can play for time only so long. What we have to do is find a way to turn imagination into evidence." He looked about him through the velvet dark. "This is an incredible place."

"Not so incredible as all that. We who have spent our lives in cities tend to forget that human beings were not meant to live in anthills. Only insects can manage to survive in such conditions. And our work does not often take us among the innocent, Alejandro. We have been over-exposed to the darker reaches of the human heart."

Hurtado continued to look out over the lake to the dwellings. "They expect the boy to remain here."

"Yes."

"They don't really think that he is Quentin Phair?"

"They don't think about such things the way we do. Because Simon is Quentin Phair's direct descendant, he partakes in his ancestor and can fulfill his destiny."

"They won't force him?"

"Alejandro," Tallis said, "this is simply something I don't want to think about tonight. It strikes me as being a far more difficult problem than finding the murderer of Propice, for which you really don't need me. As soon as you had all of the information you would have put two and two together exactly as I have done. But Theo sent for me, and I came, and I think that I came because of Simon."

"A boy you'd never heard of?"

"He needed me, Alejandro. He has been far more wounded than I, and it occurs to me that perhaps the Quiztanos are the only ones who can complete the healing."

"He appears perfectly healthy."

"He has been wounded in spirit. He attempted to hold on to an idol—and when he was forced to see him as a human being who lied and lusted and was as other men, it was like having the rug pulled out from under him. He has been exposed to murder; he has almost been killed himself; it has all been too much for him."

Hurtado said, "He has to grow up sometime."

"He is doing precisely that, Alejandro."

"What about the old lady?" Hurtado asked.

"She is dying."

"I see. Yes, it will be difficult for the boy. But surely you can't think that staying here is a possibility."

"Why not?"

"Tom, these people are—for all Vermeer says—a primitive Indian tribe."

"You do sound like a city boy. Would you want your son, had he been through what Simon has been through, to live in Caracas? Or New York? Or Charleston? Haven't you seen something healthy in this place?"

"He'll revert," Hurtado said. "He'll be no better than a savage."

"And we? How much better than savages are we?"

"Oh, have it your own way," Hurtado said. "When will you be ready to be moved?"

"By tomorrow. But I must stay here until my mind is at ease about Simon. Forty-eight hours together in the jungle can forge a close friendship."

The next day had the timeless quality of a dream for Simon. Ouldi took him through the village, through the Caring Places.

Simon stood in the cool interior of the Caring Place for the dying. There were two long rows of low beds, twelve on each side. Only two of these were empty. By most of the beds a Quiztano was seated, holding the hand of the dying person. The air was fragrant with flowers. Here was no horror, only an ineffable sense of peace.

"I'm not sure—" Simon whispered.

"Not sure of what?"

"That I'm strong enough. I'm afraid of death."

"That is all right," Ouldi said. "So am I. I have been out in the world and I have learned fear and lost faith. So I have returned to Dragonlake to lose fear and regain faith. That will happen to you, too."

Several of the Indians started to sing. "A soul is going," Ouldi said. "It is being sung into the land of the blessed. But many of those who are brought here to die do not die. They get well, and they take some of our peace and some of our caring with them."

"And my ancestor started all this?"

"With the Umara."

"Everybody here is so *good!*"

But Ouldi shook his head. "No. We are as other people. Some good, some bad. Many leave Dragonlake and choose the material goods of the world."

"Ouldi, what am I to do?"

"You will do what is right. I am trying to hide nothing from you. It is a constant struggle for us to keep to the Quiztano ways. If you become one of us it will be your struggle, too, will it not? You would not wish us to change?"

Simon shook his head. "My ancestor started these Caring Places. No, I would not want you to change, Ouldi. I would be the one to have to change."

"Not as much as you think."

"Gutiérrez—you said he turned his back on the ways of his people?"

"Not only Gutiérrez. All of that particular tribe. And they learned to like to kill. Not to eat, not for life, but to destroy."

"What's going to happen to him?"

Ouldi moved his shoulders sinuously. "He is an evil man. He will be made to pay."

Simon shuddered. "And Jan? What about Jan?"

"Jan did not kill. The Englishman knows that."

"But who did?"

Ouldi shrugged. "I do not know his name. But it is someone Jan thought of as a friend. He will be sad. Come, I still have much to show you."

The passengers stood on the promenade deck of the *Orion*, all leaning on the port rail and looking down at the dock. Geraldo had summoned them together, saying that the captain, el señor comandante Hurtado, and Mynheer Vermeer wished to speak to them. Everybody watched as a dark car drew up.

"Look!" Mrs. Smith cried. "It's Jan!"

Jan left the car, crossed the dock, and ran up the gangplank to the *Orion*. He did not look at the passengers.

Charles moved to his father. Dr. O'Keefe took his son's hand in his own.

"Daddy, Charles," Poly said, "has Jan been cleared?"

"Wait. No doubt we'll find out what's going on in a minute."

Dr. Eisenstein looked relieved. "I couldn't bring myself to believe that Jan would murder."

"Someone did," Dr. Wordsworth said, "and I would like to know who it was."

They all turned as they heard the screen door into the ship close with a light slam. Vermeer came out onto the deck, affable as usual. Dr. Wordsworth took a step toward him, then stopped.

"Ladies and gentlemen," he said. "Perhaps you all saw someone getting out of a car just now? And now you want to know what is going on, and why you have been asked to come together here. It is my sad duty to inform you that Mynheer Boon went to the captain last night and confessed to the murder of Mr. Phair."

The facts were very much as Canon Tallis had guessed. The straw that broke the back of Boon's resistance was a hint from Hurtado that Simon had been murdered. It was this last horror which finally caused Lyolf Boon to go to Van Leyden.

"How terrible for Jan!" Poly cried.

Dr. O'Keefe said, "But at least he's been completely cleared."

"But Mynheer Boon! He was Jan's friend!"

Vermeer said, "Gutiérrez threatened to kill Simon and Canon Tallis unless Boon kept his mouth shut."

Dr. Wordsworth said, "From what you have been telling us it would seem that if Boon had not killed Propice, then Propice might well have succeeded in finding a way to dispose of Simon?"

"It is quite possible."

"Then, although it wasn't exactly a murder of self-defense, it was in order to stop Simon from being murdered?"

Vermeer beamed. "That will be taken into consideration, I'm sure."

Mr. Smith asked, "But the smuggling?"

"He will have to pay for that. He was into the art racket, as Hurtado calls it. But Propice and Gutiérrez were trying to get him involved in chemicals."

"So for that, too," Dr. Wordsworth said, "he had no way out except to remove Propice?"

"He refused to deal with drugs or chemicals. Yes. Propice would undoubtedly have destroyed him one way or another had he remained alive."

"And that, too, will be taken into consideration?" Dr. Eisenstein asked.

"I would assume so."

"But there would still have been Gutiérrez," Mr. Smith said.

"There would. Mynheer Boon had—as my friend Hurtado said—painted himself into a corner."

Dr. Wordsworth asked, "Did Gutiérrez know that Boon had killed Phair?"

"He guessed. He accused him, hoping in this way to avoid what Hurtado calls the rap."

"I hate Gutiérrez!" Poly cried. "He's a beast! He didn't care whether he killed Simon and Uncle Father or not. He was just using them to hurt Mynheer Boon. Gutiérrez and Propice made Mynheer Boon do—be— somthing he never should have been."

Mr. Smith said heavily, "That first breach of honesty which can lead to so much disaster . . ."

Dr. Wordsworth reached out and took his hand with unexpected solidarity. "We've been lucky, you and I, Mr. Smith. We've managed to break away from bondage."

Mr. Theo said, "Thank God, Simon and Tom are all right. That's what we have to think about. What about the captain, Vermeer?"

"As long as Boon's smuggling was done ashore, and not on the ship, the captain cannot be implicated. The Bolivar portrait was Propice's first wedge. But we have the portrait. It was not only to implicate Jan that Boon sent it to the Quiztanos. It was the only place he could think of where it would not be taken by the art-smuggling ring he was trying to get free of. So we have the portrait, and I think the captain will have no problem. This is one of Mynheer Boon's greatest concerns."

Dr. Wordsworth asked, "What's going to be done with the portrait?"

"Miss Phair and the Quiztanos wish it to be given to the Bolivar Museum."

"Which had not been Mr. Phair's intention."

"It had not."

Poly whispered to Charles, "I sort of wished Simon could keep the portrait."

"Aunt Leonis is right about things knowing where they belong," Charles said in an exhausted and withdrawn manner.

Vermeer clapped his hands together. "Now, my dear friends, I have good news and an invitation. You are all free to go into town or wherever you would like, until five o'clock this afternoon, when you are all requested to return to the *Orion*."

Dr. Wordsworth's conditioned reflex was outrage at any curtailment of liberty. "Why?" she demanded.

Vermeer beamed on her. "Cars will be waiting to take the entire company out to the Quiztano settlement at Dragonlake, where a feast is being prepared. This will be an excitement for my fellow anthropologist, will it not, Dr. Eisenstein?" After the exclamations had died down, he said, "My dear doctors, I should count it my extreme privilege to accompany you today and be your guide if you will permit."

Dr. Wordsworth bowed graciously.

Vermeer turned his sunshine on the old Greek. "Mr. Theoto—uh—Mr. Theo, a car will come to take you to the cathedral, for as long as you desire to play the organ. Will you be ready in half an hour?"

"In five minutes," Mr. Theo said.

Poly asked anxiously, "Simon and Uncle Father are really all right, really and truly all right?"

Vermeer's smile seemed to reach completely around his head. "Really and truly." Then he looked at her father. "May I have a word with you, sir?"

"Of course. In my cabin?"

"Please." Vermeer turned to Dr. Wordsworth. "I will call for you ladies in a quarter of an hour."

Despite the heat, he shut the door to Dr. O'Keefe's cabin. "If there is anything my government can do to assist you in your investigations, Doctor, we will be glad to."

"Thank you."

"You know that there have been cases of mercury poisoning near Dragonlake?"

"Yes."

"What can you do?"

Dr. O'Keefe ran his hand worriedly through his hair. "I am a scientist and not a politician. But I will use every big gun I have. And Tallis has friends with influence who will bring their weight to bear. Even Dr. Eisenstein may be useful. People all over the world are rebelling against the results of greed. Perhaps we are ready for a test case, and the problems at Dragonlake involve at least half a dozen nations."

"The Quiztanos do not want publicity."

"We will keep it to the minimum. But they will do what has to be done to save the lake and the people of the barrio."

"Few industrial magnates in Europe or America will worry about what is happening to a small tribe of Indians most of them have never even heard about."

"We will do everything we can to stop the deterioration of the lake," Dr. O'Keefe said heavily. "I am grateful for your help."

"My Quiztano friends understand what is going on. They have an example of the problem in one of their Caring Places right now."

"Mercury poisoning?"

"Yes. A child from the barrio. Yes, they will help. I am a realistic man, Doctor; I know how difficult it is going to be, but I also believe that if just in one place we can win the battle over greed and callousness, that

one victory may swing the tide over the entire
world."

"We'll try," Dr. O'Keefe said. "We will certainly try."

The scene being enacted in the captain's quarters
was not exactly as it had been in Charles's dream, but
it was close enough. Lyolf Boon was in his summer
whites. His face was turned to Jan, a face nearly destroyed with anguish and weeping. Jan, too, wept.
Hurtado wore his most expressionless mask. Van Leyden had moved beyond tears. But the *Orion* was still
his. He was still Master of his ship. Despite his pain
over what Lyolf Boon had been forced to do, his relief
washed over him like a clean salt wave from the sea.

Throughout the entire ship there was both sorrow
and relief. It was not a happy ending to the story, but
at least it was an ending. When Van Leyden told the
crew that he alone would remain on the ship, and that
the rest of them were free to go to the festivities at
Dragonlake, the atmosphere lifted. As Van Leyden returned to the bridge he heard the sweet tone of a
flute playing a haunting minor melody.

The evening sun poured its benediction over the
Quiztano village; the water was golden, and the
greensward, too, was touched with gold. A long ray of
sunlight spotted the ancient Umara at the foot of the
great carving. She gave her blessing to the festivities
of the evening, but she herself would remain in prayers of gratitude for the return of the Phair.

The canoes were pulled up onto the beach, and the villagers were waiting for the boats bearing the passengers and sailors from the *Orion.*

Canon Tallis had graduated from his litter to a chair and a cane. Miss Leonis sat beside him. They had little need of conversation. They had moved into the companionship of mutual understanding. She knew, with gratitude, that Tallis would stay at Dragonlake until after her death. She wished that she, like the Umara, could spend the evening in solitude and prayer. —But there is an eternity awaiting me for that, she thought.

As though she had spoken aloud, Tallis rested his hand lightly on her shoulder.

A shout arose as the first boat was sighted, and then what appeared to be a small fleet appeared in the sunflecked water.

Poly was in the first boat, and she rushed ashore and flung her arms ecstatically around Canon Tallis, around Simon, around Aunt Leonis, and, without thinking, around Umar Xanai, as though he were a dearly beloved grandparent. "Oh, thank you, thank you! We were afraid we were never going to see Simon or Uncle Father again!"

The old chieftain's eyes lit with pleasure. "You are their friends. We welcome you." He looked about him until he saw Charles, who had gone to Canon Tallis and was standing silently by him. "You are the true dreamer?"

"Sometimes my dreams are—special."

"We are grateful to you."

"I haven't done anything."

"You have dreamed true." Then he spoke to the assembled company. "We have invited you to be with us tonight because you are friends of the Phair, and he has asked that you be present at our celebration of his return."

"His what!" Poly's voice rose incredulously.

"The Phair has come back to us, to make his life with us, as he promised us that he would."

"But Simon is not Quentin Phair!"

"He bears his blood. He is part of the Memory."

"Simon!" Poly cried. "No! You're not staying here, not for good!"

Canon Tallis looked down at Charles. The boy was pale. The priest took his hand, and it was cold. "Charles, are you all right?"

"I don't think I want to grow up."

"But you already have, haven't you?"

"Simon!" Poly cried. "Aunt Leonis! Explain to them!"

"Explain what?" Miss Leonis asked.

"That Simon must return with you to Pharaoh."

The old woman shook her head. "I will not be returning to Pharaoh."

"Simon's going to be a doctor!" Poly cried. "He can come live with us, we'd love to have him, wouldn't we Daddy?"

Simon held up his hand. "I have thought about this, Poly. I must stay."

"Why?"

"Because it is what I must do. I ran away from Uncle Father when we were in the jungle and the wildcat was about to attack us—"

"Simon," Canon Tallis said, "you're making too much of that."

"No. It has made me understand a lot of things. About human beings. About Quentin. About myself."

He smiled at Poly, then at Canon Tallis and Charles. "The Quentin Phair I made into a god was much less real than she is." He indicated the great carved figure. "I am learning to love him now like a real person. And that's a good thing, I think. There's also the matter of the revenge, of Cousin Forsyth's wanting to kill me. Now that he is dead, perhaps the idea of revenge will die, too. But it might not, as long as there are people like Gutiérrez left in the world. If I stay, then the Phair has returned, and the revenge will be finished. And"—he pointed to the Caring Places—"Quentin Phair started these. I have his work to continue. I'm going to be a doctor, and I have a great deal to learn. When the time comes I'll go to Caracas to medical school, or maybe back to the United States. But I have plenty to learn right here. A new language, for one thing."

Umar Xanai raised his arms. "Rejoice with us! Come, we have prepared a celebration." He drew the groups together with great embracing gestures, then led the way toward the center of the greensward, where a long colorful cloth had been spread across the grass. It was laden with bowls of fruit, platters of salads, pitchers of assorted drinks.

Dr. Eisenstein quivered with pleasure and excitement. "This is more than I dared hope for in my wildest dreams."

Dr. Wordsworth said, "It took a murder. So my Fernando has for once done a good deed."

Mrs. Smith said, "I'd like to forget him, but I'm not sure it's possible."

Mr. Theo looked at the beaming Vermeer bearing down on the group, and turned to Dr. Eisenstein.

"Will you do me the pleasure of sitting with me at this feast, Ruth?"

She glanced at Dr. Wordsworth and Vermeer, and took Mr. Theo's arm. "Thank you. Did you enjoy your time at the cathedral?"

"I have washed myself clean with music. That is a superb organ. Tomorrow evening, before we sail, the captain and Mynheer Vermeer have arranged for me to play for the passengers—for those of you who enjoy music."

"What a privilege," Dr. Eisenstein said. "I don't know much about music. My loss. And then you'll be sailing tomorrow night, Theo." He nodded. "I'll miss everybody." She sounded wistful. "But perhaps we'll be able to see the O'Keefes. You know, I'm not in the least sorry for Gutiérrez, but I feel for Boon."

"We all do. But it's a sorry lesson for us that one can seldom dabble only in the shallow waters of crime. There's always someone to pull us in deep."

Dr. Eisenstein looked at her travel companion laughing with Vermeer. "It takes a lot of courage to get out. Perhaps Boon will be able to start a new life when he has served his term."

"It's Simon who's starting the new life."

"Is this really serious?"

"Oh, yes. Simon is a serious boy."

Dr. Eisenstein looked about. "I think I envy him," she said.

Poly sat on the cool green grass between Geraldo and Jan. "It is good that you can be with your people tonight, Jan," she said.

Jan's face had a prison pallor that made it seem as

though he had been jailed for more than just over twenty-four hours. "I do not think that I could be anywhere else. I need to be healed."

Geraldo nodded solemnly, then took Poly's hand in his. "It is good that you are staying in Port of Dragons, Polyquita. You will be able to see Simon."

"Oh, Jan—Geraldo—I am so confused about Simon. Do you think he's making a terrible mistake?"

Geraldo kissed her hand. "It is not a decision the world would understand. But it is like Simon."

Poly looked gratefully at Geraldo. "Charles says Simon doesn't belong in our century."

The strain was ebbing slowly from Jan's face. "It has always seemed to me that the Quiztanos do not live in time at all. When I am here I forget clocks and bells and all the things which occupy me when I am being Dutch."

Poly looked across the greensward to where Miss Leonis was sitting. "What about Aunt Leonis?"

Jan said, "She will rest her bones in Dragonlake."

"You mean, she's dying?"

"She is an old woman, Polyquita, and her work is done." Geraldo raised Poly's fingers to his lips and kissed them gently. "It will be easier for me to let you go when we sail tomorrow night because I know that Simon will need you and Charles and your father. It will not be easy for Simon."

Jan said, "But he will become a healer, and the world is in need of healers."

"But the world won't know about him if he stays in Dragonlake!"

Jan's face relaxed into his old smile. "You think that matters, Miss Poly? I am part Quiztano, and I know the things that truly matter—and so do you."

* * *

Simon sat between Umar Xanai and Ouldi. On the old chieftain's other side was Aunt Leonis, with Mr. Theo by her. She looked as frail as old glass, and yet her expression was full of peace.

She looked at him and smiled, calmly and reassuringly.

Not everybody was seated, but Umar Xanai picked up a piece of fruit as a signal that the feast was to begin. Then he rose and spoke:

> *Power behind the stars*
> *making life from death*
> *joy from sorrow*
> *day from night*
> *who heals the heart*
> *and frees the lake*
> *of dragons and all ill*
> *come feast with us*
> *that we may share your feast*
> *with all we touch.*

Then he bowed his head silently.

When he looked up, Miss Leonis spoke:

"Thou didst divide the sea through thy power; thou breakest the heads of the dragons in the waters. Thou broughtest out fountains and waters out of the hard rocks; the day is thine, and the night is thine; thou hast prepared the light and the sun. Oh, let not the simple go away ashamed, but let the poor and needy give praise unto thy Name." She did not bow her head, but looked briefly up at the sky, then out over the lake, and closed her eyes.

"Lady, Señora Phair," Umar Xanai said, "we are as one."

All around them conversation and laughter rose like butterflies in the evening air. Above the lake the sky was flushed with color. The shadow of the mountain moved slowly over the greensward, cooling the air.

Simon looked about him at the assembled company. The intensity of the past days had broken the conventions of time and he felt that all the passengers of the *Orion* were old and treasured friends, and he was filled with love for them. He looked at Canon Tallis, sitting at the feast, with Charles between the priest and Hurtado.

—He has freed me to love Quentin as he really was, Simon thought gratefully. —So I must love him as he really is, too, and not make up another idol.

—I am older now, he thought. —And perhaps it is because I have come into the right time and place for me. Where Cousin Forsyth would have destroyed, I must learn to continue what Quentin began."

Tallis looked at the untouched plate in front of Charles. "You're not eating."

"I'm not hungry," Charles said.

Hurtado said, "My plate is already empty. You need food, Charles."

"I'll try."

"By the by, Charles, anytime you want a job in the Venezuelan Secret Service, just let me know."

Charles forced a smile. "It's not my line of work, Señor Hurtado. Dreams are not an advantage to a policeman. And I get too involved. I'm feeling very sad."

"Not as sad as Jan. Or the captain. They trusted Boon."

"I know. Jan is with Poly and Geraldo. They'll help."

"You must help, too," Tallis said.

"I know. I'll try."

"For that, then, you will need food." Hurtado piled his own plate high. "Tom, I understand that the O'Keefes have five more children at home. Surely they don't need Charles. Don't you think you could arrange to have Charles given to me?"

Now Charles's smile was real. "I'll always be your friend, Señor Hurtado."

Simon ate and drank. His responsibility to Quentin had become real, at last. Time redeemed had broken the limitations of time.

Ouldi lifted a pitcher and poured clear liquid into Simon's glass, into Umar Xanai's, then raised his own glass. "To the return of the Phair."

Simon raised his glass and drank deeply. Then he looked around until he saw Poly with Geraldo and Jan, Canon Tallis with Charles and Hurtado. They were all looking at him. So was Aunt Leonis.

In the jungle behind them a bird broke into an ecstatic trill. Water rippled gently against the shore, against the pilings of the dwellings reaching out into the lake. The breeze lifted. In the sky shadowed by the mountain a star pulsed into brightness.

Simon raised his glass to the assembled company. "It is good to be home," he said.

The Austin Family Trilogy

MADELEINE L'ENGLE

——MEET THE AUSTINS   **$1.95 (95777-X)**
Orphaned Maggy Hamilton comes to live with the Austins
in the first book about their warm, fun-loving family.

——THE MOON BY NIGHT   **$2.25 (95776-1)**
The fun and foibles of the Austin family's cross-country
camping trip are described by fourteen-year-old Vicky
Austin—who is also struggling with the fun and foibles of
early adolescence.

——A RING OF ENDLESS LIGHT   **$2.95 (97323-9)**
Vicky, now fifteen, spends a difficult summer confronting
the problems of first love and the slow death of her
grandfather.

LAUREL-LEAF BOOKS

Laurel-Leaf Books

LLOYD ALEXANDER
WESTMARK

Ever since the villainous Chief Minister Cabbarus came to power, the kingdom of Westmark has been a dangerous place indeed. When young Theo, the printer's apprentice, unwittingly defies Cabbarus by publishing a pamphlet without "royal permission," he's forced to flee Westmark and to live as a fugitive. Eventually, he teams up with the roguish but kindly Dr. Absalom, his dwarf attendant, and an urchin girl. The four embark on not-to-be-forgotten adventures which culminate in their risking their lives to save the kingdom.

$2.25

LAUREL-LEAF
BOOKS

Laurel-Leaf Books

Chilling Laurel-Leaf Mysteries